14

THROUGH THE EVER
EVER
NIGHT

VERONICA ROSSI

THROUGH THE
EVER
NIGHT

HARPER
An Imprint of HarperCollins*Publishers*

Through the Ever Night

Copyright © 2013 by Veronica Rossi

Library of Congress Cataloging-in-Publication Data is available.
ISBN 978-0-06-207206-1 (trade bdg.)
ISBN 978-0-06-224710-0 (int. ed.)

Typography by Torborg Davern
12 13 14 15 16   LP/RRDH   10 9 8 7 6 5 4 3 2 1
❖
First Edition

For Elisabeth and Flavio

PEREGRINE

A ria was here.

Perry followed her scent, moving swiftly through the night. He kept his stride even as he scanned the darkened woods, though his heart hammered in his chest. Roar had told him she was back on the outside, had even delivered a violet with a message as proof, but Perry wouldn't believe it until he saw her.

He reached a rise of boulders and dropped his bow, quiver, and satchel. Then he jumped up, leaping from rock to rock until he stood at the top. The sky was coated with a thick layer of clouds that glowed softly with Aether light. He scanned the rolling hills, his gaze stopping at a barren stretch of land. Scorched, silver in color, it was a scar left by the winter's storms. Much of his territory, two days to the west, looked the same.

Perry tensed as he spotted the tail of a campfire in the

distance. He inhaled and caught the smoky scent on a cool gust. That had to be her. She was close.

"Anything?" Reef called up. He stood some twenty feet below. Sweat glistened on his deep brown skin, running along the scar that reached from the base of his nose to above his ear, dividing his cheek, and he was breathing heavily. Just a few months ago they'd been strangers. Now Reef was the head of his guard, seldom leaving his side.

Perry climbed down, landing with a soggy crunch on a patch of melting snow. "She's due east. A mile. Maybe less."

Reef drew a sleeve across his face, pushing his braids away and wiping off sweat. Usually he kept up without any effort, but two days at a driving pace had brought out the decade between them. "You said she could help us find the Still Blue."

"She will help," Perry said. "I told you. She needs to find it, just as we do."

Reef strode up, coming to within a foot of Perry, and narrowed his eyes. "You did tell me that." He tipped his head and inhaled, the gesture bold and animal. He didn't downplay his Sense like Perry did. "But that's not why we've come after her," he said.

Perry couldn't read his own tempers, but he could imagine the scents Reef had taken in. Eagerness, green and sharp and alive. Desire, thick and musky. Impossible to miss. Reef was a Scire too. He knew exactly what Perry felt right now, moments away from seeing Aria. Scents never lied.

"It's one reason," Perry said tightly. He picked up his

things, shouldering them with an impatient tug. "Camp here with the others. I'll be back by sunup." He turned to go.

"Sunup, Perry? You think the Tides want to lose another Blood Lord?"

Perry froze and then faced him again. "I've been out here a hundred times on my own."

Reef nodded. "Sure. As a hunter." He took a water skin from his leather satchel, his movements casual and slow though he was still out of breath. "You're more than that now."

Perry stared into the woods. Twig and Gren were out there, listening and watching for danger. They'd been protecting him since he left his territory. Reef was right. Here in the borderlands, survival was the only rule. Without his guard, his life would be at risk. Perry let out a slow breath, his hope of spending a night alone with Aria vanishing.

Reef stoppered the cork on his water skin with a firm thump. "Well? What does my lord command?"

Perry shook his head at the formal address—Reef's way of reminding him of his responsibility. Like he could forget. "Your *lord* will take one hour alone," he said, and jogged away.

"Peregrine, hold on. You need to—"

"One hour," Perry called over his shoulder. Whatever Reef wanted, it could wait.

When he was sure he'd left Reef behind, Perry firmed his grip on his bow and broke into a run. Scents flashed past as he threaded through the trees. The rich, promising smell of wet earth. The smoke from Aria's campfire. And *her* scent. Violets, sweet and rare.

Perry relished the burn in his legs and the crisp air flowing through his lungs. Winter was a time for holding in place as the Aether storms wreaked havoc, and he hadn't been in the open like this for too long—not since he'd taken Aria to the Dweller Pod in search of her mother. He'd been telling himself she was back where she belonged, with her people, and he had his own tribe to take care of. Then, just days ago, Roar had showed up at the compound with Cinder and told him she was here on the outside. From that moment he could only think of being with her again.

Perry tore down a slope soft with new grass and recent rain, panning the woods. It was darker beneath the trees, the Aether light filtering softly through the canopy, but every branch and leaf stood in sharp contrast, thanks to his Night-Sighted eyes. With each step, the scent of Aria's campfire grew stronger. In a flash he remembered her game of sneaking up, silent as a shadow, and planting a kiss on his cheek. He couldn't keep the smile from coming to his lips.

Up ahead he spotted movement—a blur through the trees. Aria ran into view. Sleek. Silent. Intent as she searched the area. When she saw him, her eyes widened in surprise, but her stride didn't slow and neither did his. He shed his things, dropping them where they fell, and sprinted. Next thing he knew, she slammed into his chest, solid and fragrant in his arms.

Perry held her against him. "I missed you," he whispered

in her ear. He couldn't hold her close enough. "I should never have let you go. I missed you so much."

Words tumbled out of him. He said a dozen things he hadn't meant to say, until she drew back and smiled up at him. Then he couldn't speak at all. He took in the arch of her slender eyebrows, black like her hair, and the cleverness in her gray eyes. Fair and finely made, she was beautiful. Even more than he remembered.

"You're here," she said. "I wasn't sure if you'd come."

"I left as soon as—"

Before he could finish, her arms closed around his neck and they were kissing—a clumsy, hasty kiss. They were both breathing too hard. Smiling too much. Perry wanted to slow down and savor everything, but he couldn't find a scrap of patience. He wasn't sure if he started laughing first or if she did.

"I can do much better than that," he said, just as she said, "You're taller. I swear you've grown."

"Taller?" he said. "I hope not."

"You are," she said. She studied his face like she wanted to know everything about him. She nearly already did. During their time together, he'd told her things he'd never said to anyone. Aria's smile faded as her gaze stopped at the chain around his neck. "I heard what happened." She reached up, and the weight at his collarbone lifted. "You're a Blood Lord now." She spoke softly, more to herself than to him. "This is . . . It's stunning."

He peered down, watching her fingers run over the silver

links. "It's heavy," he said. This was the best moment he'd had since he'd taken the chain months ago.

Aria met his eyes, her temper cooling. "I'm sorry about Vale."

Perry looked across the shadowed woods and swallowed through the sudden tightness in his throat. The memory of his brother's death kept him awake nights. Sometimes, when he was alone, it kept him from breathing. Gently he took Aria's hand from the chain and slipped his fingers through hers.

"Later," he said. They had months of catching up to do. He wanted to talk to her about her mother. Had wanted to comfort her since he'd heard the news from Roar. But not now, when he'd just gotten her back. "Later . . . all right?"

She nodded, her eyes warm with understanding. "Later." She turned his hand to see the scars Cinder had given him. Pale and thick as trails of wax, they made a web from his knuckles to his wrist. "Does this still bother you?" she asked, tracing the scars with her fingers.

"No. It reminds me of you . . . of when you bandaged it." He lowered his head, bringing his cheek next to hers. "That was the first time you touched me without hating it." This close, her scent was everywhere, running through him, somehow stirring and mellowing him at the same time.

"Did Roar tell you where I'm going?" she asked.

"He did." Perry straightened and looked up. He couldn't see the currents of Aether, but he knew they were there, flowing above the clouds. Each winter, the Aether storms were growing stronger, bringing fire and ruin. Perry knew they would only get worse. His tribe's survival depended on finding a land rumored to be free of the Aether—the same thing Aria was searching for. "He told me you're looking for the Still Blue."

"You saw Bliss."

He nodded. They had gone to the Pod together in search of her mother and found it destroyed by Aether. Domes the size of hills had collapsed. Walls ten feet thick had been crushed like eggshells.

"It's only a matter of time before that happens to Reverie," she continued. "The Still Blue is our only chance. Everything I've heard points to the Horns. To Sable."

Perry's pulse quickened at the mention of the name. His sister, Liv, should have married the Horns' Blood Lord last spring, but she'd spooked and run away. Liv still hadn't appeared. He'd have to deal with Sable soon enough.

"The Horns' city is still locked in by ice," he said. "Rim won't be reachable until the pass to the north thaws. Could be a few weeks before then."

"I know," she said. "I thought it would have cleared by now. I'll go north as soon as it does."

She stepped away from him abruptly and scanned the woods, her head angling quick and sharp. He'd been there when she'd learned she was an Aud. Every sound had been a discovery. Now he watched as her attention shifted naturally to the noises of the night.

"Someone's coming," she said.

"Reef," Perry said. "He's one of my men." No way had it already been an hour. Not even close. "There are more nearby."

Perry caught the steep dive in her temper, a bracing, cool drift. In the next moment his heartbeat faltered. He hadn't felt tethered to another's emotions in months. Since he'd last been with her.

"When are you going back?" she asked.

"Soon. Morning."

"I understand." She looked from him to the chain, her expression growing distant. "The Tides need you."

Perry shook his head. She didn't understand. "I didn't come out here to see you for a night, Aria. Come back to the Tides with me. It's not safe out here, and—"

"I don't need help, Perry."

"That's not what I meant." He was too skitty to order his thoughts. Before he could say anything more, she took another step away, her hands hovering over the blades at her belt. Seconds later, Reef emerged from the woods, square shoulders hunched as he walked toward them. Perry cursed under his breath. He needed more time with her. Alone.

Reef's steps caught when he saw Aria alert and armed. Probably not what he'd expected from a Dweller. Perry noticed her wary expression too. With the scar across his face and his challenging stare, Reef looked like someone to avoid.

Perry cleared his throat. "Aria, this is Reef, head of my guard." It felt strange introducing two people who meant so much to him. Like they should already know each other.

Reef gave a tight nod, aimed at no one, and then shot Perry a hard look. "A word," he said sharply, before he stalked off.

Anger streaked through Perry at being spoken to that way, but he trusted Reef. He looked at Aria. "I'll be right back."

He hadn't gone far when Reef wheeled around, his braids swinging out. "I don't have to tell you what your temper's like right now, do I? It's the scent of *stupidity*. You've brought us out here chasing after a girl who's got you so—"

"She's an Aud," Perry interrupted. "She can hear you."

Reef jabbed a finger in the air. "I want *you* to hear me, Peregrine. You have a tribe to think about. You can't afford to lose your head over a girl—*especially* not a Dweller. Have you forgotten what happened? Because I promise you the tribe hasn't."

"The kidnappings weren't her fault. She had nothing to do with them. And she's only half Dweller."

"She's a *Mole*, Perry! One of *them*. That's all anyone's going to see."

"They'll do as I say."

"Or maybe they'll turn on you behind your back. How do you think they'll take to seeing you with her? Vale might have traded with the Dwellers, but he never brought one into his bed."

Perry shot forward, grabbing Reef by the vest. They stood, locked, inches apart. Reef's temper brought an icy burn to the back of Perry's tongue. "You've made your point." Perry let Reef go and stepped back, drawing a few breaths. Silence stretched out between them, too loud after their arguing.

He saw the problem with bringing Aria back to the Tides. The tribe would blame her for the missing children, regardless of her innocence, because she was a Dweller. He knew it wouldn't be easy—not at first—but he'd find a way to make it work. Whatever needed to be done next, he wanted her with him and it was his decision as Blood Lord.

Perry glanced to where Aria waited, then back at Reef. "You know what?"

"What?" Reef snapped.

"You're a terrible judge of time."

Reef smirked. He ran a hand over the back of his head and sighed. "So I am." When he spoke again, his voice had lost its bite. "Perry, I don't want to see you make this mistake." He nodded at the chain. "I know what that cost you. I don't want to watch you lose it."

"I know what I'm doing." Perry gripped the cool metal in his hand. "I've got this."

2

ARIA

Aria stared at the trees, listening to Perry's footsteps grow louder as he returned. She saw the gleam of the chain at his neck first and then his eyes, flashing in the darkness. They'd come together in such a rush before. Now, as he strode toward her, she took her first good look at him.

He was impressive. Much more than she remembered. He'd grown taller, as she'd first thought, and more muscular through the shoulders, settling into his lanky height. In the dim light she saw a dark coat and pants with fitted, clean lines, not the battered, patched-up clothes of the hunter she'd met in the fall. His blond hair was shorter, falling in layers that framed his face, so different from the long twisting waves she'd known before.

He was nineteen, but he seemed older than her friends in Reverie. How many of her friends had been through what he had? How many had hundreds of people to look after?

None. They came from totally different worlds. *Aether,* she thought. That was the only thing Dwellers and Outsiders had in common. It threatened them both.

Perry stopped a few feet away. Pale light fell on the strong planes of his face, and she noticed shadows under his eyes. He ran a hand over the fine scruff on his jaw. The brushing sound was so familiar, Aria could almost feel the gold bristles beneath her fingertips.

"Sorry about Reef."

"It's all right," she said, but it wasn't. Reef's words echoed in her mind. *Dweller,* he'd called her. *Mole.* Bitter insults. Words she hadn't heard in months. At Marron's, she'd fit in like she belonged.

Her gaze dropped to the ground between them. Three paces for her. Two for him. Moments ago they'd been pressed together. Now they stood apart like strangers. Like everything had just changed.

A mistake. Reef had said that, too. Was he right? "Maybe I should go."

"No—stay." Perry stepped forward and took her hand. "Forget what he said. He's got a temper. . . . Worse than mine."

She looked up at him. *"Worse?"*

His mouth lifted into the crooked smile she'd missed. "Almost worse." He shifted closer, his expression growing serious. "I didn't come here to see you for a night, or to offer to help you. I'm here because I want to be with you. It could be weeks before the pass to the north thaws. We'll wait until it does, then search for the Still Blue together." He paused, his gaze focused completely on her. "Come back with me, Aria. Be with me."

Something brilliant unfolded inside of her at the sound of those words. She memorized them as she would a song: every note, unhurried, spoken in his deep, warm timbre. Whatever happened, she'd keep those words. She wanted nothing more than to say yes, but she couldn't avoid the anxiety that swirled in her stomach.

"I want to," she said. "But it's not just the two of us anymore." He had his responsibility to the Tides, and she had her own pressures. Consul Hess, Reverie's Director of Security, had threatened Perry's nephew, Talon, if Aria didn't bring him the location of the Still Blue. It was the reason—one of the reasons—she'd come back to the outside.

Aria looked into Perry's eyes and couldn't bring herself to tell him about Hess's blackmail. There was nothing he could do. Telling him would only make him worry. "Reef said the tribe would turn on you," she said instead.

"Reef's wrong." Perry's gaze flicked to the woods in annoyance. "It may take them some time to adjust, but they will." He squeezed her hand, a smile lighting in his eyes. "Say yes. I know you want to. Roar will beat me if I show up without you, and there's another reason you should come. Maybe it'll help you decide."

He slid his hand up her arm and ran his thumb over her bicep. The feel of his archer's calluses, somehow both rough and soft, sent a thrill through her. She heard the trees rustle with a breeze, and then felt it brush cool against her cheeks. No one planted her as firmly in her skin as he did.

Perry was talking. She had to backtrack in her thoughts to catch up. "You need Markings. It's dangerous not to have them. Concealing a Sense is deceitful, Aria. People are killed for hiding them."

"Roar told me," she said. She'd been hiding out in the woods since leaving Marron's, so her lack of Markings hadn't been a problem yet. But once she went north, she'd come across other people. She couldn't deny that she'd be much safer with the Audile tattoos.

"Only a Blood Lord can warrant them," Perry said. "I happen to know one."

"You'd support me getting Markings? Even though I'm only half Outsider?"

He tipped his head to the side, blond waves falling across his eyes. "Yes. I very much want to."

"Perry, what about . . ." Aria trailed off, not sure she wanted to voice the question that had plagued her for months, but she had to know. Even if it meant hearing something that would crush her. "You told me you'd only be with another Scire, and I'm not . . ." She bit her lip and finished the sentence in the safety of her thoughts. *I'm not like you. I'm not what you said you wanted.*

Her face warmed as he watched her. No matter what she said or didn't say, he'd scent the depth of her insecurity.

He shifted closer, tracing the line of her jaw. "You changed the way I think about a lot of things. That's only one of them."

Suddenly she couldn't imagine leaving him. She had to find a way to make this work. The tribe would hate her for being a Dweller—she was sure of that. And if she and Perry arrived at the compound hand in hand, the Tides would lose all faith in his judgment. But what if she and Perry turned the focus onto something else? Onto something they both needed? An idea took shape in her mind.

"Did you tell the Tides anything about me?" she asked.

He frowned. The question seemed to catch him off balance. "I told a few people you'd help find the Still Blue."

"That's all?"

"I haven't talked about *us* with anyone, if that's what you mean." He shrugged. "It's private. . . . Between us."

"We should keep it that way. I'll go back with you as an ally, and we'll keep *us* out of it."

He laughed, the sound flat and humorless. "You're serious? You mean *lie*?"

"It wouldn't be lying. It's no different from what you just said: keeping it private. We could ease the tribe into it that way. We won't talk about us until we have a better idea of how they'll take it. Roar would keep quiet if we asked him. Would Reef?"

Perry nodded, his jaw clenched. "He's pledged to me. He'll do anything I ask of him."

The sound of a branch snapping pulled her attention to the darkened woods. Three distinct strides took form, one heavier than the others. The rest of Perry's guard was on the way. They spoke in quiet tones, yet each voice was unique to her ears, as singular as the features of a person's face. "The others are coming."

"Let them come," Perry said. "They're my men, Aria. I don't have to hide anything from them."

She wanted to believe him, but they had to be smart. As a new leader, he needed his tribe behind him. But she couldn't deny that being Marked would improve her chances of finding the Still Blue, to say nothing of the advantage Perry would provide on her journey to Rim. He was a hunter, a warrior. A survivor. More at ease in the borderlands than anyone she knew. All good reasons to go to the Tides for a few weeks before searching for the Still Blue. She and Perry would get everything they wanted if they just showed a little caution.

Perry's guards were closing in, their footsteps growing louder by the second. Aria stood on her toes, resting her hands on his chest. "This is the best way—the safest," she whispered. "Trust me."

She pressed her lips quickly to his, but it wasn't close to being enough. She took his face between her hands, feeling the soft scruff she'd missed, and kissed him again firmly, fiercely, before she backed away.

When Reef and two other men appeared, she and Perry stood several paces apart—the distance between strangers.

3

PEREGRINE

Two days later, Perry came through a stand of oaks and the Tide compound appeared, crowning the top of a slope with the thickly clouded sky at its back. Fields rolled out on either side of the dirt road, stretching to the hills that framed the valley.

Growing up, he'd imagined being Blood Lord plenty of times, but nothing compared with the feeling he had now. This was the first time he'd come home to *his* territory. Earth to sky and every person, tree, and rock in between belonged to him.

Aria appeared at his side. "Is that the compound?"

Perry shifted the bow and quiver on his back, covering his surprise. On their return, she'd paid him no more attention than she had Reef, who wouldn't look at her, or Gren and Twig, who couldn't stop staring. They'd slept across the fire from each other at night, and had hardly spoken during the days. When they had spoken, their exchanges had felt brief and cold. He hated pretending around her, but if it helped her feel comfortable coming back with him, he'd go along with it. For now.

"Right there," he said, nodding. Rain had threatened all day, and now a light drizzle began to fall. He wished the clouds would part to show the sun or the Aether—any light at all—but the sky had been overcast for days. "My father had it built in a circle—easier to defend. We have wooden walls that draw closed between the houses during raids. The highest structure . . . See the roof over there?" He pointed. "That's the cookhouse. The heart of the tribe."

Perry paused as Twig and Gren passed them. He'd sent Reef ahead that morning to make an announcement to the Tides, letting everyone know that Aria was under his protection as an ally. He wanted her arrival to go as smoothly as possible. With Twig and Gren pulling ahead, he let himself step closer to her and nodded toward the burnt stretch of land to the south.

"An Aether storm tore right through those woods in the winter. It took out part of our best farmland." A small shudder rolled through his shoulders as her temper hit him. Bright green, a scent like mint. She was alert and a little skitty with nerves. He'd forgotten what it felt like to be rendered to another person, to not only scent their tempers but feel them himself. Aria didn't know this bond existed between them. He hadn't told her in the fall, having thought then that he'd never see her again, but he'd do it soon, when he got her alone.

"The damage could've been worse, though," he continued. "We kept the fires from spreading, and the compound wasn't hit."

He watched her as she studied the horizon. The Tide Valley wasn't a large territory, but it was fertile, near the sea, and well positioned for defense. Could she see that? It was good land when the Aether left it alone. He didn't know how much longer that would be. Another year? Two, at the most, before it became nothing but scorched earth?

"It's much prettier than I imagined," she said.

He let out his breath, relieved. "Yeah?"

Aria looked at him, her eyes smiling. "Yeah." She turned away, and Perry wondered if they'd been standing too close. Couldn't they talk if they were pretending to be allies? Was a smile too much? Then he saw what she'd heard.

Willow charged toward them at full speed on the dirt path, Flea galloping at her side. The dog thundered up first, laying back his ears and baring his teeth at Aria.

"It's all right," Perry said. "He's friendly."

Aria stood her ground and rolled on the balls of her feet, ready to move quickly. "He doesn't look it," she said.

Roar had told him she'd become a skilled fighter in the past months. Perry saw the difference now. She looked stronger, quicker. More comfortable with fear.

Tearing his eyes away from her, he knelt. "Here, Flea. Give her some space." Flea inched forward and sniffed Aria's boots, his tail wagging slowly, before he pranced over. Perry scratched his wiry coat, a patchwork of brown and black fur. "He's Willow's dog. You'll never see them apart."

"Then I guess this is Willow," she said.

Perry straightened in time to see Willow blow past Gren and Twig with a hasty greeting; then she jumped into his arms the same way she'd done since she was three. At thirteen she was getting too big for that, but it made him laugh, so Willow kept doing it.

"You told me you'd only be a few days," she said as soon as Perry set her down. She was in her usual outfit—dusty pants, dusty boots, dusty shirt, and red strips of fabric braided through her dark hair, made from pieces of the skirt her mother had sewn for her over the winter but that she'd taken apart.

Perry smiled. "It was only a few days."

"Felt like forever," Willow said, and then she peered at Aria, her dark brown eyes suspicious.

When she'd first been cast out of Reverie, Aria had been hard to miss as a Dweller. She'd spoken in sharp, clipped sounds, her skin had been pale as milk, and her scent had been rancy and off. Those differences had faded away. She was noticeable for another reason now—the same reason Twig and Gren had stared at her for the past two days when she wasn't looking.

"Roar told me a Dweller was coming," Willow said finally. "He said I'd like you."

"I hope he's right," Aria said, petting Flea on the head. The dog now sat against her leg, panting happily.

Willow lifted her chin. "Well, Flea likes you, so maybe I will too." She looked up at Perry, frowning, and he scented her temper. Usually it was a bright citrus scent, but now a dark tinge blurred into the edges of his vision, telling him something wasn't right.

"What's happened, Will?" he asked.

"All I know is Bear and Wylan have been waiting for you, and they don't look happy. I thought you'd want to know." Willow's narrow shoulders lifted in a shrug; then she sped off, with Flea loping beside her.

Perry made for the compound, wondering what he'd find. Bear, a wall of a man with a gentle heart and hands permanently stained from working the earth, was lead on anything related to farming. Slight and surly, Wylan was the Tides' head fisherman. The two bickered constantly about where the Tides' resources belonged, in a never-ending battle between earth and sea. Perry hoped that it was nothing more.

Aria strode beside him with confidence as they passed through the main gates and stepped into the clearing at the center of the compound, but he scented the cool tone of her fear. He saw his home through her eyes then—a circle of cottages made of wood and stone and weathered by the salt air—and wondered again what she was thinking. It was nowhere as comfortable as Marron's, and there'd be no comparison at all to what she was used to in the Pods.

They'd arrived just before supper—unfortunate timing. Dozens of people milled around, waiting for the call to eat.

Others stood at their windows and crowded their doors, watching with wide eyes. One of Gray's boys pointed, while the other giggled at his side. Brooke rose from a bench in front of her house, looking from him to Aria and back. In a guilty flash, Perry remembered a conversation he'd had with her over the winter. He'd told Brooke they couldn't be together because he had too much on his mind. That *too much* had been Aria—the girl who, at that time, he thought he'd never see again.

Nearby, Bear and Wylan stood talking with Reef. They looked over, falling silent. Some instinct kept Perry moving toward his house. He'd deal with them soon enough. He didn't see the one person whose help he could use right now: Roar.

Perry stopped before his door and nudged aside a basket of kindling with his foot. He looked at Aria standing beside him and felt like he should say something. *Welcome? You'll be safe here?* Everything seemed too formal.

"It's small," he said finally.

He stepped inside, cringing as he saw blankets scattered across the floor and dirty mugs on the table. Clothes lay tossed in a pile in the corner, and a stack of books along the far wall had toppled over. The sea was half an hour away, but there was a dusting of sand on the floorboards beneath his feet. He supposed it could've looked worse for a house shared by half a dozen men.

"The Six sleep here," he explained. "I met them after you . . ." He couldn't say *left.* He didn't know why, but he couldn't say the word. "They're my guard now. Marked, all of them. You've met Reef, Twig, and Gren already. The rest are brothers: Hyde, Hayden, and Straggler. Seers, the three of them. Strag's name is actually Haven, but . . . you'll see. It suits him." He rubbed his chin, forcing himself to shut up.

"Do you have a candle or a lamp?" she asked.

Only then did he notice the dimness. To him, the room's lines were cut in sharp relief. To Aria—or anyone else—they'd be lost. He was always aware of being a Scire, but he forgot about his vision until times like this. He was a Seer, but the real power of his eyes was the keenness of his sight in darkness. Aria had once called it a mutation—an effect of the Aether that had warped his Sense more than others'. He thought of it more as a curse, a reminder of the Seer mother who'd died bringing him to life.

Perry opened the shutters, letting in the murky afternoon light. Outside, the clearing buzzed with gossip as news of Aria's arrival spread. Nothing he could do about it. He crossed his arms, his stomach clenching, as he watched her absorb the space. He couldn't believe she was there, in his house.

Aria came to the window beside him and studied Talon's collection of carved falcons, which rested on the sill. Perry knew he needed to see Bear and Wylan, but he couldn't move.

He cleared his throat. "Talon and I did those. His are the good ones. Mine is the one that looks like a turtle."

She picked it up and turned it in her hand. Her gray eyes

were warm as she looked up and said, "It's my favorite."

Perry's gaze moved to her lips. They were alone. This was as close as they'd stood since she'd last been in his arms.

She set the carving down and stepped away. "You're sure I can stay here?"

"Yes. You can have the room." From where he stood, he could see the edge of his brother's bed, covered with a faded red blanket. He'd rather she not stay in there, but saw no better choice. "I sleep up there," he said, tipping his head to the loft.

Aria dropped her satchel against the wall and glanced at the front door, smiling at a sound beyond the reach of his ears. A second later, Roar blew into the house in a dark flash.

"Finally!" he bellowed. He wrapped Aria into a hug, lifting her off the ground. "What took you two so long? Don't answer that." He glanced at Perry. "I think I know." He set her down and then clasped Perry's hand. "Good you're back, Per."

"What did I miss?" Perry asked, grinning.

Before Roar could answer, Wylan, Bear, and Reef arrived, crowding in as the house fell into a thick silence. They stood for a long moment, all eyes fixed on the only stranger among them. The tempers in the room sharpened, heating up and bleeding red into Perry's vision. They didn't want her there. He'd known they'd react this way, but his hands curled into fists anyway.

"This is Aria," he said, fighting the urge to step toward her. "She's half Dweller, as Reef's told you. She'll be helping us find the Still Blue, in exchange for shelter. While she's here, she'll be Marked as an Audile."

The words felt like gravel rolling from his mouth. They were true, but a partial truth, which felt more like a lie. Perry saw the questioning look in Roar's eyes.

Bear stepped forward, wringing his big hands. "Excuse my asking, Perry, but how's a Mole going to help us?"

Wylan muttered something under his breath. Aria's eyes snapped to him, and Roar tensed. Auds both, they'd heard him clearly.

Perry felt a flash of heat, and had the urge to cuff Wylan. He realized that what he felt—what gripped him—was Aria's temper. He drew a breath, grasping for control. "You have something to say, Wylan?"

"No," he answered. "Nothing to say. Just checking if her ears work." He smirked. "They do."

Reef dropped a hand on Wylan's shoulder with enough force that the smaller man winced. "Bear and Wylan were just telling me what happened while we were away," he said, changing the subject.

Perry prepared himself for their latest argument. "Let's hear it."

Bear crossed his arms over his broad chest, his thick eyebrows drawing together. "We had a fire in the storeroom last night. We think it was the boy who came back with Roar. Cinder."

Perry glanced at Roar and Aria, alarm running through him. They were the only ones who knew about Cinder's unique ability to channel the Aether. They protected Cinder's secret by unspoken agreement.

"No one saw him do it," Roar said, reading his mind. "He ran before anyone could catch him."

"He's gone?" Perry asked.

Roar rolled his eyes. "You know how he is. He'll come back. He always does."

Perry flexed his scarred hand. If he hadn't seen Cinder lay waste to a band of Croven with his own eyes, he wouldn't believe it himself. "The damage?"

Bear tipped his head toward the door. "Might be easier if I show you," he said, heading outside.

Perry paused at the threshold and looked back at Aria. She gave a small shrug of understanding. They'd been there less than ten minutes, and already he had to leave her. He hated it, but he had no choice.

The storeroom in the back of the cookhouse was a long stone room lined with wooden shelves, which were stacked with containers of grain, jars of spices and herbs, and baskets of early spring vegetables. Usually scents of food hung in the cool air, but as Perry stepped inside, the smell of burnt wood was thick. Beneath it he caught a trace of the sting of Aether—a smell that was also Cinder's.

The damage was contained to one side of the room. Part of a shelf was gone, burned to nothing.

"He must have dropped a lamp or something," Bear said, scratching his thick black beard. "We got to it quickly, but we still lost a lot. We had to throw out two bins of grain."

Perry nodded. It was food they couldn't afford to lose. The Tides were already on tight rations.

"The kid's stealing from you," Wylan said. "He's stealing from us. Next time I see him, I'll run him off the territory."

"No," Perry said. "Send him to me."

4

ARIA

"You all right?" Roar whispered as the house emptied.

Aria let out her breath and nodded, though she wasn't quite sure. Aside from him and Perry, everyone who'd stood in this room despised her because of who she was. Because of *what* she was.

A Dweller. A girl who lived in a domed city. A *Mole tramp*, as Wylan had whispered under his breath. She'd been preparing herself for that, especially after days of Reef's cold stares, but she felt shaken anyway. It would be the same if Perry entered Reverie, she realized. Worse. Reverie Guardians would kill an Outsider on sight.

She turned away from the door, her eyes drifting across the cozy, cluttered home. A table with painted chairs to one side. Bowls and pots in every color along the shelves behind it. Two leather chairs before the hearth, worn but comfortable-looking. Along the far wall she saw baskets with books and wooden toys. It was cool and quiet, and smelled faintly of smoke and old wood.

"This is his home, Roar."

"Yes. It is."

"I can't believe I'm here. It's warmer than I expected."

"It used to be more so."

A year ago, this house would've been packed with Perry's family. Now he was the only one left. Aria wondered if that was why the Six slept there. Surely there were other homes they could occupy. Maybe a full house helped keep Perry from missing his family. She doubted it. No one could ever fill the void her mother had left. People couldn't be replaced.

She pictured her own room in Reverie. A small space, spare and neat, with gray walls and an inset dresser. Her room had been home once. She felt no longing for it. Now it seemed as inviting as the inside of a steel box. What she missed was the way she'd felt there. Safe. Loved. Surrounded by people who accepted her. Who didn't whisper *Mole tramp* at her.

She had no place of her own now, she realized. No *things* like the falcon figurines on the windowsill. No objects to prove she existed. All her belongings were virtual, kept in the Realms. They weren't real. She didn't even have a mother anymore.

A feeling of weightlessness came over her. Like a balloon that had slipped free from its tether, she was floating, made of nothing more than air.

"You hungry?" Roar asked behind her, oblivious, his

tone light and cheerful as always. "We usually eat in the cookhouse, but I could bring something for us here."

She turned. Roar rested a hip against the table, his arms crossed. He wore black from head to toe, like she did.

He smiled. "Not as comfortable as Marron's, is it?"

They'd spent the past months there together while he'd healed from a leg wound. While she'd healed from deeper wounds. Little by little, one day after another, they'd brought each other back.

Roar's smile widened. "I know. You missed me."

She rolled her eyes. "It's barely been three weeks since I saw you."

"Miserable stretch of time," he said. "So, food?"

Aria glanced at the door. She couldn't hide if she wanted the Tides to accept her. She had to face them directly. She nodded. "Lead the way."

"Her skin's too smooth—like an eel."

The voice, dripping with malice, carried to Aria's ears.

The tribe had begun to gossip about her before she'd even taken a seat with Roar at one of the tables. She picked up the heavy spoon and stirred the bowl of stew in front of her, trying to focus on other things.

The cookhouse was a rough-hewn structure, part medieval hall, part hunting lodge. It was packed with long trestle tables and candles. Two massive fireplaces roared on either side. Children chased each other around the perimeter, their voices mixing with the gurgle of boiling water and the crackle of the fires. With the clanking of spoons and the slurps of people talking, eating, drinking. A belch. Laughter. The bark of a dog. All of it amplified by thick stone walls. Despite the racket, she couldn't help isolating the cruel whispering voices.

Two young women carried on a conversation the next table over. One was a pretty blonde with bright blue eyes. The same girl who'd been watching Aria as she'd entered Perry's house. That had to be Brooke. Her younger sister, Clara, was in Reverie, too. Vale had sold her off like Talon, in exchange for food for the Tides.

"I thought Dwellers died when they breathed outside air," Brooke whispered, her gaze on Aria.

"They do," said the other girl, "but I heard she's only half Mole."

"Someone actually bred with a Dweller?"

Aria's grip tightened around the spoon. They were slandering her mother, who was dead, and her father, who was a mystery. Then it hit her. The Tides would say the same things about her and Perry, if they knew the truth. They'd talk about them *breeding*.

"Perry said she's going to be Marked."

"A Mole with a Sense," Brooke said. "Unbelievable. What is she?"

"An Aud, I think."

"That means she can hear us."

Laughter.

Aria gritted her teeth at the sound. Roar, who'd been sitting quietly by her side, leaned toward her.

"Listen closely," he whispered into her ear. "This is the most important thing you need to know while you're here." She stared at the bowl of stew in front of her, her heart slamming into her ribs.

"Do *not* eat the haddock. They've been overcooking it terribly."

She jabbed her elbow into his ribs. *"Roar."*

"I'm serious. It's as tough as leather." Roar looked across the table. "Isn't it true, Old Will?" he said to a grizzled man with a shockingly white beard.

Though Aria had been on the outside for months, she still marveled at wrinkles and scars and signs of age. She'd thought them disgusting once. Now the man's leathery face almost made her smile. Bodies on the outside wore experiences like souvenirs.

Willow, the girl Aria had met earlier, sat beside him. Aria felt a weight settle on her boot and looked down to see Flea.

"Grandpa, Roar asked you something," Willow said.

The older man cocked his ear toward Roar. "What was that, pretty?"

Roar raised his voice in answer. "I was telling *Aria* here not to eat the *haddock*."

Old Will studied her, his lips pursed in a sour expression.

Aria's cheeks warmed as she waited for his reaction. It was one thing to hear whispers, but another to be shunned to her face.

"I'm seventy," he said finally. "Seventy years old and going strong."

"Old Will isn't an Aud," Roar whispered.

"I got that, thanks. Did he just call you pretty?"

Roar nodded, chewing. "Can you blame him?"

Her eyes moved over his even features. "No. I really can't," she said, though *pretty* didn't quite fit Roar's dark looks.

"So you're getting Markings," he said. "How about I vouch for you?"

"I thought Perry—Peregrine was going to?" Aria said.

"Perry will warrant them, and he'll preside over the ceremony, but that's only one part of it. The part only a Blood Lord can do."

The stout woman on Roar's opposite side leaned forward. "Someone with your same Sense needs to take an oath swearing that your hearing is true. If you're an Aud, only another Aud can do that."

Aria smiled, noting the emphasis the woman placed on the word *if*. "I am an Aud, so that'll be the case."

The woman studied her with eyes the color of honey. She seemed to decide something, because the grim set of her mouth softened. "I'm Molly."

"Molly is our healer, and Bear's wife," Roar said. "Much fiercer than the big man, though, aren't you, Molly?" He turned back to Aria. "So it should be me doing the vouching, don't you think? I'm perfect for it. I've taught you everything."

Aria shook her head, trying not to smile. Truly, Roar was the perfect choice. He *had* taught her all she knew about sounds—and knives. "Everything except modesty."

He made a face. "Who needs that?"

"Oh, I don't know. Maybe you do, pretty."

"Nonsense," he said, and tucked back into his food.

Aria forced herself to do the same. The stew was a tasty mix of barley and whitefish, but she couldn't eat more than a few bites. Not only was the tribe whispering about her, but she felt them gawking, watching every move she made.

She set her spoon down and reached beneath the table, petting Flea on the head. He blinked at her, shifting closer. He had an intelligent expression absent from dogs in the Realms. She hadn't realized animals had such distinct personalities. It was just another one of the endless differences between her old life and her new one. She wondered if the Tides would change their minds about her, as Flea had.

Aria looked up as the chatter in the hall quieted. Perry came through the door with three young men. Blond and tall, two resembled Perry in their muscular build. Hyde and Hayden, she guessed. The third, a few steps behind them and a head shorter, could only be Straggler. They all carried themselves like Seers: bows across their backs, their posture tall, and their eyes scanning.

Perry spotted her immediately. He tipped his head—a safe

acknowledgment between allies, but it left her holding her breath, wanting more. Then he took a table by the door with the brothers, disappearing into a sea of heads. Moments later, the cruel voices drifted back to her ears.

"She doesn't look real. I bet she wouldn't even bleed if you cut her."

"Let's try it. Just a little nick to see if it's true."

Aria followed the voice. Brooke's blue eyes bored into her. Aria placed her hand on Roar's wrist, grateful for his unique ability. He could hear thoughts through touch. She'd barely been fazed when she discovered that about him. It didn't feel much different from the Smarteye she'd worn her entire life, which worked by a similar process—by hearing thought patterns through physical contact.

That's Perry's girl, she thought to him. *Isn't it?*

Roar stilled, his spoon halfway to his mouth. "No . . . I'm pretty sure that would be *you.*"

She's evil. I might want to hurt her.

Roar grinned. "That I want to see."

"Look at her." It was Brooke's voice again. "She's moving in on Roar. I know you can hear me, Mole. You're wasting your time on him. He's Liv's."

Aria snatched her hand away from his wrist. Roar sighed, his eyes sliding over to her. He set his spoon down and pushed his bowl away. "Come on. Let's get out of here. I want to show you something."

She pulled her legs from beneath the table and followed him, keeping her focus on Roar's back. As she passed Perry, she slowed, allowing herself a glance. He was listening to Reef, across from him, but his eyes flicked up, meeting hers.

She wished she could tell him how much she missed him. How much she wanted to be the one sitting with him. Then she realized that through her temper, she had.

Roar led her along a trail that wove through sand dunes. Aether light filtered through the clouds, casting a glow over the path and the tall, rustling grass. As they walked, a rushing sound mixed with the low whistle of the wind. It moved through her—hiss and whisper and roar—growing louder and clearer with every step she took.

Aria stopped as they came over the last dune. The ocean stretched out before her, alive, spreading to the end of everything. She heard a million waves, each one distinct, ferocious, but together a chorus that was serene and grander than anything she'd ever known. She'd seen the ocean plenty of times in the Realms, but it hadn't prepared her for the real thing.

"If beauty had a sound, this would be it."

"I knew it would help," Roar said, his smile a white flash in the darkness. "Auds say the sea holds every sound that's ever been heard. All you have to do is listen."

"I didn't know that." She closed her eyes, letting the sound wash over her, and listened for her mother's voice. Where were Lumina's calm assurances that patience and logic would solve any problem? She didn't hear them, but she believed they were there. Aria glanced at Roar, pushing away the grief. "See? You haven't taught me everything."

"True," Roar said. "I can't run the risk of boring you."

They walked closer to the water together. Then Roar sat, leaning back on his elbows. "So what's with the act?"

Aria sat next to him. "It's for the best," she said, digging her fingers into the sand. The top layer still held the day's warmth, but beneath it was cool and damp. She drizzled it over Roar's knee. "You heard how they hate me. Imagine if they knew Perry and I were together." She shook her head. "I don't know."

"What don't you know?" Roar smiled like he was about to tease her. The moment felt utterly familiar, though they'd never been here before. How many times had they talked about Perry and Liv over the winter?

Aria poured another handful of sand on his knee, listening to the delicate drizzle beneath the crash of the surf. "It was my idea. It's the safest way, but it's strange pretending to be something different. It's like there's a glass wall between us. Like I can't touch him or . . . reach him. I don't like the way it feels."

Roar wiggled his knee, upsetting her sand pile. "Does his voice still sound like smoke and fire?"

Aria rolled her eyes. "I don't know why I told you that."

He tipped his head to the side in a gesture that was pure Perry, putting a hand over his heart, which wasn't. "Aria, your scent . . . it's like a blooming flower." He modulated his voice perfectly to sound like Perry's deep drawl. "Come here, my sweet rose."

Aria jabbed him in the shoulder, which only made him

laugh. "It's *violet*. And you're going to pay when I meet Liv."

Roar's smile vanished. He ran a hand over his dark hair and sat up, growing quiet as he stared at the breaking waves.

"Still no word?" she asked quietly. When Perry's sister had disappeared last spring, she'd left Roar heartbroken.

He shook his head. "No word."

Aria sat up, brushing off her hands. "There will be soon. She'll turn up." She wished she hadn't mentioned Liv. Roar had to feel her absence more than ever here, where they'd both grown up.

She looked across the ocean. Deep in the distance, clouds pulsed with glaring light. Aether funnels were striking. Aria couldn't imagine being out there. Perry had told her once that rogue storms were always a danger at sea. She didn't know how the Tides' fishermen found the courage to go out every day.

"You know, glass is pretty easy to break, Aria." Roar was watching her, his gaze thoughtful.

"You're right." How could she complain? She had it so much easier than he did. At least she and Perry were in the same place. "You've convinced me. I'm going to break the glass, Roar. Next chance I get."

"Good. *Shatter* it."

"I will. And you will too, when we find Liv." She waited for him to agree—wanted him to—but Roar changed the subject.

"Does Hess know you've come here?"

"No," she said. She slipped the Smarteye from a small pocket in the lining of her leather satchel. "But I need to contact him." She should've done it yesterday, their planned meeting day, but she hadn't found a chance on her journey to the Tides. "I'll do it now."

The smooth patch, clear as a water droplet and nearly as supple, struck her as something from another world after all the sun-bleached and wind-frayed edges of the compound. It *was* from another world—hers. She'd worn the device all her life without so much as a thought. All Dwellers did. It was how they moved through the Realms. She'd only recently begun to dread it. She had Consul Hess to thank for that.

Aria brought the Smarteye up, laying it over her left eye. The device suctioned to the skin around her eye socket, the pressure firm and familiar, and then the biotech plastic at the center softened, turning to liquid. She blinked a few times, adjusting to seeing through the clear interface. Red letters appeared, floating against the ocean, as the Eye powered on.

WELCOME TO THE REALMS! BETTER THAN REAL!

They faded out, and then AUTHENTICATING appeared.

She turned her head, watching the letters track with her movement.

ACCEPTED flickered up, and a familiar prickling sensation spread across her scalp and down her spine. Only one generic icon, labeled HESS, hovered against the darkness. When she'd had her own Smarteye, the screen had been filled with icons for her favorite Realms, news crawls, and messages from her friends. But Hess had programmed this Eye to only reach him.

"Are you in?" Roar asked.

"I'm in."

He lay down, resting his head on his arm. "Wake me up when you're back." To him, she'd appear to be sitting quietly on the beach. He'd have no window into the Realms the Smarteye opened to her.

"I'm still here, you know."

Roar closed his eyes. "No, you're not. Not really."

With a deliberate thought, she selected the icon, letting Hess know she was there. Moments later she fractioned, her consciousness splitting, dividing. The feeling was jarring but painless—like waking up suddenly in a strange place. In an instant she existed in two places at once: on the beach with Roar, and in the virtual construct of the Realm Hess had brought her to. She shifted her focus to the Realm and went still, momentarily dazzled by the brightness. Then she looked around, adjusting to a world turned pink.

Cherry trees spread around her in every direction. Blossoms loaded down their branches and coated the ground like a pink dusting of snow. An aimless, everywhere rustle reached her ears, and then a shower of petals drifted down in a rosy blizzard.

She found it breathtaking until she noticed the symmetry of the branches and the perfect spacing of the trees. She realized she hadn't heard the petals fall, or the creak of branches. The breeze held an empty, one-note sound. Far too aggressive for what she knew was right. *Better than Real,* they said of the Realms. She'd thought so too, once. For years she'd cruised spaces like this from within the safety of Reverie's walls, not knowing any better. Not knowing that *nothing* was better than real.

Or worse, she thought, suddenly remembering Paisley. Her best friend had only seen the terrible parts of the real world. Fire. Pain. Violence. Aria still couldn't believe she was gone. Almost all of her memories of Paisley included Paisley's older brother, too. It had always been the three of them.

How was Caleb doing in Reverie? Was he still cruising to the art Realms? Had he moved on? She swallowed against the tight feeling in her throat, missing him. Missing her other friends, Rune and Pixie, and how light life used to be. Underwater concerts and parties in the clouds. Ridiculous Realms like Dinosaur Laser Tag and Cloud Surfing and Date a Greek God. Her life had changed so much. Now, when she slept, she kept her knives within reach.

Aria looked up, and her breath caught. Through the pink branches she saw a light blue sky with no veins of Aether, no coating of glowing clouds. That had been the sky three hundred years ago, before the Unity. Before a massive solar flare had corrupted the Earth's magnetosphere, opening the door to cosmic storms. To an alien atmosphere that was unimaginably devastating. Aether. This blue sky was what she pictured over the Still Blue—bright and open and calm.

She lowered her gaze and found Consul Hess sitting at a table twenty paces away. Small, with a marble top and two iron chairs, the table belonged in a bistro in a European square. Whatever Realm Hess chose, that detail never changed.

Aria looked down at herself. A kimono had replaced her

black pants, shirt, and boots. This garment was made of thick cream brocade, patterned with red and pink flowers. It was beautiful, and far too tight.

"Is this necessary?" she asked, as always.

Hess watched in silence as she walked over. He had a severe face, chiseled, with wide-set eyes and a thin mouth that gave him a lizard-like appearance. "It befits the Realm," he said, his gaze traveling up and down her body. "And I find your Outsider clothing unsavory."

Aria sat across from him, shifting uncomfortably in the chair. She could barely cross her legs in the dress, and what was the waxy coating on her lips? She touched her finger and came away with scarlet lipstick. *Really.* This was too much.

"*Your* clothes don't *befit* the Realm," she said. Hess was in Dweller grays, as usual—clothes similar to those she'd worn in Reverie all her life, the only difference being that his grays had blue stripes along the collar and sleeves to show his position as Consul. "Neither does this table or the coffee."

Hess ignored her and poured coffee into two delicate cups as pink petals sprinkled the table. Aria studied the gurgling sound, which was clear and sharp but oddly shapeless. The fragrant, rich scent set her mouth watering. Everything was the way it'd been for the past months. A fanciful Realm. This table and chairs. Strong, dark coffee. Except Hess's hands were trembling.

He took a sip. When he set the cup down, it struck with a clack. He raised his eyes to hers. "I'm disappointed, Aria.

You're late. I thought I had impressed the urgency of your task upon you. Now I wonder if you need to be reminded of what's at stake if you fail."

"I know what's at stake," she said tightly. *Talon. Reverie. Everything.*

"And yet you've taken a little detour. Do you think I can't tell where you are? You've gone to see the boy's uncle, haven't you? Peregrine?"

Hess was tracking her movements through the Smarteye. It didn't surprise Aria, but she felt her pulse pick up anyway. She didn't want him to know anything about Perry. "I can't go north yet, Hess. The pass to the Horns is frozen."

He leaned forward. "I could have you there *tomorrow* on a Hover."

"They *hate* us," she said. "They haven't forgotten the Unity. I can't go charging in as a Dweller."

"They're Savages," he said, waving a hand dismissively. "I don't care what they think."

Aria became aware of how quickly she was breathing. Roar sat up. He watched her intently in the real, sensing her tension. *Savages.* She'd once thought of them that way too. Now Roar's presence anchored and calmed her.

"You have to let me do this my way," she said to Hess.

"I don't like your way. You're late reporting in. You're wasting time with some Outsider. I want that information, Aria. Get me coordinates. A direction. A map. Anything."

As he spoke, she noticed the shiftiness in his small eyes and the red flush creeping up his collar. In all their meetings over the winter, he'd never been this nervous and combative. Something had him worried.

"I want to see Talon," she said.

"Not until you get me what I need."

"No," she said. "I need to see him—"

Everything stopped. The cherry blossoms froze, suspending in midair around her. The sound of the wind vanished, and a sudden dead silence fell over the Realm. After an instant, the petals rose up in reverse, then seemed to catch and flitter down again, normally, floating to the ground as sounds returned.

Aria saw the shocked look on Hess's face. "What was that?" she asked. "What just happened?"

"Come back in three days," he snapped. "Don't be late, and you'd better be on your way north by then." He fractioned out, disappearing.

"Hess!" she yelled.

"Aria, what's wrong?"

Roar's voice. She shifted her focus. His eyebrows were drawn with concern.

"I'm all right," she said, quickly running through the commands in her mind to take off the Eye. Aria gripped it in her hand, rage blurring her vision.

Roar moved closer. "What happened?" he asked.

She shook her head. She wasn't entirely sure herself. Something had gone wrong. She'd never seen a Realm freeze before. Had Hess done that on purpose to scare her? But he'd been nervous too. What was he hiding? Why the sudden urgency that she go to the Horns?

"Aria," Roar prompted. "Talk to me."

"Hess knows I'm here. And he wants me to head north right away," she said, choosing her words carefully, making no mention of Talon. "He doesn't care that the pass is frozen."

"He's a bastard, Hess." Roar's gaze moved beyond her, up the beach. "But I've got good news for you. Here comes your chance to break the glass."

5

PEREGRINE

Perry walked down the beach toward Aria, aware of his every step. They'd only have a few minutes together at best, and he couldn't reach her fast enough.

He met Roar halfway. "Keep an ear out?" Perry asked.

"Of course," Roar said, cuffing him on the shoulder as he walked past.

Aria stood as he reached her. She pulled her dark hair over one shoulder. "Are you sure this is all right?" she asked, looking past him.

"For a little while," he said. "Roar's listening. Reef's farther in on the trail." It felt wrong to have men guarding him from his own tribe, but he was desperate to be alone with her.

"Did you find Cinder?"

He shook his head. "Not yet. I will, though." He wanted to reach for her, but he scented her temper. She was nervous about something. He had an idea what that was. "Twig—he's an Aud—he told me what happened in the cookhouse. What people were saying."

"It's nothing, Perry. Only gossip."

"Give them a week," he said. "It'll get easier."

She looked away and didn't answer.

Perry ran a hand over his jaw, not sure why it felt like they were still pretending around each other. "Aria, what's going on?" he asked.

She crossed her arms, and her temper cooled and cooled, turning to ice. Perry fought against the weight of it settling over him.

"Hess knows I'm here," she said at last. "He's making me leave. I need to go in a few days."

He remembered the name. Hess was the Dweller who'd thrown her out of the Pod. "Does he know it's not safe to go north yet?"

"Yes," she said. "He doesn't care."

Her fear gripped him suddenly. "Did he threaten you?" Perry asked, his mind churning.

Aria shook her head, and it hit him.

"He has Talon. He's using Talon, isn't he?"

She nodded. "I'm sorry. This is one time I really wish I could lie to you. I didn't want to burden you."

Perry fisted his hands, squeezing them until his knuckles ached. Vale had planned the kidnapping, but he still felt responsible. That wouldn't go away until Talon was home safe. His gaze moved up the beach.

47

"This is where he was taken," he said. "Right here. I watched the Dwellers kick him in the stomach and then drag him into a Hovercraft at the top of that dune."

Aria stepped toward him and took his hands. Her fingers were cool and soft, but her grip was firm. "Hess won't hurt him," she said. "He wants the Still Blue. He'll give us Talon in exchange."

Perry couldn't believe he had to *buy* his nephew. It was little different from what he would have to do to get Liv home, he realized. Vale had traded them both for food. Everything pointed to Perry going to the Horns. He needed the Still Blue—for his tribe, and for Talon. And he had to settle a debt with Sable for Liv not showing. Maybe then his sister would finally come home.

"It's sooner than I thought," he said, "but I'm going with you. We'll leave in a few days and hope the pass is clear by then."

"And if it's not?"

He shrugged. "We'd battle against the ice. It would probably take us twice as long, but we could do it. I could get us there."

Aria smiled at what he'd said. He didn't know why, but it didn't matter. She was smiling.

"All right," she said. She wove her arms around him, turning her head to his chest. Perry brushed her hair away from her shoulder and breathed her in, letting the strength of her temper bring him back. One breath at a time, his anger faded into desire.

He traced the line of her spine with his thumb. Everything about her was graceful and strong. She drew back and met his eyes.

"This . . ." He was going to tell her that this was how they should've come together, days ago in the woods. This was what he'd thought about all winter—what he'd missed. But he couldn't get past the way she felt, or the way she was looking at him.

"Yes," she said. *"This."*

Perry bent and kissed her lips. She curved against him, her sigh a warm drift against his cheek, and then nothing existed beyond her mouth and her skin and the feel of her body against his. They didn't have long. People nearby. He could barely hold the thoughts in his mind. She was everything, and he wanted more.

At Roar's warning whistle, he froze, his lips on her neck. "Tell me you didn't hear that."

"I heard it."

Again he heard Roar's signal, louder this time, insistent. Perry winced and straightened, taking her hands. Her scent was wrapped around him. The last thing he wanted was to leave her.

"We'll get your Markings done before we go. And about hiding things between us . . . let's drop it. It's killing me not being able to touch you."

Aria smiled up at him. "We're leaving soon. Can we keep it up just until then?"

"You like seeing me suffer?"

She laughed softly. "The wait will be worth it, I promise. Now *go*."

He kissed her once more, then tore himself away and ran up the beach, weightless over the sand.

Roar watched him from the top of the beach with a grin. "That was beautiful, Per. It was killing me, too."

Perry laughed, smacking him on the head as he jogged by. "Not everything's meant for your ears."

He found Reef up the trail, stalling Bear and Wylan, who'd come in search of him. As they walked back to the compound, Bear spoke of the trouble he was having with a pair of farmers, Gray and Rowan. Wylan chimed in with petty complaints every dozen paces, his voice sharp and angry, as always. No matter what Perry did or said, it was never good enough for Wylan, who'd been one of Vale's most devoted followers.

Perry listened with half a mind, doing all he could to keep himself from smiling.

An hour later, he sat on the roof of his house, alone for the first time in days. He dropped his arms over his knees and closed his eyes, relishing the cool mist on his skin. When the breeze died down and he breathed in deeply, he scented traces of Aria. She was in Vale's room now, inside the house. Laughter drifted through the crack in the roof beside him. The Six were playing a game of dice. He could hear Twig and Gren's usual banter. Auds both, they talked constantly, always arguing, competing over everything.

Lamps flickered around the compound and smoke drifted from chimneys, mingling with the salt air. This late in the night, only a few people were still about. Perry lay back, watching the Aether light sift down through the thinner patches in the clouds and listening to the volley of their voices across the clearing.

"How's the baby's fever?" Molly asked someone.

"Dropping, thank the sky," came the answer. "He's sleeping now."

"Good, let him rest. I'll bring him down to the sea in the morning. It'll open up his lungs."

Perry inhaled, letting the ocean air open his own lungs. He'd grown up under the care of many, much like the baby they spoke of. As a child, he'd crawled up into the nearest lap to sleep. When he'd had fever or a cut that needed stitches, Molly had nursed him back to health. The Tides were a small tribe, but they were also a big family.

Perry wondered where Cinder was but knew he'd come back on his own, just as Roar had said. When Perry saw him, he'd lay into Cinder for running off, and then he'd find out what happened in the cookhouse.

"Perry!"

He sat up in time to catch a wadded blanket, tossed from below.

"Thanks, Molly."

"Don't know why you're up there, and they're all warm in your house," she said, and bustled away.

But Molly did know. There were few secrets in a tribe

this small. Everyone knew about his nightmares. Up here, at least, he could pass the sleepless time by reading scents on the breeze and watching the play of light through the clouds. Such a strange spring, with a thick blanket of clouds always above. Much as he feared the Aether, part of him would have felt better if he could see it now.

Brooke fell in step with him as he left the compound at dawn, her bow and quiver over her shoulder. "Where you heading?"

"Same place you are," he said. She was a Seer, and one of the best archers in the tribe, so Perry had given her the task of teaching everyone in the Tides how to shoot a bow. Her lessons were near the same field where he was meeting Bear.

Their walk was awkward and quiet. He noticed she still wore one of his arrowheads on a strip of leather around her neck, and he tried not to think of the day he gave it to her, or what it had meant to both of them. He cared about her, and that would never change. But it was over between them. He'd told her so over the winter, as gently as he could, and hoped soon she'd see it too.

As they reached the eastern field, he found an argument already nearing a boil: two farmers, Rowan and Gray, who wanted more help in the fields than Perry could give them. Bear stood between them, massive, yet gentle as a kitten.

"Look at this," said Rowan, the young farmer whose child had had fever the night before. He lifted a boot sopping with mud. "I need a retaining wall. Something to stop the debris from coming down the hill. And I need more drainage."

Perry's gaze moved to the hillside half a mile away. Aether storms had wiped the lower portion to nothing more than ash. When the spring rains started, waves of mud and debris flowed down the slope. The whole shape of the hill was changing without the trees there to hold the earth fast.

"This is nothing," Gray said. He stood a full head shorter than Perry and Bear. "Half my land's underwater. I need people. I need use of the ox. And I need them both more than he does."

Gray had a kind face and a mild manner, but Perry often scented wrath from him. Gray didn't have a Sense—he was Unmarked, like most people—but he despised that. As a young man, he'd wanted to be a sentry or a guard, but those posts went to Auds and Seers, whose Senses gave them a clear advantage. His choices limited, Gray had been left to farming.

Perry had heard all this from Gray and Rowan before, but he needed the resources they wanted—manpower, horses, oxen—for more important tasks. Perry had ordered defense trenches constructed around the compound and a second well plumbed by the cookhouse. He was having the walls fortified and their cache of weapons bolstered. And he'd ordered every Tider—from six to sixty years old—to learn at least the basic use of both a bow and a knife.

At nineteen, Perry was young for a Blood Lord. He knew he'd be seen as inexperienced. An easy mark. He was sure the Tides would be raided in the spring by roving bands and tribes who'd lost their homes to the Aether.

As Gray's and Rowan's pleas continued, Perry arched his back, feeling his poor night of sleep. Had he become Blood Lord for this? To trudge through sopping fields so he could listen to bickering? Nearby, Brooke gave Gray's boys, seven and nine years old, their archery lesson. Far more entertaining than listening to squabbling.

He had never wanted this part of being Blood Lord. He'd never thought about how to feed nearly four hundred people when the winter stores were gone, before the spring yield arrived. He'd never imagined warranting the marriage of a couple older than he was. Or having the eyes of a mother with a feverish child on him, searching for the answer. When Molly's cures failed, they turned to him. They always turned to him when things went wrong.

Bear's voice snapped him out of his thoughts. "What do you say, Perry?"

"You both need help. I know that. But you're going to have to wait."

"I'm a farmer, Perry. I need to do what I know," said Rowan. He waved a hand toward Brooke. "I got no business shooting a bow when I have this to deal with."

"Learn it anyway," Perry said. "It could save your life, and more."

"Vale never had us do that, and we were fine."

Perry shook his head. He couldn't believe his ears. "Things are different now, Rowan."

Gray stepped forward. "We'll starve next winter if we don't seed soon."

The tone in his voice—sure and demanding—streaked Perry. "We may not be here next winter."

Rowan balked, his eyebrows drawing together. "Where will we be?" he said, his voice rising in pitch. He and Gray exchanged a look.

"You're not really serious about moving us to the Still Blue?" said Gray.

"We may not have a choice," Perry said. He remembered his brother ordering these same men, with no arguments. No convincing. When Vale had spoken, they had obeyed.

Brooke walked over, brushing sweat from her brow. "Perry, what's wrong?" she asked.

He realized he'd been pinching the bridge of his nose. A burning sensation spiked deep in his sinuses. He looked up, a curse slipping through his lips.

The clouds had broken apart at last. High above, he saw the Aether. It didn't run in lazy, glowing currents, as was normal for this time of year. Instead, thick rivers flowed above him, glaring and bright. In some places the Aether coiled like snakes, forming funnels, which would strike at the earth and unleash fire.

"That's a winter sky," Rowan said, his voice filled with confusion.

"Dad, what's going on?" asked one of Gray's sons.

Perry knew exactly what was going on. He couldn't deny what he saw—or the burn in the back of his nose.

"Get home now!" he told them, then sprinted to the compound. Where would the storm hit? West, over the sea? Or directly on them? He heard the blast of a signal horn, and then others farther away, alerting farmers to take shelter. He had to reach the fishermen, who'd be harder to alert and bring in safely.

He shot through the main gate of the compound, into the clearing. People rushed to their homes, shouting at one another in panic. He scanned their faces.

Roar ran up. "What do you need?"

"Find Aria."

6

ARIA

The rain began suddenly, carrying on a gust that hit Aria like a cold slap. She sprinted back to the compound on the trail she'd been wandering all morning, lost in thoughts of Realms that suddenly glitched and froze. Her knives drummed a reassuring rhythm against her thighs as she followed the path through the woods, the wind whipping around her.

At the sound of a horn, she skidded to a halt and looked up. Through the gaps in the rain clouds she saw thick flows of Aether. Seconds later she heard the distinctive shriek of a funnel—a ripping, high-pitched peal that sent ice through her veins. A storm *now*? The storms should've already ended for the year.

She ran again, picking up her pace. Months ago, she'd been right under a storm with Perry. She'd never forget the burn across her skin when the funnels struck close, or how her body had seized.

"River!" called a far-off voice. "Where are you?"

She froze and listened for sounds through the hissing rain. More voices. Everyone yelling the same thing, their shouts of distress sharp to her ears. She squeezed her numb hands into fists. Who was she to help? The Tides hated her. But then another voice called out—closer this time—the sound so desperate and fearful that she moved without thinking. She knew how it felt to search for someone who was gone. They might not accept her help, but she had to try.

She jogged off the trail onto thick, slippery mud, sounds guiding her to a dozen people scanning the woods. Her knees locked when she recognized Brooke.

"What are *you* doing here, Mole?" Soaked, Brooke looked crueler than usual. Her blond hair lay dark and slick against her skull, her eyes cold as marbles. "You took him, didn't you, child snatcher?"

Aria shook her head. "No! Why would I do that?" Her eyes moved to the weapon over Brooke's shoulder.

Molly, the older woman Aria had met in the cookhouse, rushed over. "You're wasting time, Brooke. Keep looking!" She waited until Brooke moved on. Then she took Aria by the arm and spoke low and close, as rain rolled down her full cheeks. "We didn't see this coming. None of us expected a storm."

"Who's missing?" Aria asked.

"My grandson. He's barely two years old. His name is River."

Aria nodded. "I'll find him."

The others were working away from the trail, heading deeper into the woods, but Aria's gut told her to search nearby. Moving slowly, she kept close to the path. She didn't call out. Instead she strained to hear the slightest sounds through the wind and the rain. Time passed with nothing but the slosh of her footsteps and the rush of water pouring downhill. The shrieks of the Aether grew louder, and her head began to pound, the noise of the storm overwhelming her ears. A humming sound stopped her in her tracks.

She moved toward it, slipping as she crept down the slope. Aria crouched before a leafy shrub. Slowly she pushed the branches aside and saw nothing but leaves. The skin on the back of her neck prickled. Whirling, she drew her knives. She found herself alone with the swaying trees.

"Relax," she muttered to herself, sheathing her blades.

She heard the humming again, faint but unmistakable. She rounded the shrub and peered inside.

A pair of eyes blinked at her less than a foot away. The boy looked so small, sitting on his knees. He had his hands pressed over his ears, and he hummed a melody, lost in his own world. She noticed he had his grandmother's round cheeks and honey-colored eyes. She looked over her shoulder. From where she knelt, Aria could see the trail back to the compound, no more than twenty paces off. He wasn't lost—he was terrified.

"Hi, River," she said, smiling. "I'm Aria. I bet you're an Aud, like me. Singing helps keep out the sound of the Aether, doesn't it?"

He stared right at her and kept humming.

"That's a good song. It's the Hunter's Song, right?" she asked, though she'd recognized it immediately as Perry's favorite. He'd sung it to her once in the fall, after much convincing, his face red with embarrassment.

River went silent. His lower lip wobbled like he was about to cry.

"My ears hurt too when it's this loud." Aria remembered her Aud cap and reached into her satchel. "Do you want to wear this?"

River's hands curled into pudgy fists. He slowly drew them away from his ears and nodded. She pulled the cap over his head and tugged the earflaps down, tying them under his chin. It was far too big for him, but it would buffer the noise of the storm.

"We need to get inside, all right? I'm going to get you home safe."

She held out her hand to help him out. He took it, and then sprang into her arms, wrapping around her ribs as snug as a vest. Holding his shaking little body close, Aria hurried, looking for Molly and the others along the trail. They came on her in a mob—soaked and enraged.

"Don't touch him!" hissed Brooke, tearing River away. Cold rushed over Aria's chest, and her balance faltered at the sudden absence of his weight. Brooke snatched the cap off his head and tossed it in the mud.

"Stay away from him!" she yelled. "Don't ever touch him again."

"I was bringing him *back*!" Aria shouted, but Brooke was already dashing for the compound with River, who'd begun to wail. The others filed after Brooke, some casting accusing looks at Aria, like it was her fault River had gotten lost.

"How did you find him, Dweller?" asked a stocky man who'd stayed behind. Suspicion lurked in his eyes. Two boys Aria guessed to be his sons stood nearby, shoulders hunched and teeth chattering.

"She's an Aud, Gray," Molly said, appearing at her side. "Now, go on. Get your boys inside."

With a final look at Aria, the man left, hurrying for shelter with his sons.

Aria picked up her Aud cap and brushed off the mud. "Brooke's not related to you, is she?"

Molly shook her head, a smile tugging at her lips. "No. She's not."

Aria shoved her cap back into her satchel. "Good."

As they hurried back to the compound together, she noticed that Molly was hobbling.

"It's my joints," Molly explained, raising her voice to be heard. The shrill sounds of the Aether funnels were growing louder. "They hurt worse when it's cold and rainy."

"Here, take my arm," Aria said. She supported the older

woman's weight. Together, they moved more quickly toward the compound.

Minutes passed before Molly spoke again. "Thank you. For finding River."

"You're welcome." Even with her body numb to the bone and her ears ringing, Aria felt oddly content to walk alongside a friend. Her first among the Tides, after Flea.

— 7 —

PEREGRINE

Perry left Roar and took the trail to the harbor faster than he had in his life, sprinting until he reached the dock. There, Wylan and Gren called to each other as they tied off a fishing skiff, their clothes flapping in the wind. The vessel struck the dock in the choppy water, shaking the planks beneath Perry's feet. His heart seized when he saw only two skiffs. Most of his fishermen were still at sea.

"How close are the others?" Perry yelled.

Wylan shot him a dark look. "*You're* the Seer, aren't you?"

Perry ran along the shore to the rock jetty that reached out like a great arm, protecting the harbor. He leaped onto the tumbled granite, then lunged from one huge boulder to the next. Geysers of seawater shot up through the gaps, soaking his legs. At the top of the jetty, he stopped and scanned the open ocean. Huge waves rolled and pitched, capped with white spray. A terrifying sight, but he also saw what he'd hoped to. Five skiffs approached the harbor, bobbing like corks in the brutal waters.

"Perry, stop!" Reef worked his way over the boulders. Gren and Wylan followed, both with lengths of rope across their shoulders.

"They're coming in!" Perry shouted. Who was left out there? The spray blurred everything. Even with his vision, he couldn't see the fishermen until the first boat drew close, moving past the jetty. Perry glimpsed the terrified looks on the men whose lives he'd sworn to protect. They weren't safe yet, but the seas weren't as rough inside the harbor as out in the open water. When the second and third boats reached the harbor, he came closer to breathing again. Closer to knowing he hadn't lost anyone.

And then the fourth skiff came in, leaving only one more at sea. Perry waited, cursing when he saw it clearly. Willow and her grandfather sat, white-faced, gripping the mast. Between them, ears pinned back, crouched Flea.

Perry leaped down the ocean side of the jetty, drawing closer to the breaking waves just as flashes burst across the horizon, freezing the moment in glaring light. The storm had broken. Funnels dropped at sea, scoring brilliant blue lines down the cloud-darkened sky. They were miles away, but he tensed on instinct and slipped, grazing his shin.

"Perry, get back here!" Reef yelled. Waves pummeled the rocks around them, a violent assault that came from every direction.

"Not yet!" Perry barely heard himself over the thundering surf.

Willow's skiff had broken off its course. It streamed right toward the jetty. She yelled something, cupping her hands around her mouth.

Gren appeared, balancing beside Perry. "They've lost the rudder. They can't steer."

Perry knew exactly what was going to happen, and the others did too.

"Abandon ship!" Wylan yelled nearby. "Get out!"

Old Will had already pulled Willow to her feet. He took her face in his hands, issuing a frantic message Perry couldn't hear. Then he embraced her hastily and helped her jump off the bow into the waves. Flea leaped in right after her, and then Old Will jumped last, his expression surprisingly calm.

Seconds passed in an instant. The swell caught the skiff, pushing it into a current. The boat came fishtailing, turning backward at the last moment, so the stern smashed against the rocks just ten paces away from Perry. It folded, splintering, sending pieces flying. His arms came up, shielding himself, debris and ocean spray pelting his forearms.

He blinked hard, clearing his eyes, and spotted Willow moving right toward the mix of broken wood and white water.

"Get a line out *now*!" Reef shouted.

Close by, Wylan threw a rope in the perfect cast of a born fisherman. Without the rope, Willow would smash against the rocks over and again, churning in the froth. With it, they had a chance of pulling her in safely.

"Willow, grab the line!" Perry yelled.

He watched her search for her grandfather, her movements jerky and frantic, and then saw her terror as she spotted Old Will farther out. A wave washed over her, and Perry's heart stopped. Willow surfaced, coughing up water and gasping for air. She swam frantically for the rope and finally grasped it.

Perry drew as low on the rocks as he dared, strength gathering in his legs as he prepared to grab her.

When the surf surged, Wylan and Gren pulled the rope. Willow came slicing toward Perry like an arrow. She knocked him back as he caught her, her forehead cracking against his chin. Pain burst across his ribs as he fell against the rocks. He held her for an instant before Reef swept her from his arms.

"Get out of there, Peregrine!" he yelled, carrying Willow higher on the jetty.

Perry didn't answer this time. He couldn't leave until they had Old Will.

Wylan threw another line. It dropped near Old Will, but the fisherman struggled, swimming in place with his head tipped up, barely above the water.

"Move, Will! Swim!" Perry yelled.

Funnels lashed down, closer now, and waves that had been five and six feet high minutes ago doubled into monstrous surges that spilled over the jetty.

"Grandpa!" Willow screamed suddenly, like she knew.

Like she'd had some sense of what would come next.

Old Will disappeared beneath the water.

Perry covered the distance between him and Wylan in four leaps. He grabbed hold of the rope. Behind him, Gren's and Reef's voices boomed, "No!" just as he pushed off the rocks and dove.

The quiet beneath the water shocked him. Perry took up slack on the rope, firming his grip, and kicked away from the jetty. His foot struck something hard—a board? A rock?—as he came up. Waves rose in huge, rolling walls around him. He could only see water until a swell lifted him out of the trough. His stomach lurched as he rose up, and then he was at the crest, able to see the rocks where he'd just stood. Only seconds, and he was nowhere near where he thought he'd be.

Perry swam toward where he'd last seen Old Will. The current was brutally strong, pulling him back toward the jetty. He spotted movement in the water. Flea paddled twenty yards off. Nearby, Old Will thrashed in place, his silvery hair blending with the whipped sea foam.

The fisherman's skin was ghastly white when Perry reached him. "Hang on, Will!" Perry tied the rope around him. "Go!" he yelled toward shore, waving his arms.

Seconds passed before the fibers of the rope stretched taut beneath his hands. He was pulled forward, but barely. Another tug and he couldn't deny that together they were too heavy for Wylan. He caught another glimpse of the jetty, seeing the dark granite boulders flash white for an instant. The Aether storm was closing on them.

Perry let go of the rope, and Old Will surged away from him. He swam after, demanding more from his tired muscles. Every stroke felt like he was lifting his own weight. He could hear Reef's and Gren's shouts as he neared the jetty. He pushed himself. Peered up through whipping spray. A few more yards.

A sudden current gripped him like a hook, pulling him away, back toward the open water. Just as suddenly, the tide shifted, and he saw the jetty closing fast. He covered his head and pulled his legs up. His feet struck hard; then he whipped sideways and crashed into the rocks.

Pain speared through him. Spine cracking. Everywhere. The ache solidified in his right shoulder. He reached up, not recognizing his own shape. His shoulder jutted the wrong way, dislodged from the socket.

This couldn't be happening. He swam with his good arm and begged more from his legs, but every movement sent stabbing pain across his shoulder. Through the crashing surf, he caught another glimpse of the jetty. Bear and Wylan pulled the rope hand over hand, bringing in Old Will. Willow and Flea stood nearby, shaking and soaked. Reef and Gren perched on the rocks, yelling for him, ready to hoist him out of the water. Perry kicked harder, but his legs wouldn't answer. Wouldn't move the way he wanted them to. He was coughing up seawater and couldn't catch his breath.

There was only one way out of this. He stopped swimming and plunged underwater. He grabbed his wrist and took an instant to shore up his resolve. Then he pulled it across his body. Spots of red burst before his eyes. It felt like he was ripping his own muscles, the pain an explosion inside his shoulder, but the joint wouldn't spring back into place. He let go of his arm. Couldn't try again. Was sure he'd pass out if he did.

He pushed up, cutting through the churning water, his breath running out. He kicked harder, searching for the surface. Searching.

Searching.

Suddenly he couldn't tell which way was up. Fear threatened to overtake him, but he forced himself to swim with calm strokes. Panic would mean the end. Long seconds later, his lungs screaming for oxygen, panic came anyway, and he felt himself thrashing wildly in the water, his body moving beyond his control.

He knew he couldn't breathe. That he wouldn't draw in air. No matter how he fought against it, he couldn't stop himself. The ache in his lungs and his head was bigger than the pain in his shoulder. Bigger than anything.

He opened his mouth and inhaled. An explosion of cold shot down his throat. In the next instant, he pushed it back out. The bright red bursts came back, and his chest convulsed, pulling, pushing. Needing, rejecting.

He slipped down into colder water, where it grew darker and quieter and darker still. He felt his limbs relax, then an aching sorrow spread through him, replacing the pain.

Aria. He'd just gotten her back. Didn't want to leave.

Didn't want to hurt her. Didn't want—

Something slammed into his throat. The Blood Lord chain . . . strangling him. He grasped for it, and then he realized someone was above, tugging him upward. The chain loosened, but now he felt an arm around his chest, and he was moving, being towed.

He broke the surface and retched seawater, convulsing with his entire being. He felt a rope being tied around his ribs, and then Gren and Wylan were hauling him up to the rocks while someone pushed him from behind. It could only be Reef.

Bear grabbed for his arm, cursing as he almost slid into the water.

"Shoulder!" Perry gritted through his teeth.

Bear understood, wrapping his arm around Perry's waist and carrying him beyond the reach of the crashing waves. Perry kept going after he was set down. He clambered across the jetty, desperate, until he reached sand. Then he sank and folded around the pain in his gut—in his shoulder—in his throat. His lungs felt like they'd been beaten blue.

A circle formed around him, but he kept coughing, struggling to find his breath. Finally he swiped the saltwater from his eyes.

Shame hit him hard. He was on his back, broken in front of his people.

Gren shook his head, like he couldn't believe what had just happened. Old Will stood with Willow tucked into his side. Reef's chest heaved, the scar across his cheek bright red. Above, the Aether turned in massive, vengeful wheels.

"His arm's out of its socket," Bear said.

"Pull it up and then across," Reef said. "Slow and firm, and don't stop, no matter what. And be quick about it. We need to get inside."

Perry shut his eyes. Huge hands closed over his wrist; then he heard Bear's deep voice above him. "You won't like this, Perry."

He didn't.

Body shaking with nerves and cold, Perry climbed up to his loft, clutching his arm to his side. Awkwardly, hissing at the ache in his shoulder, he pulled his sopping shirt over his head and flung it across the room below. It landed with a splat on the fireplace mantel, hanging there. He lay back and drew breath after breath into his battered lungs as he watched the Aether through the open sliver in the roof. Rain dripped through it, tapping on his chest. Rolling to the mattress beneath him.

Just a few minutes. He needed some time alone before he had to face the tribe.

He closed his eyes. All he could see was Vale, making speeches. Vale, sitting at the head table of the cookhouse, calmly overseeing everything. His brother had never so much as tripped in front of the Tides. And what had Perry just done?

It was the right thing, going after Old Will. So why couldn't he slow down his breathing? Why did he feel like punching something?

The door swung open, banging against the stone wall with a crack and letting in a cold gust.

"Perry?" someone said from below.

Perry winced in disappointment. It wasn't the voice he wanted to hear. The only one he'd listen to right now. Had Roar found her?

"Not now, Cinder." Perry listened for the sound of the door closing. Seconds passed with nothing. He tried again more forcefully. "Cinder, go."

"I wanted to explain about what happened."

Perry sat up. Cinder stood below, soaking wet. He was holding his black cap in his hands. He looked determined and calm.

"You want to talk now?" Perry heard his father's angry tone in his own voice. He knew he should stop himself, but he couldn't. "You show up when you want to, and run when you don't? Which is it going to be? If you're staying, I'd appreciate you not burning our food."

"I was trying to help—"

"You want to *help*?" Perry jumped down from the loft, muffling a curse as pain lanced through his arm. He strode up to Cinder, who stared up at him with wide, piercing eyes. He waved toward the open door. "Then why don't you do something about *that*?"

Cinder glanced outside, then back at him. "That's why you want me here? You think I can stop the Aether?"

Perry caught himself suddenly. He wasn't thinking straight. Didn't know what he was saying. He shook his head. "No. That's not why."

"Forget it!" Cinder backed away, moving toward the door. The veins at his neck had begun to glow blue, like the Aether. It seeped like branches beneath his skin, spreading up over his jaw, across his cheeks and his forehead.

Perry had seen him this way twice—on the day Cinder had burned his hand, and when he'd laid waste to a tribe of Croven—but it stunned him again.

"I never should have trusted you!" Cinder yelled.

"Wait," Perry said. "I shouldn't have said that."

It was too late. Cinder spun, and shot outside.

8

ARIA

R oar ran up a short while later, as Aria approached the compound with Molly. "I've been looking for you everywhere," he said, wrapping Aria in a quick hug. "You made me worry."

"Sorry about that, pretty."

"You should be. I hate worrying." He clutched Molly's free arm, and together they pulled her as quickly as she could manage to the cookhouse.

Inside, the tribe was packed together, crowding at the tables and along the walls. Molly left to check on River, and Roar went to see Bear. Aria spotted Twig, the lanky Aud who'd been with her on the journey there. She slid onto the bench beside him and scanned the buzzing hall. People were in a panic over the storm, talking over one another in brittle voices, their faces tight with fear.

She wasn't surprised to see Brooke a few tables over with

Wylan, the fisherman with dark, shifty eyes who'd cursed her under his breath at Perry's house. She saw Willow nestled between her parents, with Old Will and Flea nearby, and the rest of the Six, who never strayed far from Perry's side. As her gaze moved from one person to the next, a sense of dread rolled through her, making her fingertips tingle. She didn't see Perry.

Roar walked over and dropped a blanket over her shoulders. He edged Twig aside and sat beside her.

"Where is he?" she asked plainly, too anxious for caution.

"At his house. Bear said he knocked his shoulder out of joint. He's fine." Roar's dark eyes flicked to her. "But it was close."

Aria's stomach clenched. Her ears latched onto Perry's name drifting across the tables in a wave of whispers. She sifted through the din and grabbed onto Wylan's spiteful tone, her eyes finding him again. A group of people had gathered around him.

". . . he jumped in like an idiot. Reef had to fish him out. Almost didn't get to him in time, either."

"I heard he saved Old Will," someone else said.

Wylan's voice again. "Old Will wouldn't have drowned! He knows the sea better than any of us. I was gonna get him on the line on my next cast. Right now I'd feel better if Flea were wearing that damned chain."

Aria touched Roar's arm. *Do you hear Wylan? He's horrible.*

Roar nodded. "He's all bluster. You're the only one who's actually listening to him, trust me."

Aria wasn't sure about that. She wove her hands together, her leg bouncing beneath the table. Both the hearths blazed, warming the hall. It smelled of damp wool and mud, and the sweat of too many bodies. People had brought treasured belongings from their homes. She saw a doll. A quilt. Baskets packed with smaller items. An image appeared in her mind of the falcon carvings on the sill in Perry's house. Then of Perry, there alone. She should be with him.

Aether funnels struck outside, their distant shrieks carrying to her ears. Faint tremors vibrated up through the soles of her boots. She wondered if Cinder was out in the storm, but she knew that—of anyone—he'd be safe under the Aether.

"Do we just sit here?" she asked.

Roar ran a hand over his wet hair, making it spike. He nodded. "A storm this close, this is the safest place to be."

At Marron's, the storms hadn't been nearly as frightening. Everyone in the compound retreated deep underground to the old mining caves of Delphi. There Marron had provisions at the ready. Even diversions, like music and games.

Another deep rumble thrummed through the floorboards. Aria looked up as dust shook loose from the rafters, sprinkling the table in front of her. In the cooking area, pots rattled softly. Nearby, Willow hugged Flea, her eyes shut tight. Aria hardly heard anyone talking now.

She reached for Roar again. *You need to do something. They're petrified.*

Roar lifted an eyebrow. "*I do?*"

Yes, you. Perry's not here, and I can't. I'm a Mole, remember?

No, wait. I'm a Mole tramp.

Roar stared at her, seeming to weigh his options. "All right. But you owe me." He crossed the room to a young man with a cobra tattoo that wove around his neck, and nodded to the guitar leaning against the wall. "Can I borrow that?"

After a moment of surprise, the young man handed over the instrument. Roar returned and sat up on the table, propping his feet on the long bench. He began testing the strings, his eyes narrowing in concentration as he adjusted the tension. He was meticulous, as she would've been. They both heard in perfect pitch. Anything less would've grated on their nerves.

"So," he said, satisfied. "What are we singing?"

"What do you mean *we*, Roar? You're doing it."

He smiled. "But it's a duet." He played the opening notes to a song by her favorite band, Tilted Green Bottles. Over the winter he couldn't get enough of the song. "Arctic Kitten," a ballad, was supposed to be sung overly romantically, which made the lyrics more ridiculous than they already were.

Roar had the romantic part down. He strummed the first riffs, his dark brown eyes intent on her, his lips pulled in a subtle, seductive smile. He was joking, but it was almost enough to make her blush. Aria felt the attention of everyone on them now.

When he sang, his voice was smooth and rich with humor. "Come thaw my frozen heart, my little arctic kitten."

Unable to resist, Aria jumped in and picked up the next line. "No chance, my yeti man, I'd rather be frostbitten."

"Let me be your snowman. Come live in my igloo."

"I'd rather freeze to death than hibernate with you."

Aria couldn't believe they were singing such a stupid song to people who were wet and scared stiff—who had Aether funnels pounding down around them. Roar bought into it fully, his hands beating a cheerful rhythm out of the strings. She forced herself to match his enthusiasm as they kept on, back and forth.

She expected the Tides to throw mugs or shoes at her at any moment. Instead she heard a muffled snort, and then, from the corner of her eye, she caught a few smiles. When they sang the chorus together—which involved some melodic purring—a few people laughed openly, and she finally relaxed, letting herself enjoy something she did well. *Very* well. She'd been singing all her life. Nothing felt more natural.

After Roar plucked the last notes, there was a beat of perfect silence before the sounds of the storm filtered back in and the chatter of the hall returned. Aria peered at the faces around her, picking up snatches of conversation.

"Barmiest song I've heard in all my life."

"Funny, though."

"What's a yeti?"

"I've got no idea, but the Mole sings like an angel."

"I heard she was the one who found River."

"You think she'll sing something else?"

Roar bumped his shoulder into hers. He raised an eyebrow. "So? Will she sing again?"

Aria straightened her back and filled her lungs. They thought "Arctic Kitten" was something special? They hadn't heard anything yet.

She smiled. "Yes. She will."

9

PEREGRINE

For the first time in months, no one noticed Perry as he stepped into the cookhouse. All eyes were fixed on Aria and Roar. He pulled himself into the shadows and leaned against the wall, gritting his teeth at the pain that shot down his arm.

Roar sat on top of one of the trestle tables at the center of the hall, playing a guitar. Beside him, Aria sang, with a relaxed smile on her lips and her head tipped to the side. Her black hair hung in wet strands that spilled over her shoulder.

Perry didn't recognize the song, but he could tell she and Roar had sung it before by the way they were in pitch sometimes and sometimes apart, twining like birds in flight. He wasn't surprised to see them singing together. Growing up, Roar had always turned unlikely things into songs to make Liv laugh. Sounds connected Roar and Aria, just as scents connected Scires. But another part of him couldn't stand seeing them having fun, right after he'd almost drowned.

Across the hall, Reef and Gren saw him and came over, drawing Aria's attention. Her voice broke off, and she gave Perry an uncertain smile. Roar's hands stilled over the guitar, an anxious look crossing his face. The entire hall noticed Perry now, a stir sweeping across the crowded tables.

His pulse picked up, and he felt his cheeks warm. He had no doubt they knew what had happened at the jetty. That *everyone* knew. Perry saw the disappointment and worry in their expressions. Scented it in the rancy tempers that filled the hall. The Tides had always called him rash. His dive after Old Will would only reinforce that.

He crossed his arms, pain stabbing deep in his shoulder socket. "No need to stop." He hated the hoarseness of his voice, raw after coughing and retching seawater. "Will you sing another?"

Aria answered right away, never taking her eyes off him. "Yes."

She sang a song he knew this time—one she'd sung to him when they'd been at Marron's together. It was a message from her. A reminder—here among hundreds of people—of a moment that had been theirs alone.

He let his head rest against the wall. Closed his eyes as he listened, pushing back the urge to go to her. To bring her close. He imagined her fitting right beneath his shoulder. Imagined the aches fading, along with the shame of having been fished out of the sea, mangled before his tribe. He imagined until it was just the two of them, alone on a roof-top again.

Hours later, Perry rose from his spot in the cookhouse. He stretched his back and rolled his shoulder, testing it. He swallowed, and confirmed that every part of him still hurt.

Morning sunlight filtered through the open doors and windows, falling in golden shafts across the hall. People lay everywhere—in piles along the walls, beneath tables, in the aisles. The quiet seemed impossible for such a large crowd. His gaze went to Aria for the thousandth time. She slept by Willow, Flea curled into a ball between them.

Roar woke, rubbing his eyes, and then Reef climbed to his feet nearby, pushing his braids back. The rest of the Six stirred to life, sensing Perry needed them. Twig nudged Gren, who shoved back while still half-asleep. Hyde and Hayden rose, sweeping their bows across their backs in unison and abandoning Straggler, who was still pulling on his boots. Quietly they moved past the sleeping tribe and followed Perry outside.

Apart from the puddles and branches, and the broken roof tiles scattered across the clearing, the compound looked the same. Perry scanned the hills. He didn't see any fires, but the pungent stench of smoke hung in the damp air. He'd lost more land, he was certain. He only hoped it wasn't more farmland or pasture, and that the rain had contained the damage.

Straggler pushed his way forward and wrinkled his nose,

looking up. "Did I dream that last night?"

The Aether flowed calmly, blue sheets between wispy clouds. A normal spring sky. No blanket of glowing clouds. No spools of Aether churning above.

"Was the dream about Brooke?" Gren said. "Because then the answer is yes. And me too."

Straggler shoved him in the shoulder. "Idiot. She's Perry's girl."

Gren shook his head. "Sorry, Per. I didn't know."

Perry cleared his throat. "It's all right. She's not anymore."

"Enough, both of you," Reef said, glaring at Strag and Gren. "Where do you want us to start, Perry?"

More people filed out of the cookhouse. Gray and Wylan. Rowan, Molly, and Bear. As they looked around the compound and up to the sky, Perry saw the worried looks on their faces. Were they safe now, or would they see another storm soon? Was this the beginning of Aether year-round? He knew the questions were on all their minds.

Perry got them moving through the compound first, assessing damage to roofs, checking the livestock in the stables, and then working out to the fields. He sent Willow and Flea in search of Cinder, regretting last night. He'd been out of his mind, and he needed to find Cinder to apologize. Then he headed northwest with Roar. An hour later they stood before a smoldering field.

"This won't help," Roar said.

"It's hunting land only. Not the best we had."

"That's sunny of you, Per."

Perry nodded. "Thanks. I'm trying."

Roar's gaze moved to the edge of the field. "Look, here comes cheerfulness himself."

Perry spotted Reef and smiled. Only Roar could entertain him at a time like this.

Reef gave him a report of the rest of the damage. They'd lost forestland to the south, adjacent to areas leveled by fires they'd had over the winter. "It just looks like a bigger stretch of ashes now," Reef said. Every last one of the Tides' beehives had been destroyed, and the water from both of the wells at the compound had been tainted and now tasted like ash.

With Reef's report finished, Perry couldn't avoid what had happened at the jetty any longer. Roar was spinning his knife in his hand, a trick he did when he grew bored. Perry knew he could say anything in front of him, but he still had to force his next words out.

"You saved my life, Reef. I owe you—"

"You don't owe me anything," Reef interrupted. "An oath is an oath. Something you could stand to learn."

Roar slid the knife back into the sheath at his belt. "What's that supposed to mean?"

Reef ignored him. "You swore to protect the Tides."

Perry shook his head. Wasn't Old Will part of the tribe? "That's what I did."

"No. What you did is almost got yourself killed."

"Should I have let him drown?"

"Yes," Reef said sharply. "Or let me go in after him."

"But you didn't."

"Because it was suicidal! Try and understand something, Peregrine. *Your life* is worth more than an old man's. More than mine, too. You can't just go diving in like you did."

Roar laughed. "You don't know him at all, do you?"

Reef spun, pointing a finger at him. "You should be trying to talk some sense into him."

"I'm waiting to see if you'll ever shut up," Roar said.

Perry shot between them, pushing Reef back. "Go." The fury in Reef's temper shimmered red at the edge of his vision. "Take a walk. Cool off."

Perry watched him stride away. Beside him, Roar cursed under his breath.

If this was happening between the two people most loyal to him, what was going on with the rest of the Tides?

On the way back, Perry spotted Cinder at the edge of the woods. He was waiting by the trail, fidgeting with his cap.

Roar rolled his eyes as soon he saw him. "See you later, Per. I've had enough," he said, jogging off.

Cinder was toeing the grass as Perry walked up.

"I'm glad you came back," Perry said.

"Are you?" Cinder said bitterly, without looking up.

Perry didn't bother replying. He crossed his arms, noticing that his shoulder felt better than it had that morning. "I shouldn't have yelled at you. It won't happen again."

Cinder shrugged. After a few moments, he finally looked up. "Is your shoulder . . . ?"

"It's fine," Perry said.

"I didn't know about what happened when I came to see you. The girl—Willow—she told me this morning. She was real scared. For herself and her grandfather. And for you."

"I was scared too," Perry said. It almost seemed unbelievable to him now. A day ago he'd been underwater, seconds away from dying. "It wasn't my best day. I'm still here, though, so it wasn't the worst."

Cinder flashed a smile. "Right."

With Cinder's temper finally settling, Perry saw his opportunity. "What happened in the storeroom?"

"I just got hungry."

"In the middle of the night?"

"I don't like eating during supper. I don't know anybody."

"You spent the winter with Roar," Perry said.

"Roar only cares about you and Aria."

And Liv, Perry thought. It was true that Roar had few loyalties, but they were unbreakable. "So you snuck into the storeroom."

Cinder nodded. "It was dark in there, and so quiet. Then all of a sudden I saw this beast with yellow eyes. It scared me so bad I dropped the lamp I was holding, and next thing I knew there was fire burning across the floor. I tried to put it out, but I was only making it worse, so I ran."

Perry was stuck on the first part of the story. "You saw a *beast*?"

"Well, I thought so. But it was just the stupid dog, Flea. In the dark he looks like a demon."

Perry's mouth twitched. "You saw Flea."

"It's not funny," Cinder said, but he was fighting a smile too.

"So Flea, the demon dog, scared you, and the lamp was what made that fire? It wasn't . . . what you do with the Aether?"

Cinder shook his head. "No."

Perry waited for him to say more. There were a hundred things he wanted to know about Cinder's ability. About who he was. But Cinder would speak when he was ready.

"Are you going to make me leave?"

"No," Perry said immediately. "I want you here. But if you're going to be part of things, you need to be a part of *all* of it. You can't run off whenever something goes wrong, or take food in the middle of the night. And you need to earn your way like everyone else."

"I don't know how," Cinder said.

"How to what?"

"Earn my way. I don't know how to do anything."

Perry studied him. He didn't know how to do *anything*? It wasn't the first time Cinder had said something peculiar like that.

"Then we've got a lot of ground to cover. I'll have Brooke

get you a bow and start you on lessons. And I'll talk to Bear tomorrow. He needs all the help he can get. One last thing, Cinder. When you're ready, I want to hear everything you have to say."

Cinder frowned. "Everything I have to say about what?"

"You," Perry said.

10

ARIA

You have a good way with pain," Molly said.

Aria looked up from the bandage in her hand. "Thank you. Butter is a good patient."

The mare blinked lazily in response to her name. Last night's storm had triggered her flight instinct. Butter had kicked her stall in panic and suffered a gash along her front leg. To help Molly, whose hands were bothering her, Aria had already cleaned the wound and applied an antiseptic paste that smelled like mint.

Aria resumed rolling the bandage around Butter's leg. "My mother was a doctor. A researcher, actually. She didn't work with people often. Or with horses . . . ever."

Molly scratched the white star at Butter's forelock with fingers as gnarled as roots. Aria couldn't help but think of Reverie, where ailments like arthritis had been cured through genetics long ago. She wished there were something she could do.

"Was?" Molly said, peering down.

"Yes . . . she died five months ago."

Molly nodded thoughtfully, watching her with warm, soulful eyes the same color as Butter's chestnut hair. "And now you're here, away from your home."

Aria looked around, seeing mud and straw everywhere. The smell of manure hung in the air. Her hands were cold and reeking of horse and mint. Butter, for the tenth time, nuzzled the top of her hair. This couldn't have been more different from Reverie. "I'm here. But I don't know where home is anymore."

"What of your father?"

"He was an Aud." Aria shrugged. "That's all I know."

She waited for Molly to say something fantastic, like, *I know exactly who your father is, and he's right over here, hiding behind this stall.* She shook her head at her own silliness. Would that even help? Would finding her father take away the airy, gossamer feeling inside her?

"Shame to not have family at your Marking Ceremony tonight," Molly said.

"Tonight?" Aria asked, glancing up. She was surprised Perry had scheduled it, right in the aftermath of the storm.

Butter gave an irritated snort as Wylan walked into the stable.

"Look at this. Molly and the Mole," he said, leaning

back against the stall. "You put on a good show last night, Dweller."

"What do you need, Wylan?" Molly asked.

He ignored her, his focus locked on Aria. "You're wasting your time going north, Dweller. The Still Blue's nothing more than a rumor spread by desperate people. Better watch yourself, though. Sable's a mean bastard. Cunning as a fox. He's not sharing the Still Blue with anyone, let alone a Mole. He *hates* Moles."

Aria stood. "How do you know that—from rumors spread by desperate people?"

Wylan stepped closer. "As a matter of fact, yes. They say it goes back to the Unity. Sable's ancestors were Chosen. They were called into one of the Pods, but they were double-crossed and left outside."

In school, Aria had studied the history of the Unity, the period after the massive solar flare that had corroded the earth's protective magnetosphere, spreading Aether across the globe. The devastation in the first years had been catastrophic. The polarity of the Earth had reversed over and over again. The world was consumed by fires. Floods. Riots. Disease. Governments had rushed to build the Pods as the Aether storms intensified, striking constantly. *Other*, scientists had called the alien atmosphere when it first appeared, because it defied scientific explanation—an electromagnetic field of unknown chemical composition that behaved and looked like water, and struck with a potency never seen before. The term evolved to *Aether*, a word borrowed from ancient philosophers who'd spoken of a similar element.

Aria had seen footage of smiling families, walking through Pods just like Reverie, admiring their new homes. She'd seen their ecstatic expressions when they'd first worn Smarteyes and experienced the Realms. But she'd never seen footage of what had happened outside. Until a few a months ago, Aether *was* something other to her—as foreign as the world beyond the safety of Reverie's walls.

"You're saying Sable hates Dwellers because of something that happened three hundred years ago?" she said. "Everyone couldn't fit in the Pods. The Lottery was the only way they could make it fair."

Wylan snorted. "It wasn't fair. People were left to die, Mole. You really believe in fairness when the world is ending?"

Aria hesitated. She'd seen the survival instinct enough times now, and she'd felt it herself. A force that had pushed her to kill—something she'd never thought she'd do. She remembered Hess tossing her out of the Pod to die in order to protect Soren, his son. She could imagine that in the Unity, fairness wouldn't have counted for much. What had happened *wasn't* fair, she realized, but she still believed in it. Believed that fairness was something worth fighting for.

"Did you come here to be a nuisance, Wylan?" Molly asked.

Wylan licked his lips. "I was just trying to warn the Mole—"

"Thanks," Aria interrupted. "I'll make sure not to ask Sable about his great-great-great-great-grandparents."

He left with a greasy, curling smile. Molly went back to scratching the mare's white star. "I like her, Butter. How about you?"

Late in the afternoon, Aria went to Perry's house, wanting a few minutes alone before the Marking Ceremony. Vale's room—where she'd spent her first night—was much tidier than the rest of the house. A red blanket lay across the foot of the bed, and there was a chest and a dresser, but nothing more. She'd never met Perry's brother, but she sensed his presence in the room. The intensity she imagined he'd possessed left her feeling uneasy.

She grabbed Perry's turtle-falcon from the sill in the other room and set it on the nightstand, smiling at the simple solution. Then she changed into a white undershirt with thin straps, sat on the edge of the bed, and looked at her arms. In some ways, getting Markings would feel like an acceptance—an *official* one—of herself as an Outsider. As an Audile. As her father's daughter. Had he broken her mother's heart? Or had they been torn apart for another reason? Would she ever know the answer?

Outside, people gathered in the clearing. Their animated voices drifted in through the window. A drum pounded a deep heartbeat rhythm. She'd been at the Tide compound two nights now. On the first, she'd provided the tribe with a source of gossip. Last night, she'd entertained them. What would tonight bring?

Aria found her Smarteye in her satchel and held it in her palm. She wished she could use it to reach her friends. What would Caleb think of her getting Markings?

The front door opened and then closed with a solid clunk. Aria stuffed her Smarteye back into her satchel and rose from the bed, listening to the floorboards creak as someone approached. Perry appeared at the door, his green eyes intent and serious. They stood looking at each other, his expression growing softer, her pulse pounding harder.

Perry's gaze moved to the figurine on the nightstand, honing in on the small change in the room. "I'll put it back," she said.

He stepped inside and picked it up. "No. Keep it. It's yours."

"Thank you." Aria glanced through the door behind him, to the other room. She felt that strange and unsettling distance between them again—the glass wall keeping them apart, in case someone came into the house.

He set the falcon down and nodded to her satchel. "I thought we'd leave tomorrow at first light."

"Are you sure you should leave? I mean, after what happened?"

"Yes, I'm sure," he said sharply. Perry winced. Then he let out a slow breath and rubbed a hand over his face. "I'm sorry. Reef's been . . . Never mind. Sorry."

The shadows beneath his eyes seemed darker, and his broad shoulders had a tired slant.

"Did you sleep at all?" she asked.

"No . . . I can't."

"You mean you couldn't?"

"No." His smile was faint and humorless. "I mean I can't."

"How long?" she asked.

"Since I slept a full night?" He lifted his shoulders. "Since Vale."

She couldn't believe it. He hadn't slept a decent night in months?

"Aria, this room—" Perry stopped abruptly. He turned and pulled the door shut behind him. Then he leaned against it, hanging his thumbs on his belt, and watched her, waiting, like he expected her to object.

She should have. She'd heard snatches of gossip all day. The Tides were unsettled by the storm, and by what had almost happened to Perry. She didn't want to add to that. She could just imagine Wylan or Brooke calling her the Mole tramp who had seduced their Blood Lord. But she didn't care about any of that now. She just wanted to be with him.

"This room?" she said, prompting him.

He relaxed against the door, but his eyes were intent, shining like the chain around his neck. Night was falling outside, and murky blue light seeped through the half-open shutter.

"Was my father's," he said, picking up where he'd left off. "He was hardly ever here, though. He left before dawn and spent the day in the fields or at the harbor. Sometimes, when he could, he'd go hunting. He liked to keep moving. I guess it's one way we're alike.

"At supper, he talked with the tribe. He was careful, always, to give equal time to everyone. I liked that he did that. . . . It was something Vale never did. Afterward, he'd come home with us, and he wasn't Jodan the Blood Lord anymore. He was ours. He'd listen to us, and read to us, and we'd wrestle and play around." His lips pulled up in a crooked smile. "He was huge. Tall as I am, but strong as an ox. Even with the three of us trying, we could never bring him down." His smile faded. "But then there were other times . . . the times he'd show up here with a bottle." He tipped his head. "You know some of this already."

Aria nodded. She could hardly breathe. Perry's father had blamed him for his mother's death during childbirth. Perry had only spoken of it once to her, with tears in his eyes. Now she stood in the very house where he'd been beaten for something that wasn't his fault.

"On those nights, usually he'd be yelling within the first hour. It got worse from there. Vale hid in the loft. Liv crawled under the table. I bore it. And that was how it went. Everyone knew, but no one did anything. When I was broken and blue, they accepted it. *I* accepted it. I told myself there was no better way. We needed him as Blood Lord. And he was the only parent we had. Without him, we wouldn't have had anything."

She knew too well how that felt. Every day since her mother had died, she'd struggled with the idea that she didn't have anything.

Perry shook his head. "Maybe this won't make sense, but

I feel like the Aether's the same way. We think we need this . . . this land. This house. This room. . . . But it's not the right way to live. We lost acres last night to fires, and a man I've known my entire life almost died. I almost did."

She closed the space between them in a shot and took his hands, holding on as tight as she could. As tight as she would have if she'd been at the jetty. He let out a slow breath, staring into her eyes, his grip just as tight as hers.

"We lose and lose, but we're still here. Shaking in place, afraid of doing something. I'm tired of settling for this because I don't know if something better exists. It has to. What point is there otherwise? I can do something about it now. And I will."

He blinked, the intensity in his eyes vanishing as he shifted back to the present. He laughed at himself. "That was a lot. Anyway . . ." He lifted an eyebrow. "You're pretty quiet."

She wrapped her arms around his waist, hugging him. "Because there isn't a word for how perfect that was."

Perry tucked her closer, his shoulders molding around her. They clung to each other, his chest solid and warm against hers. After a moment, he bent by her ear and whispered, "Was it champ?"

It was a word from her world, and she could tell he was smiling.

"Very. It was *very* champ." She drew back and stared into his eyes. As much as he kept to himself, he cared so deeply for others. He was a force. He was *good*. "You amaze me."

"I don't know why. You're getting Talon back. And you're

helping your people. It's no different from what I'm doing."

"It's different. Hess is—"

He shook his head. "You'd be doing all the same things even if he weren't blackmailing you. Maybe you're not sure about that, but I am." His hand brushed past her cheek and slid into her hair. "We're the same, Aria."

"That's the best thing anyone's ever said to me."

He smiled and leaned down, kissing her softly, tenderly. She knew she should step away. This was a risk, but she didn't care about anything except him just then. She wove her arms around his neck and parted his lips with hers, stealing a taste of him. Tenderness could wait for another time.

Perry went still for an instant; then he cinched her close, momentum sending them thudding into the door behind him. He sank against it, bringing himself closer to her height, kissing her with a sudden urgency. With a hunger that she matched. His lips moved to her neck and trailed up to her ear, and the world fell away. She gasped and dug her fingers into his shoulders, pulling him closer—

His *shoulder.*

She remembered, and her hands relaxed. "Which shoulder was it, Perry?"

A grin spread over his lips. "Right now I have no idea."

His eyes were heavy with desire, but she saw something else. A gleam that made her suspicious.

"What?" she asked.

His hands slid to her hips. "You're incredible."

"That's not what you were thinking."

"Was so. I always think that." He leaned in, twisting a strand of her hair around his finger as he kissed her bottom lip. "But I was also wondering what you were doing around Butter today."

Aria laughed. That was attractive. She smelled like horse. "Do you ever miss anything?"

Perry smiled. "You, all the time."

11

PEREGRINE

Perry drew the blade across his palm, slicing his skin. Making a fist over the small copper pot on the table, he let a few drops of his blood fall.

"On my blood as Lord of the Tides, I recognize you as an Audile and warrant that you should be Marked."

Perry didn't recognize the sound of his own voice—sure and formal—or the words he spoke, which had always belonged to Vale or his father. He lifted his gaze and scanned the crowded hall. Against Reef's advice, he'd ordered all the regular trappings of a Marking Ceremony. Incense at each table put off fragrant cedar smoke to represent Scires. Torches and candles blazed, washing the cookhouse in light to honor the Seers. For the Auds, drummers beat a steady rhythm at the far end. Unlike last night's cold and wet and fear, now the hall was filled with the comfort of tradition. He'd been right to do this. The Tides needed it as much as he and Aria did.

Aria stood just a few paces in front of him. She'd pulled her black hair up, and her neck looked slender and delicate. Her cheeks were flushed pink, whether from nerves or the heat of the hall, Perry wasn't sure.

Did she think this ritual was savage? Did she want Markings, or were they just a necessity to get the location of the Still Blue? He hadn't had the chance to ask earlier, and now it was too late. He couldn't tell how she felt. With the cedar and smoke and hundreds of people, her scent was lost to him.

Perry handed the knife to Roar, who gave the blade a quick, showy twirl before he swore his own oath, recognizing Aria as an Audile. As one of his own. "May sounds guide you home," he finished, adding his blood to the pot.

The tattoo ink would be added next. When Aria received her Markings, she'd receive part of him and Roar as well, their blood sealing their promises to shelter and protect her should she ever be in need. The ceremony would end with him and Roar making that oath to her. Perry couldn't wait. He already felt that way, and he wanted her to know.

"Bear will do the Markings now," he said. For years it had been Mila's role. His sister-in-law had done the falcon on his back and both of his Markings—Scire and Seer. Molly was his next choice, but her hands were bothering her. The only other person left who'd ever done them was Bear.

Perry stood a moment longer, fighting the urge to kiss Aria's cheek. Much as he wanted to be open about them to the tribe, a show of his feelings seemed wrong now. With a final glance at the flawless skin along her arms, he headed for the head table at the rear of the hall. The Markings would take hours, and he didn't want to hover. Getting inked wasn't terrible, but he knew any discomfort she felt would pain him.

He took Vale's old seat at the head table on a platform at the end of the hall. With Roar and Cinder at his sides and the Six filling in around them, he felt too much like the Blood Lord his brother had been, one for ceremony and appearances. But tonight *was* for ceremony.

Across the table, a stringy-haired man smiled, showing more gaps than teeth. "Well, well . . . what a *sight* you are, Peregrine."

The trader, who'd arrived earlier in the afternoon, came around every spring selling trinkets. Coins, spoons, rings, and bangles hung from his necklaces and coat, messy as seaweed. They had to weigh as much as he did. But the goods were just a cover for his real trade—gossip.

Perry nodded. "Shade." With the Marking underway and time to kill, this was a good opportunity to learn news before he left with Aria tomorrow morning.

"You've grown into such a *shining* young lord," Shade said. He lingered over the word, drawing the sound from it like he was sucking marrow from a bone. From the corner of his eye, Perry caught the grin that spread across Roar's face. Perry was already looking forward to hearing his best friend's imitation.

"How *much* you resemble your brother and your father,"

Shade continued. "He was a great man, Jodan."

Perry shook his head. His father, a great man? Maybe to some. Maybe in some ways.

He glanced toward the hearth. Bear sat at a table with Aria. With a piece of willow charcoal, he drew the Audile's curving lines on her bicep, preparing to ink them into her skin. Aria stared at the fire, her gaze distant. Perry exhaled through his teeth, not sure why he was worried. He'd seen Markings done a dozen times.

"On with it, Shade," he said. "Let's have your news."

"It seems patience is missing from your *formidable* list of virtues," Shade said.

"True," Perry said. "I lack restraint as well."

A smile spread over the gossipmonger's face. One of his front teeth sat sideways, like an open door. "So I understand. You know, I admire you *tremendously*, and I'm not alone. News of your challenge has spread far and wide. How very difficult it must have been to spill your brother's blood. Few men have the strength to commit such a merciless—pardon me—such a *selfless* act. All done for your nephew, I heard. A dear child, Talon. Dear, dear boy. Word says you took down a band of sixty Croven as well. Such a young lord, and yet you're making quite a mark, Peregrine of the Tides."

Perry had the urge to cuff him, but Reef moved first, setting his foot on the bench next to Shade with a solid *thunk*. He leaned over the ratty man. "I could speed this up."

Shade winced, his gaze traveling to Reef's scar. "No—no need. Forgive me. I meant no offense. Your time must be so precious, especially with the storm last night. You're not the only one seeing the Aether this late, you know. The southern territories are suffering. Fires burn everywhere, and the borderlands are *crawling* with dispersed. The Rose and Night tribes were both forced from their compounds. Word says they've joined together and gone in search of a stronghold."

Perry looked to Reef, who nodded, their thoughts aligning. The Rose and the Night were two of the largest tribes anywhere, each numbering in the thousands. The Tides barely reached four hundred in number, and that included children. Infants. Elderly. Perry had been preparing the Tides for raids, but against those odds, they wouldn't have a chance.

He drew an unsatisfying breath, warm and heavy with scents. This far back in the hall, the air festered. "Any sign where they're going?"

"No." Shade smiled. "No sign of that."

Perry looked over the sea of heads, finding Aria again. Bear took a thin copper rod from the wooden box with the Marking supplies. He held it over a candle, heating the fine tip. In moments he would jab it into Aria's skin to form her Marking. Used the wrong way, the instrument could be lethal. Perry shook his head, pushing away the thought.

"What else?" he asked. Nausea had begun a steady creep up his throat, and a bead of sweat ran down his spine. "What of the Still Blue?"

"Ahh . . . much talk of the Blue out there, Peregrine.

Tribes are striking out in search of it. Some going south, across the Shield Valley. Some east, beyond Mount Arrow. The Quince tribe took to the north, beyond the Horns, and came back with nothing more than empty stomachs. Lots of talk, see, but none of it sticks."

"I hear Sable knows where it is," Perry said.

Shade shrank back, his clothes jingling. "He says so, yes, but I'm no Scire, like you are, Peregrine. I can't know if he speaks the truth. If he does know, he's not telling a soul about it. Word says there's a boy who can control the Aether— you might want to know that. Such a child would be worth something in a time like this."

Perry kept still despite the jolt to his pulse. How much did Shade know? From the corner of his eye, he saw Cinder pull his hat down. "That's not possible."

"Yes, well . . . it is hard to believe." Shade seemed disappointed to not have drawn any interest, because his next bit of information came readily. "The thaw came early to the north this spring. The pass to Rim is clear. You can go see Olivia now."

Liv. Perry was caught off guard by the mention of his sister. "She didn't go to the Horns. She never made it there."

Shade lifted his eyebrows. "Didn't she?"

Perry froze. "What do you know about Liv?"

"More than you, it seems." Shade smiled. He seemed pleased to have information to bargain with now. But he hadn't counted on Roar.

Perry turned in time to see his friend leap over the table

in a dark blur. There was a sudden loud tumble and a rattling of spoons and rings and trinkets. Reef and Gren drew their knives, and then everything stopped. Perry climbed over the table to see Roar pinning Shade.

"Where is she?" Roar hissed, pressing his blade to Shade's throat.

"She went to the Horns. That's all I know!" Shade looked at Perry, terrified. "Tell him, Scire! It's the truth. I wouldn't lie to you."

The hall grew quiet as all eyes turned to the commotion. Perry's legs felt unsteady as he climbed down. He brought Roar to his feet and caught his friend's temper, a searing scarlet color.

"Walk." He pushed Roar toward the door. Air. They both needed air before they dealt with Shade. He didn't need bloodshed tonight.

"Sable found her." Roar's eyes darted everywhere as Perry shepherded him across the hall. "He had to have. The bastard tracked her down and hauled her back. I have to go there. I need—"

"*Outside*, Roar."

They left a wake of questioning stares as they made their way across the hall. Perry focused on the door, imagining the cool night air outside.

Roar stopped and turned so abruptly that Perry almost crashed into him. "Perry . . . *look*."

He followed Roar's gaze to Aria. Bear drove the rod into her arm in quick, short stabs, Marking her with the ink. Aria was sweating, and her hair clung to her neck. She looked over, meeting his eyes. Something was wrong.

He was in front of her in a heartbeat. Seeing him, Bear startled and yanked the rod back. A line of blood dribbled down Aria's arm. Too much blood. Far too much. Part of the Marking was done, the flowing lines of the Aud tattoo reaching halfway across her bicep. The skin around the inked skin was red and swollen.

"What is this?" Perry demanded.

"She has thin skin," Bear said defensively. "I'm doing it the way I know."

Aria's face was ghostly pale, and she was slumping. "I can handle it," she said weakly. She wouldn't look at him. She kept her gaze on the fire.

Perry's eyes locked on the inkpot just as he smelled something off. He picked up the small copper bowl and brought it to his nose. He inhaled. Beneath the ink he caught a musty, mousy odor.

Hemlock.

For an instant, his mind couldn't fit the information together. Then it hit him.

Poison.

The ink was poisoned.

The copper pot clacked against the hearth before he realized he'd thrown it. Ink splattered across the mantel, the wall, the floor.

"What did you do?" Perry yelled. The drums stopped. Everything stopped.

Bear's eyes darted from the rod to Aria's arm. "What do you mean?"

Aria pitched forward. Perry dropped to his knees, catching her just before she toppled off the bench. Her skin burned beneath his hands, and her entire weight lay against him, heavy and limp. This couldn't be happening. He didn't know what to do. Couldn't make a decision. Nausea and fear coursed through his body, freezing him to the spot.

He picked her up, pulling her into his arms. Next thing he knew, he was in his house. He barreled into Vale's room and set her on the bed. Then he yanked his belt off, his knife falling to the floor with a clunk. Perry tied the belt above her bicep, cinching it tight. He had to stop the poison from flowing to her heart.

Then he took her face in his hands. "Aria?" Her pupils were so dilated that he could hardly see the gray of her irises.

"I can't see you, Perry," she murmured.

"I'm right here. Right beside you." He knelt by the bed and took her hand. If he held on tight enough, she'd be fine. She had to be. "You're going to be all right."

Roar appeared, setting a lamp on the bedside table. "Molly's on her way. She's getting what she needs."

Perry stared at Aria's arm. The veins around her Marking looked corded and deep purple. With every second that passed, her face grew paler. He ran a shaking hand over her forehead and thought of the medical facility at Marron's. He had nothing here. Never in his life had he *felt* primitive until now.

"Perry," she breathed.

He squeezed her hand. "Right here, Aria. I'm not going anywhere. I'm right—"

Her eyes drifted closed, and he was plunged deep underwater again, in the cold darkness, where there was no up. No air to draw into his lungs.

"She's still breathing," Roar said behind him. "I hear her. She's just unconscious."

Molly arrived, carrying a jar with a chalky white paste used for poison rashes.

"That won't work," Perry snapped. "It's *inside* her skin."

"I know," Molly said calmly. "I hadn't seen the wound yet."

"What do we do? Should I cut the skin off?" The words had hardly left Perry when his stomach seized.

Roar's hand came down to his knife. "I can do it, Perry."

He looked at Roar, who was blinking fast, ashen, and couldn't believe they were talking about cutting into Aria's arm.

"That won't help," Molly said. "It's already in her bloodstream." She set another glass jar on the nightstand. Leeches cut swiftly through the water, agitated and eager. "These might, if they take to the spoiled blood."

He fought off another wave of nausea. A belt around her arm. *Leeches.* Was this the best he could do for her? "Do it. Try them."

Molly plucked a writhing leech from the jar and placed it over Aria's Marking. When it latched onto her skin, Roar let out a loud exhale, but Perry still couldn't breathe. Molly took another leech from the jar, and on it went, every second an eternity, until six leeches clung from Aria's arm. On perfect skin he'd run his fingers across just hours ago.

Perry shifted his grip on her hand, threading their fingers together. Aria's hand tightened, just a faint twitch before it relaxed again. Wherever she was in the unconscious, she was telling him she'd fight.

He watched the leeches grow dark purple, filling with blood. They had to be working. They had to be drawing the poison out of her. Then he couldn't watch anymore. He put his head down on the bed, his knees aching from kneeling, and felt the passing of time in snatches. From the room outside, Bear's deep voice, swearing his innocence. Then Cinder, pleading desperately with Reef to let him in. Silence. Then Molly shifting nearby, pulling the blanket over Aria and resting her hand briefly on his head. And silence again.

Finally, Perry looked up. Though Aria still hadn't stirred, he sensed her returning. He stood, swaying in place, his legs stiff. Relief coursed through him, blurring his eyes, but it was overshadowed quickly.

He looked at Roar, who held his knife by the blade.

"Go," Roar said, handing it over. "I'll stay with her."

Perry took it and strode to the cookhouse.

12

ARIA

Aria fractioned to a vast dome, feeling weak and dizzy. Sterile white rows stretched back hundreds of feet. Vegetables and fruits sprouted from them—ordered, perfect bursts of color.

Her heart began to pound. This was Ag 6—one of the farming domes in Reverie. She'd been here before in search of information about her mother. Soren had attacked her not far from where she now stood.

Paisley had died here.

Aria's gaze traveled up. High above, black smoke hissed from the irrigation pipes, tumbling down and pooling around her. She tried to run for the airlock door. Her legs wouldn't move.

A voice broke the silence. "You can't get out, remember?"

Soren. She didn't see him, but she recognized his taunting

voice. "Where are you?" The smoke reached her, stinging her eyes and making her cough, but she couldn't see anyone else in the dome.

"Where are *you*, Aria?"

"You can't hurt me in here, Soren."

"You mean in a Realm? Is that what you think this is? And you're wrong. I can hurt you."

A wave of dizziness sent her stumbling. Her knees buckled, and she went down, grabbing her head. Why was her head pounding? What was wrong with her?

A burning pressure grew stronger and stronger at her bicep. She looked down. Smoke poured out of her skin, seeping into the air. There was fire inside her. Her blood was burning. She yanked and tore at her skin, but invisible hands trapped her.

"Enough, Molly! Get them off her arm!"

It was Roar's voice, but where was he?

Soren's muscular form appeared above her. "You won't get away this time."

She struggled to tear her arms free. She needed to fight him, but she couldn't break loose. "I'm not afraid of you!"

"You sure about that?" He darted for her, grabbing her around the waist.

"It's me, Aria! It's all right. It's me."

Roar's voice. Soren's face. Soren's hands wrapped around her.

Aria struggled against his grip. She didn't know what to

be afraid of. She had no idea what was real, or why her blood felt like boiling water in her veins. She fell back against the farming rows, kicking, fighting, as her vision turned gray and then black.

13

PEREGRINE

Perry entered the cookhouse and found Wylan standing on a table, facing a small crowd. It was late—only a few stray lamps were lit across the shadowed hall—and most of the tribe had gone to their homes for the night.

"He's a hothead; that's all he's ever been," Wylan said. "He's *with* the Dweller. He was keeping that from us. Now he says he's going north for the Still Blue, but don't believe that, either. I wouldn't be surprised if he never comes back!"

"I'm back," Perry said. He felt cold. Completely focused. As sharp as the knife in his hand.

Wylan whirled and nearly fell off the table. Around Perry, people gasped, their eyes dropping to the blade at his side.

Bear put up his hands. "I had no idea, Perry. I didn't. I would never do—"

"I know." Bear's temper proved his innocence. He'd been just as shocked as Perry had been earlier. Perry inhaled deeply, slashes of blue edging his vision. "Who was it?" He searched the faces around him.

No one answered.

"Do you think silence will protect you?" He walked past Rowan and Old Will, moving through the crowd, pumping air into his lungs. Inhaling.

Sifting.

Searching.

"Do you have any idea how loud guilt is to me?"

He caught it: the rancid reek of fear. He grabbed the scent like a line and followed it. The tribe recoiled, terrified, stumbling into benches and tables. All except Gray, who stood fixed as a tree. Perry's vision tunneled, focusing only on him. On the farmer, who shook his head, his face pulled taut with terror.

"She's a *Mole*! She's not even one of us! She has *no right* to be Marked!"

Perry lunged, slamming into Gray. They fell together, knocking into people and crashing into the floor. Someone kicked his hand, and the knife tore from his fingers. Hands fell on his shoulders, but they didn't stop him. He was pure intent. Pure focused power—all the fear inside him releasing through his fist

one—

two—

three times before Reef and Bear wrenched him away. Perry fought his way back, cursing, struggling. He'd heard bones crack, but it wasn't enough. Not enough, because

Gray was still alive. Still moving on the floor.

Bear lifted him off his feet, throwing him backward. "*Stop!* He's got sons."

Perry crashed into a table. Reef appeared in front of him, jamming a forearm into his neck, stunning him. "Look at me, Peregrine!"

He forced himself to meet Reef's eyes.

"Let him disperse," Reef said. "Let him go."

Perry's gaze went to the two boys, standing in the crowd. Yesterday in the fields they'd been laughing, taking shots with Brooke's bow. Now they stood pressed together, crying.

Reef stepped back, releasing him.

Gray lay on his side a few feet away. Dark blood streamed from his nose and pooled on the floorboards.

"Pick him up," Perry said. Hyde and Straggler hauled him off the floor and held him upright. Gray couldn't stand on his own. "Why?" Perry asked. "Why did you do it?"

"She doesn't deserve Markings! She's not even one of us. *I am.*"

"Not anymore," Perry said. "You lost that right. Be off my land by tomorrow morning."

As Hyde and Strag dragged Gray away, Perry put his head down and spit out the warm pool of blood in his mouth. He'd taken a punch at some point. Out of the corner of his eye, he caught a flash of Shade's messy, jangling coat. The gossipmonger had scored a victory tonight.

"You're a liar, Peregrine."

Perry looked up and followed the bitter voice until he found Wylan, buried in the crowd. "You want to come here and say that, Wylan?"

"If I do, will you beat me, too?" Wylan shook his head. "You're worse than Vale," he said under his breath, and left.

Twig shoved Wylan as he passed by. A cheap shot—surprising for someone as honorable as Twig. Perry's gaze moved across the hall. Hayden braced nearby, and Gren had his knife in his hand. Reef scanned the crowd, a warrior assessing the enemy.

They weren't the enemy. These were his people. Perry looked around the hall, scenting pity and fear and rage.

Finally, Reef spoke. "Go on, all of you. It's over," he said.

But Perry knew he was wrong.

14

ARIA

Searing pain in Aria's arm woke her. She blinked in the darkness. Her tongue was stuck to the roof of her mouth, and her head pounded so intensely she was afraid to move. She was on the bed in Vale's room. Aether light seeped through a small crack between the shutters, blue and cool, like the glow of a full moon.

She looked down, moving her head slowly. A strip of cloth was tied tightly around her bicep. She knew the dark stains on it were blood. Her hand shook wildly as she reached up and touched it. She felt scalded. Not just along her skin but deep inside her veins.

She remembered the ceremony. Bear prodding her arm with the rod, and the terrible sting she'd felt spreading into her muscle. Then the fading of sounds, of voices and drums, and a tilting, tilting hall.

She'd been poisoned.

She pressed her eyes closed. It was so unbelievably *medieval* that she'd laugh if she could, but then rage and fear collided inside of her. The shaking in her hands spread to the rest of her body as the reality of what had happened sank in. She didn't know how she could feel so cold with her blood burning, searing inside her veins. Rolling onto her side, she tucked into a ball and squeezed every muscle tight as chills shook her.

Who had done this? Brooke? Wylan? Was it Molly? Could it have been the one person she'd begun to trust here? Aria remembered the night she'd sung with Roar in the cookhouse. So many people had smiled at her then. Had they smiled while she'd been poisoned, too?

She licked her dry lips. The bitterness she tasted—was that poison? Her eye caught on the falcon figurine sitting on the nightstand, its small, blunt lines painted blue with Aether. She stared at it as sleep came and swept her away.

When she woke again, someone had lit a candle by the bedside. She squinted, the brightness of the flame hurting her eyes. Perry was speaking in the next room, his voice hoarse and anxious. Her pulse immediately picked up.

"I knew something was wrong," he said. "I felt sick in there. But I didn't know it was because of her."

Reef responded with no trace of surprise. "You're rendered to her." Aria heard the creak of a floorboard and then his soft curse. "I thought you might be. I've been praying I was wrong."

Aria stared at the door, struggling to understand. Perry had rendered *to her*?

"You think that's the last time her tempers are going to affect you?" Reef said. "Because it won't be. You're rendered to a girl no one wants around. I can't think of anything worse than that. She's clouding your judgment—"

"She's not—"

"She *is*, Perry. She can't stay. You have to see that. And after what you just did, the Tides sure as hell won't accept her now. You just chose *her* over one of *them*."

"That's not what I did. I can't allow murder under my nose, no matter who's involved."

"Of course not," Reef said, "but people see what they want to see. They'll come after her again, or worse, they'll come after you. And don't tell me you're going north. The Tides need you *here*."

She waited for Perry to disagree. He didn't.

A moment later the door opened, and he walked in, his fingers pressed to his eyes. He looked up, freezing when he saw her awake. Then he shut the door and came to the bed. He took her hand, his green eyes filling with tears.

"Aria . . . I'm sorry. I'm so sorry. There's no way for me to tell you how sorry I am."

She shook her head. "Not you. Not your fault." She couldn't find the strength to talk. A red bruise spread over one side of his jaw, and his lower lip was swollen. "You're hurt."

"It's nothing. It doesn't matter."

It did matter. He was hurt because of her. It *mattered*.

"What time is it?" She had no idea if an hour had passed. A day. A week. Every time she woke, it was dark in the room. Night outside. That was all she knew.

"Almost dawn."

"Have you slept?" she asked.

Perry lifted his eyebrows. "Sleep?" He shook his head. "No . . . haven't even tried."

She was too tired. Too weak to say what she wanted. Then she realized it would only take one word. She patted the bed. "You."

He lay down, gathering her close. Aria slumped against him, turning her ear to his chest. She listened to his heart-beat—a good, solid sound—as the warmth of his body melted into her. She'd been in a fog earlier. Hallucinating and searching for what was real. She found it in him. He was real.

"We're together now," he whispered against her forehead. "The way we should be."

She closed her eyes and relaxed her breathing, seeking calm. He was rendered to her. Maybe he'd feel it too. "Sleep, Perry."

"I will," he said. "With you right here, I will."

~ 15 ~

PEREGRINE

P erry, wake up!"

Perry's eyes flew open. He was in Vale's room. He'd never spent a night there in his life. Aria slept soundly, pressed against his chest. He tightened his arms around her as the scents of sweat and blood brought last night crashing back.

Roar stood at the door. "You better come outside. *Now.*"

Taking care not to wake her, Perry slipped from the bed and followed Roar outside.

He found the entire tribe in the clearing—a crowd of hundreds. People were crying, yelling insults at each other. On the roof of the cookhouse he saw Hyde and Hayden with their bows nocked, ready to fire. Reef appeared at Perry's side with his knife drawn, Twig a second later.

"What's going on?" Cinder asked.

Perry didn't know. Didn't understand until Gray came through the crowd.

His face was so swollen it was nearly unrecognizable. He carried a heavy bag over his shoulder. "You chose wrong," he said simply, and then walked out of the compound. His two sons followed, crying, wiping at their faces.

Then Wylan came forward with his own bag across his back. "You killed Vale for dealing with the Dwellers. How's that any different from what you did?"

Perry shook his head. "Talon and Clara are gone because of what Vale did. He betrayed the tribe. I'll *never* do that."

"What was last night? I swear those were your fists on Gray's face. You're a fool, Peregrine. But we were bigger fools to think you could lead us."

He spat in Perry's direction and strode off. Wylan's mother followed after him, staring straight ahead, her gait slow and uneven. Perry wanted to stop her. With a lame leg, she wouldn't survive the borderlands for long.

Then Wylan's cousin came through the crowd. A strong Aud of fourteen who Perry liked. One of Wylan's uncles followed. And then the rest of his family.

They kept leaving, one after another. Ten, then twenty, and still more. So many that Perry began to imagine himself standing in an empty clearing. The idea filled him with giddy relief, gone in an instant. He was meant to be there. He was meant to lead the Tides.

When they finally stopped leaving and the clearing settled, he looked around, waiting a few moments to be sure he hadn't imagined what had just happened. The crowd looked thinner, like it'd been pruned.

At least a quarter of his tribe was gone.

He looked at the faces of all the people loyal to him, who had stayed. Among them he saw Molly, Bear, and Brooke. Rowan and Old Will. He searched for the right words, wishing for Vale's ease with speeches, but failed to find them.

He'd look weak if he thanked them for their loyalty, though he was grateful. And he wouldn't apologize for what he'd done. This was his land. It was his duty to protect everyone there: Dweller, Outsider, or anything in between.

When the tribe—what was left of it—settled into their regular work, Perry met with Bear and Reef in the cookhouse. They sat at the table closest to the door and listed the names of everyone who had dispersed and the tasks they'd handled for the tribe. Bear wrote slowly—the pen looking like a piece of straw in his massive hands as he moved it over the page. Every name felt like a fresh betrayal.

Perry didn't know how he'd gone wrong. Was it diving in after Old Will during the storm? Fighting Gray last night? Was it his plan to go north to find the Still Blue with Aria? Everything felt justified. Right. He didn't understand how he'd failed them.

When they finished the tally, they sat in silence. Bear had written the names of sixty-two people, but the number didn't tell the whole truth. As Perry had suspected, a large share were Marked. Even the Unmarked who'd dispersed were able-bodied, trained fighters. The young, old, and weak seldom left by choice.

Reef sighed, crossing his arms. "We culled the dissidents. I'm damned glad to be rid of a few of them. It'll make us stronger in the long run."

Bear set down the pen and ran a hand over his beard. "It's the short run I'm worried about."

Perry looked at him. What could he say? It was the truth. "We'll be more open to attack once news of this spreads. Shade's probably out there now, telling whoever he comes across what happened."

"We should double the night watch," Reef said.

Perry nodded. "Do it." He looked across the hall. In two days, the Tides had seen a rogue Aether storm, an attempt on Aria's life, and a rebellion. Was a raid next? He knew it would happen. Double the night guard or not, they were too vulnerable. It wouldn't surprise him to see Wylan return to make a play for the compound.

The clearing felt too quiet and empty as Perry returned home. He was anxious to check on Aria. Was she well enough to go north? Reef's words from last night echoed in his mind. *The Tides need you here.* How could he leave them now? How could he stay, when the answer to their safety might be out there?

He entered his house and found Gren and Twig yelling at each other in front of Vale's bedroom. They quieted when they saw him.

"Per . . . ," Twig said, guilt flashing across his face. "We searched everywhere—"

Perry shoved past them, bursting into the room. He saw

the bed. The rumpled blanket. He looked to the nightstand and didn't see the falcon carving. Didn't see Aria's satchel. Didn't see her.

"Roar's gone too," Twig said. He stood at the door with Gren, both of them watching him.

Cinder slipped between them, his hat dropping to the floor. "I saw them leave. They said to tell you they'd take care of Liv and the Still Blue."

Perry stood, absorbing the truth, his ears roaring with the sound of rushing blood.

They had left without him, but he could track them. They'd only be hours ahead. If he ran, he'd catch up to them, but he couldn't bring himself to move.

Reef shouldered his way inside. He looked around the room, cursing. "I'm sorry, Perry."

Unexpected and sincere, the words snapped Perry out of his trance.

She was gone.

Pain edged in past the numbness. Perry pushed it back. Pushed with everything in him, until he'd buried it. Until he was back to numbness.

He walked to the door and picked up Cinder's hat.

"You dropped this," he said, handing it back.

Then he went outside and stepped into the clearing, heading nowhere.

16

ARIA

Here. Have some water."

Aria shook her head, pushing away the water skin. She took breath after breath through pursed lips until the urge to vomit passed. The grass rolled in waves before her eyes. She blinked until it stopped. She didn't know how she could feel worse than just hours ago, but she did. With poison still flowing through her veins, her body rebelled against every step.

"It'll be all right soon," Roar said. "It'll leave your system."

"He's going to hate me."

"He won't."

Aria straightened, keeping her arm tight to her side. They stood on a hill that overlooked the Tide Valley. More than anything, she wanted to see Perry striding toward her.

That morning, she'd woken to the tribe's shouts in the clearing. The Tides were splintering. People were leaving, yelling at Perry. Yelling obscenities about her. She'd stepped out of Vale's room, panicked to get out of there quickly, before Perry lost everything. She'd found Roar with his satchel packed. Liv was at the Horns. He was leaving, too. It'd been easy to escape unnoticed. With dozens of people streaming out of the compound, she and Roar had simply crept the other way.

She wished she could've seen Perry before she'd gone, but she knew him. He wouldn't have let her leave without him. That decision would've cost him the Tides. She couldn't let that happen.

"We should keep going, Roar." If they didn't keep moving, she'd change her mind.

She walked in a daze through the afternoon, her legs shaking, her arm burning beneath its bandage. *This is for the best,* she told herself over and over. *Perry will understand.*

At night they found shelter under an oak tree, a steady rain creating a blanket of quiet noise around them. Roar offered her food, but she couldn't eat. Neither could he, she noticed.

He moved next to her. "Let me check that."

Aria bit her lip as he took the bandage off her arm. The skin at her bicep was swollen and red, crusted with dried blood and smeared with ink. It bore the ugliest Marking she'd ever seen.

"Who did it?" she asked, her voice shaking with anger.

"A man named Gray. He's Unmarked. He's always been envious of us."

A face appeared in Aria's mind. Gray was the stocky man she'd seen in the woods during the Aether storm when she'd found River. "A Mole was getting Markings and he couldn't bear it," Aria said. "He couldn't let that happen."

Roar rubbed the back of his neck, nodding. "Yeah. I guess that's about it."

Aria touched the scabbed skin on her arm. "A half Marking for a half Outsider." She'd meant to make light of it, but her voice wobbled.

Roar watched her in silence for a moment. "It'll heal, Aria. We can have it finished."

She pulled her sleeve down. "No . . . I wasn't even sure I wanted to be Marked."

She had no idea where she belonged. Out here? In Reverie? Hess had banished her in the fall, and now he was using her. The Tides had tried to kill her yesterday. She didn't fit anywhere.

She scooted closer to the fire and lay down, pulling her blanket around her shoulders. She'd been cold all day, racked with chills. Time would help, she told herself. The poison would work itself out of her blood, and her skin would heal. She needed to focus on her goal now. She had to get north and find the Still Blue. For Perry and Talon. For herself.

As tired as she was, she couldn't stop thinking of the way Perry had felt against her that morning, warm and safe. Was he sleeping on the roof tonight? Was he thinking about her?

After an hour, she sat up, giving up on sleep. Though Roar's eyes were closed, she could tell he wasn't asleep either. His expression was too strained.

"Roar, what is it?"

He looked over, blinking tiredly at her. "He's a brother to me . . . and I know how he's feeling right now."

Aria gasped as it struck her: by running away with no explanation, she'd done exactly to Perry what Liv had done to Roar. "It's different . . . isn't it? Perry will know I left to protect him—won't he? You saw how many people left the Tides because of me. None of this would have happened if I hadn't been there in the first place. I *had* to leave."

Roar nodded. "It's still going to hurt."

Aria pressed the heels of her hands to her eyes, keeping back the tears. Roar was right. When it came to pain, reasons didn't matter. She took her hands away. "I did the right thing." She wished she could convince herself.

"You did," Roar agreed. "Perry needs to be there. He can't leave now. The Tides can't afford it." He sighed, resting his head on his arm. "And you're safer out here with me. I can't watch you come that close to dying again."

The rain had stopped when Roar woke her at dawn for another day of walking. They'd had a reprieve from the Aether after the storm, but now she saw thick streams of it running behind a scrim of gray clouds. The blue light filtering down gave the day an underwater quality.

"We'll keep an eye on it," Roar said, looking up beside

her. They were traveling in the open. If another storm built, they'd need to find shelter in a hurry.

Apart from the soreness in her arm, Aria had recovered. They'd leave Perry's territory behind soon, and she needed to be alert to danger. Every step took her closer to the city of Rim. To what she needed.

Late in the afternoon, she stood at the lip of a valley and looked south to the rolling hills stretching to the horizon. Last fall, she'd camped with Perry somewhere out there. She'd worn book covers for shoes. She'd lost her best friend. And she hadn't known it yet, but she had lost her mother, too.

Aria reached into her satchel and found the falcon figurine. She'd grabbed it as she left Perry's house, needing something real to remind her of him.

"I was there when he made that," Roar said. He sat against a tree, watching her with bloodshot eyes.

"You were?"

Roar nodded. "Talon and Liv were there too. We were starting a collection for Talon, each of us making a different one for him. Liv nicked her finger barely five minutes in." He smiled faintly, lost in the memory. "She's a brute with the knife. No finesse at all. She and I quit after a few minutes, but Perry kept at it for Talon."

Aria ran her thumb over the smooth surface. Every one of them, at one time, had held the falcon resting in her palm. Would they ever be together—all of them?

She spent the next hour adjusting to the sounds of the

woods, staring at the figurine in her hand, taking the first watch as Roar drifted asleep. There were wolves out here. Bands of drifters and cannibals. She picked out the patterns in the wind and the rustle of animals, listening until she was sure they were safe. Then she put the falcon away and found her Smarteye.

Three days had passed since she'd contacted Hess on the beach. She glanced at Roar, asleep, and then applied the device. The Eye attached as the biotech activated, and her Smartscreen popped up.

She chose the Hess icon and then felt the familiar tug of fractioning, that moment when her mind adjusted to being here *and* here. She'd appeared at a café in a Venetian Realm. Gondolas glided along the Grand Canal just steps away, roses floating in the sparkling, clear water. It was a beautiful, sunny day, golden and warm. Somewhere, a string quartet played, the notes thin and brittle.

Hess appeared across the small table. He had modified his clothing this time, wearing an ivory-colored suit with light blue pinstripes and a red tie. He'd given himself a tan, but the effect was odd. He looked strangely older—or, rather, closer to his true age of well over a hundred—and his skin was orange. So unlike Perry's bronze skin.

Hess frowned at her clothes. Before she could utter a word, she felt a jolt, like her entire body had blinked. She looked down. A royal-blue silk dress clung to her like a second skin.

Hess smiled. "That's better."

Her heart started drumming with anger. "Much," she said.

A waiter arrived with a tray of coffees. Dark-eyed and handsome, he could have been Roar's brother. He smiled as he set the drinks on the table. A warm breeze blew past, carrying the spicy scent of cologne and shifting Aria's hair on her bare back. It was all so normal and safe and charming. A year ago, Paisley would've been kicking her under the table over the waiter's smile. Caleb would have looked up from his sketchbook and rolled his eyes. She was suddenly furious at how *difficult* life was now.

Hess sipped his coffee. "Are you well, Aria?"

Did he know she'd been poisoned? Could he tell through the Eye? Through her body chemistry? "I'm terrific," she said. "How are you?"

"Terrific," he said, matching her sarcasm. "You're on your way now. Are you traveling alone?"

"What do you care?"

Hess's eyes narrowed on her. "We detected a storm near you."

Aria smirked. "I detected it too."

"I can imagine."

"No, you really can't. I need to know if something's happening in Reverie, Hess. Were you hit by the storm? Has there been any damage?"

He blinked at her. "You're a smart girl. What do you think?"

"It doesn't matter what I think. I need to *know*. I need proof that Talon is all right. I want to see my friends. And I want to know what you're going to do when I give you the location of the Still Blue. Are you moving the entire Pod? How will you do that?" Aria leaned across the table. "I know what *I'm* doing, but what about *you*? What about everything *else*?"

Hess tapped his fingers on the marble tabletop. "You're quite fascinating now. Life among the Savages suits you."

Suddenly the Realm plunged into silence. Aria looked to the canal. The gondola had frozen on water that was as still as glass. A flock of pigeons hung in the air above, caught in mid-flight. People looked around them, panic on their faces; then the Realm snapped back, sound and movement returning.

"What *was* that?" she demanded. "Answer me, or we're done."

Hess took another sip of coffee and watched the traffic in the Grand Canal like nothing had just happened. "Do you think you can fraction if I don't want you to?" He looked back at her. "We're done when I say so."

Aria grabbed her coffee and flung it at him. The dark liquid splattered over his face and his pale suit. Hess jerked back, gasping, even though it hadn't hurt him. Nothing in the Realms could inflict true pain. The most he would feel was warmth, but she'd surprised him. She had his attention now.

"Still want me to stay?" she asked.

He disappeared before she'd finished speaking, leaving her to stare at an empty chair. Though she knew it would be pointless, she tried to shut off the Eye. She was ready to be back—completely—in the real.

UNAUTHORIZED COMMAND flashed on her Smartscreen.

Now what? The waiter peered through the café window, interest sparking in his eyes. Aria turned away, looking toward the canal. A couple embraced at the top of the ornate cement bridge, watching the water traffic below. She tried to imagine that she was the one pressed against the rail. That it was Perry brushing her hair aside and whispering in her ear. Perry had hated the Realms. She couldn't form the picture in her mind.

A time counter appeared at the upper corner of her Smartscreen. It ticked down from thirty minutes. Aria braced herself. Hess was up to something.

In the next moment, she fractioned to another Realm, appearing on a wooden pier. The ocean lapped gently below, and gulls cried overhead, the sounds garish parodies of their real versions. A boy sat at the very end of the pier. He faced out to sea, but Aria knew exactly who he was.

Talon.

She felt sick. She'd wanted to know that Perry's nephew was well, but she wasn't sure she wanted to *know* him. She didn't want to care any more than she already did. And what was she supposed to say to him? Talon didn't even know her. She looked down at herself. At least she was back in her usual black clothes.

The time counter now read twenty-eight minutes. She'd been standing there for two minutes. She shook her head at herself, and went to him.

"Talon?"

He leaped to his feet and faced her, his eyes wide with surprise. She'd never met Talon, but she'd seen him once before. Months ago, when Perry had visited Talon in the Realms, she'd been watching on a wallscreen. He was a striking boy, with curling brown hair and serious green eyes, their color darker, richer than Perry's.

"Who are you?" he asked.

"A friend of your uncle's."

He glared at her suspiciously. "Then how come I don't know you?"

"I met him after you were brought into Reverie. I'm Aria. I was with Perry when he came to see you in the Realms last fall. . . . I was helping him from the outside."

Talon wedged his fishing rod between the slats on the wooden pier. "So you're a Dweller?"

"Yes . . . and an Outsider, too. I'm half of both."

"Oh. . . . *Where* are you? Outside or in Reverie?"

"Outside. I'm actually . . . I'm sitting next to Roar."

Talon's eyes brightened. "Roar's there?"

"He's asleep, but when he wakes, I'll tell him you said hello." Another pole rested by the pier. Talon was using two. He was a Tider, she realized. He'd probably fished for all of his eight years. "Can I join you?"

He didn't look happy about it, but he said, "Sure."

Aria picked up the extra rod and sat next to him. She couldn't believe that after a few days in a fishing settlement, she was now fishing in the Realms. She studied the wooden pole in her hands, realizing she had no idea how to cast it. She'd gone fishing in another Realm before. A Space Fishing Realm, where you fired hooks at fish as you floated through the cosmos. This was fishing as the ancients had done it.

"Umm . . . here," Talon said, taking the rod from her hand. He cast out slowly, so she could see what he was doing, then handed it back.

"Thanks," she said.

He shrugged without looking at her and began swinging his legs over the edge of the pier. Kicking left and right, left and right, left and right. *Being still makes me tired,* Perry had once told her. Apparently it ran in the family.

"We use nets more at home," Talon said after a while.

"Oh, really?" She fumbled for a follow-up question. The timer read twenty-three minutes. "Do you like fishing better or hunting?"

He looked at her like she was crazy. "I love them both."

"I could've probably guessed that. You look like you're good at both." He was sturdier now, healthier than when she'd seen him in the fall.

Talon scratched his nose. "I can catch them and catch them, but this Realm doesn't let you cook them. I tried a few times. I gathered some wood and I tried to start a fire, but it doesn't work. There's no fire in the Realms. I mean there is, but it's like a pretend kind of fire?"

Aria bit her lip, nodding. She knew that too well.

"You have to go to a cooking Realm to cook fish, but

those are barmy. And then even when you eat them, it doesn't fill your stomach after you leave the Realms. It's not as fun catching them when there's no point."

Aria smiled. When he talked, his legs stopped swinging, and a crease appeared between his eyebrows. "I'm sure there are places where you can compete," she suggested.

"For what?"

"For, you know, rankings. You could be first place."

"Does first place mean I get to cook and eat what I catch?"

Aria laughed. "Probably not."

"Maybe I'll try them anyway." He looked out at the ocean and swung his legs for a while before he spoke again. "I want to go home. I want to see my uncle."

She felt her throat tighten. He hadn't asked for his father. She wondered if he'd figured out what had happened between Vale and Perry, but it wasn't her place to ask. It dawned on her that he no longer had parents. He was an orphan like she was.

"Are you unhappy in Reverie?" she asked.

He shook his head. "No. I just want to go home. I'm better now. The doctors here made me better."

"That's good, Talon." She remembered Perry telling her that Talon had been ill on the outside. "I'm going to get you out, and back home to the Tides. I promise."

He scratched his knee but didn't say anything.

"Do you ever fish with a friend?"

"Clara used to come with me. She's Brooke's sister. Do you know Brooke?"

Aria swallowed back a laugh. "Yes, I know Brooke. Why did Clara stop fishing with you?"

"She got bored. She thinks this Realm is too slow now. No one likes to fish this way."

"I like it. Maybe we could do this again sometime?"

Talon gave her a sidelong glance and smiled. "All right."

For the rest of their time together, Talon told her about all the fish he'd caught here. Using what sort of bait. At what time of day. Under what weather conditions.

He tipped his head to the side when his voice grew softer. His legs never stopped swinging over the edge of the pier. A few times, when he smiled, she had to look to the sea and breathe; he was so much like his uncle. She hugged him as the counter wound down to zero, promising she'd come see him again soon.

Aria fractioned into another Realm—an office. Hess sat at a sleek gray desk with a glass wall behind him. Through it she saw Reverie's Panop—her home her entire life—with its circular levels coiling up. The view stole her breath and beckoned her forward. She'd been in the Realms dozens of times with Hess since she'd been cast out, but she hadn't seen the Pod, her physical home, until now.

Hess spoke before she'd taken a step. "Pleasant visit," he said. "He's not suffering, as you saw. I hope we can keep it that way."

17

PEREGRINE

Pledge, Vale," Perry said, as he held the knife to his brother's throat. His voice sounded too harsh, like his father's voice, and his hands shook so badly he couldn't hold the blade steady. He had Vale pinned to the grass in an empty field.

"Pledge to you? You can't be serious. You have no *idea* what you're doing, Perry. Admit it."

"I know what I'm doing!"

Vale started laughing. "Then why did they leave you? Why did *she* leave you?"

"Shut up!" Perry pressed the blade against his brother's throat, but Vale only laughed harder.

Then it wasn't Vale. It was Aria. Beautiful. So beautiful beneath him, on Vale's bed. She laughed as he held the knife to her throat. Perry couldn't take the blade away. It trembled in his hand as he pressed it against the smooth skin at her neck, and he couldn't stop himself and she didn't care. She just kept laughing.

Perry lurched out of the nightmare and shot upright in his loft. He cursed loudly, unable to keep it quiet. Sweat rolled down his back, and he was out of breath.

"Easy. Easy, Perry," Reef said. He was perched on the ladder, brow furrowed with worry.

The house was dim and deathly silent. Perry didn't hear the usual snores of the Six. He'd woken everyone up.

"You all right?" Reef asked.

Perry turned toward the shadows, hiding his face. Two days. She'd been gone two days. He reached for his shirt and pulled it on.

"I'm fine," he said.

Bear was waiting for him when he stepped outside. "We're leaner than ever, Perry, I know that. But I need my people rested. It's too much, asking them to work a whole day in the fields and then do the night watch. Some of us need sleep."

Perry tensed. He slept even less lately, and everyone knew it. "We can't afford to be raided. I need people on watch."

"*I* need help clearing drainage ditches, Perry. I need help tilling and seeding. What I don't need is people snoring when they should be working."

"Make do with what you have, Bear. Everyone else is."

"I will, but we won't get more than half of what we need done."

"Then do the half! I'm not pulling men off watch."

141

Bear went still, as did several people around the clearing. Perry didn't understand how *they* didn't understand. Almost a quarter of the tribe had dispersed. Of course they couldn't get everything done. He'd hoped to build up food rations for the tribe's journey to the Still Blue, but after the damage from the Aether storm and the loss of manpower, it was all he could do to keep them fed every day. They were overworked and underfed, and he needed a solution.

He considered his options throughout the day as he cleared drains for Bear and checked the Tides' defense measures. Reef worked beside him, close as his shadow. When Reef wasn't there, one of the Six took his place. They wouldn't leave him alone. Even Cinder seemed in on it, joining Perry if he walked off in search of a few minutes to himself.

He didn't know what they expected from him. The initial shock had worn off, and now he saw the situation for what it was. Roar and Aria had left; they would go to the Horns to find Liv and the Still Blue. Soon they'd return, and that was all. It had to be. He wouldn't let himself think beyond that.

Supper was late that night—they'd lost three cooks to Wylan's group—and the cookhouse was strangely empty and quiet. Perry didn't taste his food, but he ate because the tribe watched him. Because he had to show them that things might have changed but tomorrow would still come.

Reef fell in step with him as he left the cookhouse and headed for the eastern lookout. Perry sensed Reef working up the courage to say something as they walked. Hands curling into fists, he waited to be told he needed sleep, or more patience, or both.

"Terrible supper," Reef said at last.

Perry let out a breath, the tension seeping out of his fingers. "Could've been better."

Reef looked up to the sky. "You feel it?"

Perry nodded. The sting in the back of his nose warned him that another storm wouldn't be far off. "Almost always now."

The Aether flowed, corded and angry, giving the night a blue, marbled glow. After the storm, the calm skies had only held for a day. Now there was little difference between day and night anymore. Days were darkened by clouds and the blue cast of Aether. Nights were brightened by the same. They flowed together, the edges blurring into an endless day. An ever night.

He looked at Reef. "I need you to send a message."

Reef raised his eyebrows. "To?"

"Marron." Perry didn't want to ask for help from him again—he'd done it only months ago when he'd sought refuge there with Roar and Aria—but the Tides' position was too weak. He needed food and he needed people. He'd ask for a favor before he saw his tribe starve or lose the compound in a raid.

Reef agreed. "It's a good idea. I'll send Gren first thing tomorrow."

Even after he and Reef showed up to relieve them, Twig and Gren remained at the watch post, huddled at the edge of a rocky overlook. The four of them sat together in comfortable silence as a fine mist began to fall.

Hyde and Hayden arrived soon after, Straggler trailing behind them. They had the night off watch, all three. Perry had seen Hyde yawn half a dozen times during supper. They settled themselves along the lookout, watching as the mist thickened to rain. Still no one spoke, or left.

"Quiet night," Twig said finally. "We're quiet, I mean. Not the rain." His voice sounded raspy and hoarse after the long stretch of silence.

"You eat a frog, Twig?" Hayden asked.

"Maybe there were frogs in the soup tonight," said Gren.

Hyde grunted. "Frogs taste better than that tripe."

Twig cleared his throat. "You know I almost did eat a live frog once," he said.

"Twig, you *look* like a frog. You have froggy eyes."

"Show us how high you can jump, Twig."

"Shut up and let him croak the story."

The story itself wasn't much. As a boy, Twig had been on the brink of kissing a frog, on a dare from his brother, when it slipped through his fingers and jumped into his mouth. It was the wrong story for Twig to tell. At twenty-three, he had yet to kiss a girl, and the Six knew it, as they knew nearly everything about one another. A massacre followed, as they took shots at Twig, saying things like maybe he was worried that after the frog, a girl would be a letdown, and that they supported his quest to find a prince.

Perry listened, smiling at the better jabs, feeling more

himself than he had in the past two days. Eventually it grew quiet again, except for the rhythm of a few snores. He looked around him. The rain had stopped. Some slept. Others breathed steadily, focused on the night. No one spoke, but Perry heard them clearly. He understood why they'd been shadowing him and why they sat with him now, staying when they didn't have to.

Given any choice, they wouldn't leave. They'd stand by him.

18

ARIA

"We made better pace today." Aria wrung her hair out, scooting closer to the fire. Spring had come in force, with days of steady rain. They'd left the Tides three days ago, and her strength had finally returned. "Don't you think we made up some ground?"

Roar lay against his satchel, his legs crossed at the ankle, his foot tapping to a beat she couldn't hear. "We did."

"Good fire, too. We got lucky to find dry wood."

Roar looked over, raising an eyebrow. She realized she'd been staring not at him, but through him.

"You know what's worse than mute Aria? Small-talking Aria."

She picked up a stick and jabbed at the fire. "I'm just sparing you."

They had traveled in near silence most of the day, despite Roar's attempts at conversation. He wanted to discuss their plan for when they reached the Horns. How would they discover information about the Still Blue? How would they negotiate for Liv's return? But Aria hadn't wanted to discuss anything. She'd needed to stay focused on moving forward. On pushing harder when she felt the urge to turn back. And speaking might get her *speaking*.

She worried about Talon. She missed Perry. There was nothing she could do about either except race to the Horns. Now, feeling a little guilty over her silence, she was trying—lamely, it was true—to make up for it.

Roar frowned. "You're *sparing* me?"

"Yes, sparing you. All I've got right now is anxious nonsense. I'm exhausted, but I can barely sit still. And I feel like we should keep going."

"We can travel through the night," he said.

"No. We need to rest. See? I'm not making any sense."

Roar watched her for a moment. Then he looked up at the tree branches above them, his expression growing thoughtful. "Have I ever told you about the first time Perry tried Luster?"

"No," she said. She'd heard stories about Perry, Roar, and Liv all winter, but she'd never heard this one.

"We were on the beach, the three of us. And you know how Luster is, how it sweeps you up. Anyway, Perry got a little carried away. He decided to strip down to nothing and go for a swim. This was right in the middle of the day, by the way."

Aria smiled. "He did not."

"He did. While he was out whooping in the waves, Liv took his clothes and decided it was a good time to get all the girls in the tribe to come down to the beach."

Aria laughed. "Roar, she's worse than you are!"

"You mean better."

"I'm scared to see you two together. So what did Perry do?"

"He swam down the coast, and we didn't see him until the following morning." Roar scratched his chin, smiling. "He told us he snuck into the compound during the night wearing seaweed."

"You mean he wore a . . . a *seaweed skirt*?" Aria laughed. "I would give anything to have seen that."

Roar shuddered. "I'm glad I didn't."

"I can't believe you never told me that story before."

"I was saving it for the right moment."

She smiled. "Thanks, Roar." The story had pulled her from her worries for a little while, but they returned too quickly.

Gingerly, she pulled up her sleeve. The skin around the Marking was still red and scabbed, but the swelling had gone down. In some places it looked like ink had been smudged *inside* her skin. It was a mess.

She reached out and rested her hand on Roar's forearm. For some reason, this seemed easier. Maybe it took less courage to just let herself think than to speak her worries aloud.

What if this was a sign? Maybe I'm not supposed to be an Outsider.

He surprised her by taking her hand and threading his fingers through hers. "You already *are* an Outsider. You fit everywhere. You just don't see it yet."

She stared at their hands. He'd never done that before.

Roar gave her a droll look. "It's just odd having you lay your hand on my arm all the time," he said, responding to her thoughts.

Yes, but this feels intimate. Don't you think it does? I don't mean that I think we're being too intimate. I guess I do. Roar, sometimes it's really hard to get used to this.

Roar flashed a grin. "Aria, this isn't intimate. If I *were* being intimate with you, trust me, you'd know."

She rolled her eyes. *Next time you say something like that, you should toss a red rose and then leave with a swish of your cape.*

He gazed off like he was imagining it. "I could do that."

They fell into silence, and she realized how comforting it felt being connected to him this way.

"Good," Roar said. "That's the idea."

His smile was encouraging. *The last time I saw my mother, it was terrible,* she admitted after a while. *We were fighting. I said all the wrong things to her, and I've been regretting it since then. I think I always will. Anyway, I didn't want to do that with Perry. I thought it would be easier to just leave.*

"And I'm guessing you were wrong?"

She nodded. *Leaving is never easy.*

Roar watched her for a long moment, the hint of a smile in his eyes. "That's not anxious nonsense, Aria. It's what's happening. It's truth." He squeezed her hand and let go. "Please don't ever spare me that."

When Roar fell asleep, she dug her Smarteye out of her satchel. It was time to check in with Hess again. For days, she'd been picturing Talon with his legs swinging over the pier. Now her stomach tightened as she remembered Hess's threat. She chose the Hess icon on her Smartscreen and fractioned. When she saw where she was, every muscle in her body went rigid.

The Paris Opera House.

From her spot at center stage, she stood in stunned silence, absorbing the familiar opulence of the hall. Tiers of gilded balconies wrapped around a sea of red velvet seats. Her eyes traveled higher, to the colorful fresco nestled in the domed ceiling, lit by the brilliant grand chandelier. She'd been coming here since she was just a young girl. This Realm—more than anywhere—felt like home.

Her focus moved beyond the orchestra pit to the seat directly in front of her.

Empty.

Aria closed her eyes. This had been her place with Lumina. She could imagine her mother there, in her simple black dress, her dark hair pulled back in a tight bun, a gentle smile on her lips. Aria had never known a more reassuring smile. A smile that said, *Everything will be all right* and *I believe in you.* She felt that now. A stillness. A certainty. Everything would work out. She clung to the feeling, locking it in her heart.

Then slowly she opened her eyes, and the feeling seeped away, leaving questions that burned in the back of her throat.

How could you leave me, Mom? Who was my father? Did he mean anything to you?

She'd never have answers. She would only have an ache that stretched backward and forward and kept going as far as she could see.

The stage lights clicked off, and then the audience lights. Suddenly she stood in blackness so complete that her balance wavered. Her ears thrummed to their full power, ready to seize any small sound.

"What is this, Hess?" she said, annoyed. "I can't see."

A spotlight sliced through the darkness, blinding her. Aria lifted her hand, shielding her eyes from the light and waiting for them to adjust. She could just make out the dark void of the orchestra pit below and the rows of seats beyond. High above, thousands of crystals from the grand chandelier twinkled.

"A bit theatrical for you, isn't this, Hess? Are you going to sing *Phantom of the Opera* to me?" On a whim, she sang a few lines of "All I Ask of You." She'd only meant to play around, but the lyrics swept her up. The next thing she knew, she was thinking of Perry and *singing*.

She'd missed the way the hall amplified her control and power. This stage had never been mere boards on which to stand. It was alive—shoulders that propped her up and lifted her higher. When she finished, she had to cover her emotion with a smile. "No applause? You're hard to please."

His silence was going on too long. She pictured the small marble-topped table, the delicate saucers filled with coffee—all absent for the first time—just as an arrogant voice broke through the silence.

"It's good to see you again, Aria. It's been a while."

Soren.

Dead ahead, roughly four rows back, she saw a shadowed figure silhouetted against the darkness. Aria rolled onto the balls of her feet and breathed steadily as images flashed before her eyes. Soren, chasing her as fire raged around them. Soren, on top of her, crushing her throat with his hands.

This was the Realms, she reminded herself. *Better than Real.* No pain. No danger. He couldn't hurt her here.

"Where's your father?" she asked.

"Busy," Soren answered.

"So he sent *you*?"

"No."

"You hacked your way in."

"Hacking is something you do with a machete. This was a minor incision with a scalpel. Your mother would've liked that analogy. This is where you used to come with her, isn't it? I thought you'd like coming back."

The amusement in his voice made her stomach churn with anger. "What do you want, Soren?"

"A lot of things. But right now I want to see you."

To see her? She doubted it. Revenge seemed more likely. He probably blamed her for what happened that night in Ag 6. She wasn't going to wait around to find out. Aria tried to fraction out of the Realm.

"That won't work," Soren said, just as a message appeared on her screen, telling her the same. "Nice try, though. I liked the song, by the way. Touching. You've always been amazing, Aria. Really. Sing some more. I like that story. There's a horror Realm about it."

"I'm not singing to you," she said. "Turn the lights back on."

"He's deformed, isn't he? The Phantom?" Soren continued, ignoring her. "Doesn't he wear the mask to hide how hideous he is?"

There was another way out of the Realms. Aria shifted her focus to the real and curled her fingers around the edges of the Smarteye. She knew the pain of ripping off the device. A shocking ache that burned in the back of her eyes and ran like fire down her spine. She wanted out of there, but she couldn't bring herself to tear it off.

Soren's voice pulled her back to the Realm. "By the way, that blue dress in Venice was deadly. Thoroughly sexy. And champ move with the coffee. You shocked the hell out of my father."

"You've been *watching* me? You're disgusting."

He snorted. "If you only knew."

He'd toy with her as long as she allowed it. Aria took a few steps to the side, beyond the reach of the spotlight. Darkness settled over her—a relief this time. There. Now they were even.

"What are you doing? Where are you going?" Soren's

voice climbed in panic, spurring her on.

"Stay there, Soren. I'll come down to you." She wasn't, really. Aria couldn't see beyond the tip of her nose. But let him imagine her lurking in the darkness for a bit.

"*What?* Stop! Stay where you are!"

She heard a resounding *thump-thump*, like limbs sprawling. Then the lights came back—all of them—lighting up the lavish hall.

Soren had stumbled into the center aisle. He stood there, keeping his back turned to her. His breath was ragged, and his thick shoulders strained against his black shirt. He'd always been solid muscle.

"Soren?" One second passed. Two. "Why aren't you facing me?"

He grasped the seat beside him like he needed to steady himself. "I know my father told you. Don't act like you don't know what happened to my jaw."

She remembered and finally understood. "He told me it had to be reconstructed."

"Reconstructed," he said, still facing away from her. "That's such a *tidy* way to describe the *five fractures* and *burns* that needed to be fixed on my face."

Aria watched him, fighting the pull she felt to go to him. Finally she cursed herself for being too curious, and climbed down the stairs. Her heart beat wildly as she walked past the pit and up the aisle. She made herself keep going until she stood in front of him.

Soren stared down at her with brown eyes that swam in

rage, his lips pulled in a tense, grim line. He was holding his breath, just as she was.

He looked the same. Tan. Big-boned. Handsome in a harsh way, the angles of his face just a little too sharp. He held his chin at a condescending tilt. She couldn't help but compare him to Perry, who never seemed to look down at people despite being much taller.

Soren hadn't changed except for one significant difference. The set of his jaw was slightly off, and a scar ran through his bronzed skin, from the left corner of his mouth down to his jawbone.

Perry had given him that scar. That night in Ag 6 he had stopped Soren from strangling her. She'd be *dead* if Soren didn't have that scar. But she knew he hadn't been in his right mind. He'd been affected by Degenerative Limbic Syndrome—a brain disease that weakened basic survival instincts. It was the same disease her mother had studied.

"It doesn't look that bad," she said. She knew what it was like in Reverie. No one had scars. No one even had scratches. But she couldn't believe what she was saying. Was she really consoling *Soren*?

His Adam's apple bobbed as he swallowed. "Not bad? When did you get to be so funny, Aria?"

"Recently, I guess. You know, they're all scarred on the Outside. You should see this one guy, Reef. He's got this deep scar across his cheek. It's like a zipper running through his skin. Yours is . . . I mean, you can barely see it."

Soren narrowed his eyes. "How'd he get it?"

"Reef? He's a Scire. Those are Outsiders who . . . never mind. I don't know for sure, but my guess is that someone tried to cut his nose off."

Her voice rose at the end, making it sound like a question. She was trying to seem unfazed, but the brutality of the outside world seemed even more pronounced in such an elegant place. Aria studied his scar more closely. "Can't you get your father to hide that for you in the Realms? Wouldn't it just be simple programming?"

"*I* could do it, Aria. I don't need my father to do anything in here." His voice rose almost to a yell. Then he shrugged. "Anyway, why bother? I can't hide it in the real. Everyone knows I look like this. They know, and they won't ever un-know it."

Soren wasn't the same at all, she realized. His usual smug expression looked forced, like he was trying too hard to keep it there. She remembered that Bane and Echo—his closest friends—had died in Ag 6 the same night as Paisley.

"I can't talk about what happened that night, to anyone," he said. "My father says it would threaten the safety of the Pod." He shook his head, pain flitting across his face. "He blames me for what happened. He doesn't understand." Soren looked down at his hand, still gripping the seat beside him. "But you do. You know I didn't do anything to you on purpose . . . don't you?"

Aria crossed her arms. As much as she wanted to blame him for what he'd done to her, she couldn't. She'd learned about the disease in her mother's research files. After hundreds of years in the Realms and the safety of the Pod, some people, like Soren, had lost the ability to cope with real pain and stress. He'd behaved the way he had in Ag 6 because of DLS. She understood—but she also couldn't let him off easy.

"I feel like that was an apology in disguise," she said.

Soren nodded. "Maybe," he said, sniffing. "Actually, it was."

"Apology accepted. But don't *ever* touch me again, Soren."

His eyes flicked up, the look in them relieved, vulnerable. "I won't." He straightened and ran a hand over his head. The softness she'd seen vanished, replaced by a smirk. "Did you know not everyone has DLS? I'm part of the crazy group. How's that for luck? Doesn't matter. I'm getting the meds. A couple of weeks and I'll be ready."

"What *meds*? And ready for what?"

"Experimental cures so I won't go mental again. And immunization to outside diseases. They give them to Guardians who work on external repairs in case their suits rip or break. Once I have them, I'm coming out there. I'm done with this."

Aria gaped at him. "Out *here*? Soren, you have no idea how dangerous it is. It's not like going to a Safari Realm."

"Reverie's *breaking*, Aria," he snapped. "We're all coming out there sooner or later."

"What are you talking about? What's happening to Reverie?"

"Promise to help me on the Outside and I'll tell you."

Aria shook her head. "I'm not helping—"

"I could show you Caleb and Rune. Even the Savage kid you're always asking about." Suddenly his back straightened. "Gotta go. Time's up on the scramble."

"*Wait.* What's wrong with Reverie?"

He grinned, tipping his chin up. "If you want to know, then come back," he said, and fractioned out.

Aria blinked at the space where he'd been standing, and then at the empty opera hall. An icon flashed up on her Smartscreen, taking the spot next to the one for Hess.

It was the white mask of the Phantom of the Opera.

19

PEREGRINE

I t's been a week," Reef said. "You ever going to talk about it?"

Perry leaned his elbows on the table. The rest of the tribe had cleared out of the cookhouse after supper hours ago, leaving only the two of them. The sound of crickets chirping at the night carried to his ears, and shafts of cool Aether light slanted into the darkened room.

Perry ran his finger across the top of the candle between them, playing with the flame. When he went too slowly, it hurt. The trick was to go quickly. To not stop.

"No. I'm not," Perry answered, keeping his gaze on the flame.

Over the past days, he'd cleaned and gutted fish until the smell of the sea seeped into his fingers. He'd stayed out on night watch until his eyes grew bleary. He'd fixed a fence, then a ladder, and then a roof. He couldn't ask the Tides to work night and day if he didn't do so himself.

Reef crossed his arms. "The tribe would've turned against you if you'd left with her. And they would've turned if she'd stayed. She was smart. She saw that. Couldn't have been an easy decision for her. She did the right thing."

Perry looked up. Reef's gaze was direct. In the candlelight, the scar on his face looked deeper. It made him look cruel. "What are you doing, Reef?"

"Trying to draw out the poison. You've got it inside you, just as she did that night. You can't keep carrying this around, Perry."

"Yes. I can," he shot back. "I don't care what she did, or why, or whether it's wrong or right, understand?"

Reef nodded. "I understand."

"There's nothing more to say." What good did sitting around and talking ever do? It wouldn't change anything.

"All right," Reef said.

Perry sat back. He took a drink and grimaced. The well water hadn't recovered since the storm; it still tasted like ash. The Aether had a way of invading everything. It destroyed their food and burned their firewood before it ever reached their hearths. It even seeped into their water.

He'd done what he could by sending word to Marron. Now he had no move to make. No way to get Talon out of Reverie. Nothing to do except wait for Aria and Roar to come back and try to keep his people from starving. That didn't sit right with him.

Perry rubbed a hand over the back of his head and sighed.

"You want to know something?"

Reef nodded. "Sure."

"I feel like an old man. I feel how you must feel."

Reef smiled. "Not easy, is it, pup?"

"Could be easier." Perry's gaze drifted to his bow, leaning against the wall. When was the last time he'd used it? His shoulder had healed, and he had time now. He could find some food the way he always had.

"You want to hunt?" he asked, a surge of energy running through him. Suddenly nothing sounded better.

"Now?" Reef said, surprised. It was late, nearing midnight. "Thought you were tired."

"Not anymore." Perry pulled the Blood Lord chain over his head and dropped it into his satchel. He waited for Reef to object, and had his answers ready. It would be too loud if he had to run after prey, and too bright if he had to go unseen. But Reef just stood, a grin spreading over his face.

"Then let's hunt."

They loaded their quivers and jogged out beyond the compound. After checking in with Hayden, Hyde, and Twig, who sat watch on the eastern post, they slowed to a walk and moved off the trails into dense, untouched woods. Putting a hundred paces between them, they began to track.

Relief loosened Perry's limbs as he moved away from the compound. He inhaled deeply, catching the sting of the Aether. Looking up, he saw the same glowing currents that had hovered threateningly above all week. They bathed the woods in cool light. An offshore breeze swept toward him, perfect for bringing him the scent of game and for keeping his own scent hidden. He treaded softly, scenting, scanning the woods, feeling more energized than he had in weeks.

The wind died down, and he became aware of the night's stillness and the loudness of his footsteps. He looked up, expecting a storm, but the currents hadn't changed. He found Reef, who walked up shaking his head.

"I got nothing. Squirrels. A fox, but only an old trail. Nothing worth—Perry, what is it?"

"I don't know." The wind had risen again, moving through the trees with a soft hiss. On the cool air, he caught human scents. Fear blasted through him, sparking in his veins. "Reef—"

Beside him, Reef cursed. "I got it too."

They ran back to the eastern post. The rocky perch would give them the high ground. Twig reached them before they got there, his eyes frantic. "I was coming after you. Hyde's warning the compound."

"Do you hear them?" Perry asked.

Twig nodded. "They've got horses, and they're coming at a full gallop. Thunder's quieter."

Perry pulled his bow off his shoulder. "We'll make a stand here and slow them down." A swift approach in the middle of the night meant one thing: an attack. He needed to buy the tribe some time. "Take the near range," he told Hayden and Reef. "I'll take the long." He was the strongest archer among them, his eyes best suited to the dimness.

They spread out, finding cover among the trees and rocks along the overlook. His heart felt like a fist pounding inside his chest. The grassy meadow below looked as smooth and calm as a moonlit lake.

Was Wylan returning with a larger band to fight for the compound? Were the Rose and Night tribes attacking with their thousands? Suddenly he thought of Aria, lying on the bed in Vale's room, and then Talon, snatched away into a Hovercraft. He hadn't protected either of them from harm. He couldn't fail the Tides.

His thoughts disappeared when the earth began to rumble beneath his feet. Perry nocked an arrow, instinct taking over as he drew his bow. Seconds later the first riders broke through the trees. He aimed for the man at the center of the charge and loosed the bowstring. The arrow struck the man in the chest. By the time he twisted sideways and fell from the horse, Perry had another arrow nocked. He aimed and fired. Another rider down.

The cries of the attackers broke the silence, raising the hair on his arms. He saw roughly thirty mounted raiders below, and now he heard the whistle of arrows flying past him. Ignoring them, he focused on finding the nearest man and firing. One after another, until he'd gone through his quiver and then Reef's, with only one arrow that corkscrewed left and missed its mark because of damaged fletching, he was sure.

He lowered his bow and looked at Hayden, who was sighting down an arrow, scanning the field below for raiders.

No one else came into view, just their horses, galloping off, riderless.

It wasn't over, though. Seconds later a flood of people emerged from the woods, charging on foot.

"Hold them back as long as you can," Perry ordered Hayden and Twig. Then he tore for home with Reef. They dug in, feet churning over the earth, pushing themselves to run faster. The compound appeared ahead—already crawling with the movements of people climbing to the rooftops and pulling the gates between the houses closed.

Perry sprinted into the clearing and spotted Brooke on top of the cookhouse, bow in hand.

"Archers up!" she yelled. "Archers up now!"

People pumped water from the well into buckets, preparing for fires. They'd brought the animals within the protection of the walls. Everyone moved as they should, as they'd practiced.

Perry tore up to the roof of the cookhouse. Against the pale tinge of dawn on the horizon, he saw the swarm of raiders tearing upslope. He put them at less than a half a mile away, and two hundred in number. The Tides had the fortified position, but as he saw the horde of people streaming toward the compound, he didn't know if the tribe could hold them off.

The first arrows soared toward them, cracking roof tiles around him with sharp pops. Twig appeared at his side with a full quiver and a shield, giving him cover. Perry took his bow and set to defending his home. He'd done this plenty of times before, but never as the one in charge. The realization came on him like a quiet madness, slowing time, making his every move complete, efficient, sure.

Fire lit bright points of light against the rising dawn. A blazing arrow sliced past him, landing on the crates by the cookhouse. Perry adjusted his aim to the archers trying to set fire to the compound. His arrows—and those of Brooke and the Tides' other archers—sheared through the charging mob. Some raiders fell into the trenches he'd had excavated and covered, but still they kept coming, too many in number. He watched as they split into smaller bands, swinging wide to circle the compound.

Men were climbing the gates, chopping at them with axes. Perry fired his last arrow, spearing one of them through. Not enough. Too late. He heard a splintering crash and saw the gates split open. They'd been breached—and they were burning. Smoke wafted from the stables, and from the crates by the cookhouse.

Perry climbed down from the roof, drawing his knife as he leaped off the ladder. He drove it into a man's gut as he ran past. Voices he recognized screamed around him. He heard them faintly, no thought in his mind but finding the next attacker, the moment of hesitation, the false step, and seizing it.

In flashes, he saw Reef fighting nearby, his braids swinging in a blur. He saw Gren and Bear. Rowan, who'd resisted learning a weapon. Molly, whose life had been spent healing wounds.

Perry caught the glimpse of a black hat moving across the clearing. Cinder. A man with braided hair like Reef's snagged him by the shoulder, yanking him off his feet. Perry watched him cower, powerless, though he wasn't. Not a person there had more power, but Cinder wilted and didn't fight back. Willow darted forward suddenly and plunged a dagger into the man's leg. She took Cinder's hand and pulled him away, running into the nearest house.

A raider with metal studs around his eyes spotted Perry and charged forward, ax held high. Perry had a knife—no weapon to challenge an ax. With only steps left between them, an arrow struck the raider's head, lifting him off his feet. The impact sounded like stone roof tiles cracking. The man's body and the ax thudded to the dirt. Looking up, Perry saw Hyde on the roof above, the string of his bow still quivering.

He spun and plunged back into battle, losing time until someone yelled, "Pull back!" Around the clearing, others picked up the call. He saw the crowd grow thinner, no longer a thrashing, clanging mass.

Stunned, he watched the raiders retreat over the field they'd crossed no more than an hour before. Some carried sacks with them—food or other provisions. From the rooftops, Hyde and Hayden fired at them, forcing them to drop their stolen goods to run.

When the last of them had gone, Perry scanned the compound. Fires needed to be put out. The crates burning beside the cookhouse worried him most. He gave that work to

Reef, then sent Twig to track the raiders and make sure they weren't doubling back. Then he looked around the clearing. Bodies lay strewn everywhere.

Perry made his way around, finding each of the wounded, calling Molly over to those hurt the worst. He counted twenty-nine dead. All raiders. None of them his. Sixteen people had been wounded, ten of them Tiders. Bear had a gash on his arm, but he would live. Rowan needed a cut on his head sewn together. There were more injuries—a broken leg, smashed fingers, welts and burns—but nothing fatal.

At that point, knowing they'd all survived, he stepped over the broken main gate and walked beyond the compound until the flood of relief forced him to his knees. Digging his hands into the dirt, he felt the pulse of the earth move through his body, steadying him.

When he rose, a knot of brightness caught his eye to the east, and then another, just north. They were the glowing slash of funnels dropping from the sky. For a moment he watched the storms in the distance, absorbing the fact that his land was burning. He'd protected the compound from human attack, but the Aether was an enemy too powerful to fight off. He wouldn't let that weigh him down now. Today, he had won. Nothing could steal that away.

He returned to the clearing and organized the handling of the slain raiders. First they stripped the valuables from the dead. The tribe would reuse weapons, belts, and shoes. Then they loaded the bodies on horse carts, making one trip after another over the sandy trail. At the beach, wood was stacked to form a pyre. When it was ready, he dropped the torch that lit the wood, speaking the words that would release the souls of the dead to the Aether. He did this with some amazement at himself. Here, in the aftermath of battle just as during, neither his voice nor his hands wavered.

It was well into afternoon by the time he took the path back through the dunes to the compound, his legs shaking with fatigue. Perry slowed his pace, and Reef matched him. They let the others pull ahead.

Bloodstains covered Perry's shirt, his knuckles throbbed, and he was pretty sure he'd broken his nose again, but Reef had managed to come through the raid without a scratch on him. Perry didn't know how he'd done it. He'd seen Reef fighting as hard as he had been, maybe harder.

"What'd you do this morning?" he asked.

Reef smirked. "Slept late. You?"

"Read a book."

Reef shook his head. "I don't believe you. You look worse after you read." He was quiet for a moment, the humor disappearing from his face. "We got lucky today. Most of those people had no idea how to fight."

He was right. The raiders had been desperate and disorganized. The Tides wouldn't be that lucky twice. "Any idea where they were from?" Perry asked.

"South. They lost their own compound a few weeks ago. Strag got it out of one of the injured before he drove them off Tide land. They were after shelter. My guess is they got word of our weak numbers and decided to take a chance.

They won't be the last ones to try." Reef tipped his chin at Perry. "You know you probably wouldn't be standing here if you'd been wearing the chain? They'd have targeted you. Take the leader down and the rest is easy."

Perry stopped. He reached up, feeling the absence of the weight around his neck, and then noticed that Reef was carrying his satchel.

"It's in here," he said, handing it over. "Strange thing about you, Peregrine. Sometimes it's like you know things are going to happen before they do."

"No," Perry said, taking it. "If I could predict the future, I'd have avoided a lot of things." He slipped the chain out of the leather pack. For an instant he held it in his hand and felt a connection to Vale and his father through it.

"They're calling you a hero for this," Reef said. "I've heard it a few times already."

Were they? Perry pulled the chain over his head. "First time for everything, I guess," he joked, but it made no sense to him. What he'd done today felt no different from trying to rescue Old Will during the storm.

As he walked up, he found the tribe waiting at the compound. They spread into a circle around him. The clearing had been washed down with buckets of water, but the mud beneath his feet held traces of ash and blood. At his side, Reef muffled a grunt, reacting to the scent that hung in the afternoon air. Pure fear was hard on the nose.

Perry knew they wanted to be reassured—to be told that it was safe now, that the worst was over—but he couldn't do it. Another tribe would raid them. Another Aether storm would come. He couldn't lie and tell them that everything was fine. Besides, he was terrible at speeches. If there was something genuine and important to be said, he needed to look a person in the eye and say it.

He cleared his throat. "We can still put in the better part of a day's work."

The Tides looked at one another, unsure, but after a few moments they broke off to fix the protective walls and the roof tiles, and make all the other repairs that were needed.

Reef's voice was quiet beside him. "Well done."

Perry nodded. The tasks would help put them at ease. Repairing the compound would calm them more than any speech he could give.

Then it was time for him to do his own work. He started from the western edge of his territory and made his way east. He found the Tides, every one, in the stables, in the fields, at the harbor, and looked into their eyes and told them he was proud of what they'd done today.

Late that night, with the compound silent, Perry climbed up to his roof. He gripped the heavy links around his neck until the cool metal warmed between his fingers. For the first time, he felt like their Blood Lord.

20

ARIA

Ready?" Aria asked Roar.

They'd made camp by the Snake River, which would lead them the rest of the way to the Horns. Branches were strewn across the harsh, gravelly banks, and the wide river ran smooth as a mirror, reflecting the swirling Aether sky. They'd moved swiftly through the afternoon, keeping ahead of an Aether storm. The distant shriek of the funnels carried to her ears, prickling the skin on the back of her neck.

Roar leaned back against his satchel and crossed his arms. "I've been ready since the day I woke up and Liv wasn't there. You?"

They'd spent the past week climbing Ranger's Edge, a frigid mountain pass bordered by sharp, soaring peaks that looked like shredded metal. Between her ears and Roar's, they'd steered clear of encounters with other people and wolves, but they hadn't been able to escape the constant wind that sliced through the pass, trapping it in what felt like perpetual winter. Aria's lips had chapped and cracked. Her feet had blistered, and her hands were numb, but tomorrow, two weeks after they'd left the Tides, they'd reach Rim at last.

"Yes. Ready," she answered, trying to sound more confident than she felt. The magnitude of her task was hitting her. How was she going to discover protected information from Sable—a Scire who despised Dwellers? A Blood Lord who trusted no one with the secret he guarded?

She pictured Talon's legs swinging over the pier. If she failed, how would she get him out? Would it be the end of Reverie? Aria shook her head, pushing away the worries. She couldn't let herself think that way.

"You think Sable will want to bargain?" she asked. They planned to tell him that they'd come on behalf of Perry, who, as new Blood Lord of the Tides, wanted to rescind the betrothal Vale had arranged a year earlier. They'd also try to buy the information of the Still Blue's location.

Roar shook his head. "I don't know. The Tides already accepted the first half of the dowry. The only way Perry can repay him is in land, but with the Aether getting worse, that might not be enough. Who would take on new territory just to watch it burn?" He lifted his shoulders. "It's a long shot, but it might work. From what I know, Sable's greedy. We'll try it first."

Their second tactic was to snoop around and figure out

the Still Blue's whereabouts, get Liv, and run.

As they fell into silence, Aria reached into her satchel for the falcon carving. She ran her fingers over the dark wood, remembering Perry's smile as he'd said, *Mine is the one that looks like a turtle.*

"If he's hurting her, or forcing her in any way—"

She looked up. Roar was staring at the campfire. His dark eyes flicked to hers before moving back to the flames. He hunched down into his coat, firelight dancing on his handsome face. "Forget I said that."

"Roar . . . it'll be all right," she said, though she knew it wouldn't bring him any comfort. He was trapped in the pain of not knowing. She remembered feeling the same way when she'd been searching for her mother. A cycle of hoping, and then the *fear* of hoping, and then just fear. There was no way out except to learn the truth. At least he'd have that tomorrow.

They fell into another stretch of quiet before Roar spoke again. "Aria, be careful around Sable. If he scents you're nervous, he'll ask until he learns why."

"I can hide my nerves on the surface, but I won't be able to stop feeling them. It's not something that can be turned off and on."

"That's why you should keep away from him as much as possible. We'll find ways to look around quietly for the Still Blue."

She scooted her feet closer to the fire, feeling the heat soak into her toes. "So I'm supposed to stay away from the one person I'm trying to get close to?"

"Scires," Roar said, like it explained everything.

In a way, it did.

After a few hours of restless sleep, she woke at dawn and slipped her Smarteye out of her satchel. She'd seen Hess twice during the week, but he'd kept their meetings short. He wanted news, and apparently walking day and night with freezing hands and feet didn't qualify. He'd refused to let her see Talon again. Refused to tell her anything about Reverie's condition. Whenever she asked, he fractioned, leaving her abruptly. Now she decided she'd had enough of being kept in the dark.

With Roar sleeping nearby, she applied the Smarteye and called the Phantom.

Seconds after she selected the white mask, Aria fractioned. Her heart leaped as she recognized the Realm. It was one of her favorites, based on an ancient painting of a gathering along the Seine River. Everywhere, people in nineteenth-century dress strolled or lounged, enjoying the sunshine as boats glided through the calm water. Birds twittered cheerfully, and a gentle breeze rustled the trees.

"I knew you wouldn't be able to stay away from me."

"Soren?" Aria asked, scanning the men around her. They wore top hats and suits with coattails, while the women wore bustled skirts and held colorful parasols. She looked for thickset shoulders. The aggressive tip of a chin.

"I'm here," he said. "You just can't see me. We're invisible.

People think you're dead. If anyone saw you, there's no way I could keep that from my father. Even I have limits."

Aria looked down at her hands. She didn't see them—or any part of herself. Panic washed over her. She felt like she was nothing more than a floating pair of eyes. In the real, she wiggled her fingers to shake off the feeling.

Then she heard a voice she'd known all her life.

"Pixie, you're blocking my light."

She followed the sound to the source, her heart thudding in her chest. Caleb sat on a red blanket just a few paces away, sketching in a notebook. His tongue poked out of the corner of his mouth—a habit he had when swept away by his creations. Aria took in his gangly limbs and ruddy hair as he moved a pencil across the page. He looked so much like Paisley. She'd never realized how alike they were until now.

"Can he hear me?" she whispered, her voice high and thin.

"No," Soren said. "He has no idea we're here. You've been saying you wanted to see him."

She wanted much more than that. Aria wanted hours, days to spend with Caleb. Time to tell him how sorry she was about Paisley and how much she missed spending every day with him. Caleb was there with other people now. Pixie sat beside him in silence, watching him sketch, her jet-black hair trimmed shorter than Aria remembered. Aria wondered how Soren felt seeing her. Less than a year ago, they'd been dating. Rune was there as well with the Tilted Green Bottles' drummer, Jupiter. They were tangled in a passionate kiss, oblivious to anyone else.

Something about them—about all of them—seemed distant and desperate.

"Congratulations," Soren said. "You're officially nothing."

She panned the empty space beside her. It was strange hearing his voice and not being able to see him. "Soren, this is eerie."

"Try it for five months, then tell me how you feel."

"Is this . . . is this really how you spend your time?"

"You think I like skulking around? My father *banned* me, Aria. You think you were the only one he sold out after that night?" He made a snorting sound, like he regretted his last words. "Anyway . . . whatever." He sighed. "Check it out. Jupiter and Rune are, like, mega into each other. Saw that coming. Jup's a good man. Decent pilot, too. We used to have fun racing D-Wings before . . . you know. Before. And Pixie, she and I were . . . I don't know. I don't know what we were. But *Caleb*, Aria. What do you *see* in him?"

She saw a thousand things. A thousand memories. Caleb used words like *audacious* and *lethargic* to describe colors. He loved sushi because it was beautiful. When he laughed, he covered his mouth. When he yawned, he didn't. He was the first boy she'd ever kissed, and it'd been a disaster—nothing like the breathless thrill of kissing Perry. They'd been on a Ferris wheel in a carnival Realm. Caleb's eyes had been open, which she hadn't liked. She'd kissed his bottom lip, which he'd found odd. But the main problem, they'd decided, was that the kiss had lacked meaning. Or *gravitas*, as Caleb had called it.

Now when she looked at him, all she saw was meaning. All she felt was sadness. For him. For how they'd been. Things would never be the same.

Aria's attention moved to his drawing, curious to see what absorbed him. The sketch was a side view of a skeletal figure in a tight crouch, knees and arms bent, head down. It reached to the very edge of the page, so the figure looked trapped in a box. The drawing was somber, menacing, and nothing like his usual loose sketches.

Suddenly, silence closed over the Realm. Aria looked up. The trees were still. No sounds drifted up from the river. The Realm was as motionless as the painting it'd been modeled after, except for the anxious, subtle shifting of the people. Caleb's gaze lifted from his sketchbook. Pixie squinted at the sky and then at the river like she couldn't believe her eyes. Rune and Jupiter drew apart and looked at each other with confusion.

"Soren—" Aria began.

"It usually comes right back."

He was right. A second later, the sound of birdsong returned, and a breeze stirred the leaves above her. Out on the lake, sailboats resumed their progress over the water.

The Realm had unlocked, but it hadn't returned to normal. Caleb snapped his sketchbook shut, sticking his pencil over his ear. A man nearby cleared his throat and adjusted his tie, resuming his walk along the path. Slowly, conversations around them picked up again, but they seemed forced, a little too enthusiastic.

Aria had never dreamed until she'd been cast out of Reverie. Now she saw how similar the Realms were. A good dream was something you clung to until the last moment before waking. Caleb was clinging. They all were. Everything about this place was good, and they didn't want to see any hint of it ending.

"Soren, can we get out of here? I don't want to watch this any—"

They fractioned back to the opera hall before she'd finished speaking. Aria looked down, relieved to see herself.

Soren stood with her onstage. He crossed his arms and raised an eyebrow. "What do you think of your old life? Different, right?"

"That's putting it lightly. The glitch just now—how often is that happening?"

"A few times a day. I looked into it. Power surges. One of the domes that houses a generator was compromised this winter, so things are . . . glitchy."

A wave of numbness rolled through her. It was the same thing that had happened to Bliss, the Pod where her mother had died. "Can't they fix it?"

"They're trying. It's what they've always done. But with Aether storms getting worse, they can't patch the damage fast enough."

"That's why your father is pressuring me for the Still Blue."

"He's desperate—and he should be. We have to get out of here. It's just a matter of time." He smiled darkly. "That's where you come in. You wanted to see them, and I told you what's happening in Reverie. Now you have to help me when I come out there."

She studied him. "You're really ready to leave everything?"

"What *everything*, Aria?" He glared at the audience seats. "You want to know what I'm leaving? A father who ignores me. Who doesn't even *trust* me. Friends I can't see, and a Pod that's an Aether storm away from ruin. You think I'm going to miss any of that? I'm *already* on the outside." He took a deep breath and closed his eyes, exhaling slowly. Calming himself. "Do we have a deal or not?"

He was a long way from the cocky, controlling Soren she remembered. That night in Ag 6 had transformed both of them. "Things aren't any easier out here."

"Does that mean yes?"

She nodded. "But only if you look after someone until you come out here."

He froze. "Caleb? Done. Even though he's a worthless piece of—"

"I wasn't talking about Caleb."

Soren blinked at her. "You mean the Savage's nephew? The Outsider who *broke* my *jaw*?"

"He did it because you were attacking me," she snapped. "Don't forget that part. And you better think again if you're coming Outside for revenge. Perry would destroy you."

Soren put his hands up. "Easy, tigress. I was just asking. So what do you want me to do—babysit the kid?"

She shook her head. "Make sure Talon stays safe—no matter what. And I want to see him."

"When?"

"Right now."

Soren worked his jaw side to side as he stared down at her. "Fine," he said. "I'm curious. Let's go see the little Savage."

Ten minutes later, Aria sat on the pier and watched as Talon taught Soren how to cast out. Athletic and competitive, Soren actually wanted to learn, and Talon picked up on that. As she watched them prattle on about bait, she felt unexpectedly optimistic. Somehow the two castoffs were getting along.

Soren had a fish on the line as she left them and moved through the commands to shut off the Eye. Aria slipped it back into her satchel and woke Roar.

It was time to meet Sable.

21

PEREGRINE

A week after the raid, Perry woke in the darkness. The house was still, his men lay scattered in slumbering mounds across the floor, and the first tinge of daylight bled through the cracks in the shutters.

He'd dreamed of Aria. Of the time months ago when she'd convinced him to sing to her. His voice rough and breaking, he'd sung the words of the Hunter's Song while she listened, nestled in his arms.

Perry pressed his fingers to his eyes until he saw stars instead of her face. He'd been such a fool.

He pulled himself to his feet and wove past the Six to the loft. Gren still hadn't returned from the journey to Marron's, and as Perry had feared, the Tides were going hungry. He saw it in the new angles in Willow's face. Heard it in the sharp edge in the Six's voices. A constant ache had settled in his gut, and yesterday he'd needed to cut a new notch in his belt. He didn't feel it yet, but he worried that weakness would come next.

Perry couldn't spend any more effort on fields that might end up burning. Between overhunting and Aether storms, tracking game was nearly impossible. So they relied on the sea more than ever and managed, most of the time, to fill the cooking pots at the end of the day. No one complained about the taste of food anymore. Hunger had done away with that.

Their position by the coast was an advantage other tribes wanted. Reports came daily from his patrol of bands sniffing at the edge of his territory. Perry knew he couldn't wait for Marron's help anymore. He couldn't wait for the next storm or the next raid. He needed to do something.

He climbed a few rungs until he could see into the loft. Cinder lay sprawled across the mattress, snoring softly. The night of the raid, he'd scurried up there, terrified and teary, and it had been his place ever since. His eyes twitched in sleep, a bead of drool slipping down the side of his mouth. His black wool cap was crumpled in his hand.

Perry was reminded of Talon then, though he wasn't sure why. He guessed Cinder to be about five years older than Talon, and they were nothing alike in temperament. Perry had been with Talon every day of his life until he'd been kidnapped. He'd held Talon in his arms and watched him drift asleep, and seen him unfold, day by day, into a child who was gentle and wise.

He knew next to nothing about Cinder; the boy hadn't

breathed a word about his past, or his power. When he did speak, it was often to snap and bite. He was guarded and reactive, but Perry felt a bond with him. Maybe he didn't *know* Cinder, but he understood him.

Perry jostled him lightly. "Wake up. I need you to come with me."

Cinder's eyes flew open, and then he climbed down with a clumsy, noisy thump.

Reef and Twig woke. Hyde and Hayden too. Even Strag did. They looked at one another, and then Reef said, "I'll go," and rose to follow Perry.

It was just as well. Perry had planned to ask Reef along anyway.

Since the raid, the Six were as protective over him as ever. Perry let them be. He grabbed his bow by the front door, glimpsing the scars Cinder had given him. Like everyone, Perry was made of flesh and bone. He burned and bled. He'd survived the raid and the Aether storm, but how many times would he cheat death? There was a time for risk and a time for caution. Always he struggled to choose between them, but it was something he was learning.

Aether spread across the sky in waves, blue and glowing. Thicker than he'd ever seen, even in the harshest winters. The sun would rise and the day would brighten a bit, but they would still be in the blue, marbled light.

With Cinder and Reef at his sides, Perry took to the northern trail beyond the compound, passing a field of dead wood that tickled his nose with fine ash and left Reef sneezing.

Neither of them asked where Perry was taking them—for which he was grateful. With every step, his pulse beat faster.

He glanced at Cinder, who was anxious, his temper vibrant and green. They hadn't talked about what had happened in the raid. Perry had taken him aside a few minutes a day and showed him how to shoot a bow. Cinder was terrible—skitty and impatient—but he tried. And he seemed to have grown closer to Willow, who'd likely saved his life. They sat together in the cookhouse now, and a few days ago Perry had run into them on the harbor trail and seen Willow wearing Cinder's cap.

The dirt path narrowed as it wove farther away from the compound. The earth was uneven and rocky here, no good for farming, but it was a good place to hunt—it had been, when that was how he spent his days. After an hour, the trail cut west and brought them to a cliff overlooking the sea. Below, the bluff wrapped around a small cove. Black rocks of every size jutted up along the beach and out on the water.

Perry glanced back at Reef and Cinder. "There's a cave down there that I need you to see."

Reef pushed his braids back, looked at him with an expression he couldn't decipher. Perry could've searched for his temper, but chose not to. He climbed down the craggy slope, over rocks and hard sand and tussocks of grass. He'd done this a hundred times with Roar and Liv and Brooke. This climb had meant freedom then. An escape from the never-ending chores at the compound, and the closeness of tribe life. Now, instead of feeling eagerness to reach a hideaway, he felt like he was heading into a trap.

Skitty with nerves, he realized he was moving too quickly, and had to force himself to slow down and wait for Cinder and Reef, who were upsetting small avalanches behind him.

When they reached the sand, he was out of breath, but not from the climb. The steep walls of the bluff curved around him in the shape of a horseshoe, and he could already feel the weight of the rock inside the cave pressing down on him. The surf crashed against the shore. It felt like it pounded inside his chest. He couldn't believe what he was doing. What he was about to say—and show them.

"This way." He led them to the narrow cleft in the rock face—the entrance to the cave—and slipped inside before he could change his mind. He had to lean at an angle to fit along the narrow crevice until the way opened into the vast main cavity inside. Then he stood and made himself breathe, in and then out, in and then out, as he told himself the walls wouldn't fold on him. Wouldn't crush him beneath unknown tons.

It was cold and damp in the dim cavern, but sweat ran down his back and along his ribs, dripping from him. A brackish smell flowed into his nose, and a hollow silence roared in his ears. His chest was tight—as tight as it'd been under the churning water the day of the Aether storm. No matter how many times he'd been there, it was always this way at first.

Finally he found his breath, and looked around.

Daylight streamed in behind him, enough for him to see

the vastness of the space—of the wide, open belly of the cave. His gaze moved to a stalagmite in the distance: a formation shaped like a jellyfish, with dripping, melting tendrils. From where he stood, it looked small and only fifty yards off. It was actually many times his height and a hundred yards away. He knew, because he'd shot arrows at it from there. He and Brooke had. A year ago, he'd stood in the same spot with her while Roar whooped loudly, laughing at the way the sound echoed, and Liv wandered off, exploring the deeper reaches of the cave.

Reef and Cinder stood in silence beside him, eyes wide and scanning, glinting in the low light. He wondered if they could see what he saw.

Perry cleared his throat. It was time for him to explain. To justify something he hated and didn't want to admit.

"We need a place to go if we lose the compound. I won't wander the borderlands with the tribe, searching for food, for shelter from the Aether. This is big enough to fit us all. . . . There are tunnels that lead to other caverns. And it's defensible. It won't burn. We can fish from the cove, and there's a freshwater source inside."

Every word that came out of him felt like an effort. He didn't want to say any of this. He didn't want to bring his people underground, to this dark place. To live like the ghostlike creatures from the deep sea.

Reef looked at him for a long moment. "You think it will come to this."

Perry nodded. "You know the borderlands better than I

do. You think I want to take River and Willow out there?"

He pictured it. Three hundred people under an open, roiling sky, surrounded by fires and bands of dispersed. He imagined the Croven—cannibals in black capes and crow masks—surrounding them like they were a herd and picking them off one by one. He wouldn't let it happen.

Cinder shifted his weight, watching them silently.

"We have to be prepared for the worst," Perry continued, his voice echoing in the cavern. He wondered how it would be with hundreds of voices in there.

Reef shook his head. "I don't see how you're going to do this. It's . . . a *cave*."

"I'll find a way."

"This isn't a solution, Perry."

"I know." It was a last resort. Coming there would be like standing on the prow of a ship as it sank. It wasn't the answer. The answer would have to come with Roar and Aria. But this would buy time as the waters rose.

"I wore a chain once," Reef said, after a long moment. "Much like yours."

Surprise moved through Perry. Reef had been a Blood Lord? He had never said anything, but Perry should've seen it. Reef was so determined to teach him, to keep him from failing.

"It was years ago. A different time than this. But I know something of what you're facing. I'm behind you, Peregrine. I would be, even without having sworn an oath to you. But the tribe will resist this."

Perry knew that too. It was the reason he'd brought Cinder. "Give us a few minutes," he told Reef.

Reef nodded. "I'll be right outside."

"Did I do something wrong?" Cinder asked when Reef had left them.

"No. You didn't."

Cinder's scowl faded. "Oh."

"I know you don't want to talk about yourself," Perry said. "I understand that. Pretty well, actually. And I wouldn't ask you unless I had to. But I do have to." He shifted his weight, wishing he didn't have to press. "Cinder, I need to know what you can do with the Aether. Can you tell me what to expect? Can you keep it away? I have to know if there's any alternative—any way at all to avoid this."

Cinder was still for a moment. Then he took his cap off and slipped it through his belt. He walked deeper into the cave and turned, facing Perry. The veins at his neck took on the glow of the Aether, which seeped up over his face like water snaking through a dry river. His hands came alive. His eyes became bright blue points in the darkness.

Aether burned in the back of Perry's nose, and his heart raced. Then, as gradually as it had brightened, the glow in Cinder's veins faded away, the sting receding, leaving just a boy, standing there again.

Cinder pulled on his cap back, tugging it down and brushing wisps of straw-colored hair away from his eyes. Then he went still and watched Perry for a few moments, his gaze direct and open, before he spoke at last.

"It's harder to reach it in here," he said. "I can't call it as easily as when I'm outside, right under it."

Perry moved closer to him, eager to learn what he'd wondered for months. "What does it feel like?"

"Most of the time, like right now, I feel hollow and tired. But when I call it, I feel strong and light. I feel like fire. Like I'm part of everything." He scratched his chin. "I can only hold on to it a little while before I have to push it. That's all I can do is just bring it to me, and then push it away. I'm not very good, though. Where I'm from—Rhapsody—there were kids who were better at it than me."

Perry's heart thudded. Rhapsody was a Pod hundreds of miles away, past Reverie. "You're a Dweller."

Cinder shook his head. "I don't know. I don't remember much from before I broke out of there. But I guess . . . I guess I could be. When I met you in the woods and you were with Aria? It didn't seem like you hated her. That's why I followed you. I thought maybe you'd be all right with me, too."

"You thought right," Perry said.

"Yeah." Cinder smiled, a flash in the dimness that faded quickly.

A hundred questions buzzed Perry's mind about how Cinder had escaped Rhapsody. About the other kids, who were like him. But he knew to tread lightly. He knew to let Cinder come to him.

"If I could help you with the Aether, I would," Cinder said, the words sudden and blunt. "But I can't . . . I just can't."

"Because it makes you weak afterward?" Perry asked, remembering the way Cinder had suffered after their encounter with the Croven. By calling the Aether, Cinder had destroyed the band of cannibals. He'd saved Perry's life, and Aria and Roar's too, but the act had left him cold as ice and drained to the point of unconsciousness.

Cinder looked past him, like he was worried Reef would be there.

"It's all right," Perry said. He could trust Reef with secrets—Cinder's scent probably already had Reef suspicious—but Perry knew Cinder would only be at ease with him. "Reef's outside, and he'll stay there. It's just us."

Reassured, Cinder nodded and replied, "Every time, I feel worse afterward. It's like the Aether takes part of me away with it. I feel like I can barely breathe, it hurts so much. One day it'll take everything. I know it will." He brushed away a tear from his cheek with an angry swipe. "It's all I have," he said. "It's the only thing I can do, and I'm scared of it."

Perry exhaled slowly, absorbing the information. Every time Cinder used his power, he gambled with his life. Perry couldn't ask that of him. It was one thing to take chances with his own life. But he couldn't put an innocent boy in that position. Not ever.

"You're well if you don't use it?" he asked.

Cinder nodded, his eyes downcast.

"Then don't. Don't call the Aether. Not for any reason."

Cinder peered up. "Does that mean you're not streaked at me?"

"Because you can't save the Tides for me?" Perry shook his head. "No. Not at all, Cinder. But you're wrong about something. The Aether isn't the only thing you have. You're part of this tribe now, no different from anyone else. And you've got me. All right?"

"All right," Cinder said, fighting off a smile. "Thanks."

Perry thumped him on the shoulder. "Maybe one day you'll let me borrow your hat, if it's all right with Willow."

Cinder rolled his eyes. "That was . . . that wasn't . . ."

Perry laughed. He knew exactly what it was.

Twig ran up on the trail as they returned to the compound. "Gren is back," he said, panting for breath. "He's brought Marron with him."

Marron was *here*? It didn't make sense. Perry had sent Gren for provisions. He hadn't expected his friend to deliver them personally.

He stepped into the clearing and saw a filthy, weather-beaten group, roughly thirty in number. Molly and Willow were giving them water, and Gren stood with them, his face tight with worry.

Perry clasped his hand. "Good you're back."

"I ran into them on my way," Gren said, "and brought them with me. I knew it was what you'd want."

Perry scanned the crowd and almost missed Marron. He was a different person. Dirt coated his tailored jacket, the ivory silk shirt beneath rumpled and stained with sweat. His blond hair—normally perfectly combed—was matted and darkened by grease and dirt. His face was windburned and had lost all of its roundness. He had withered.

"We were overpowered," Marron said. "There were thousands." He took a gulping breath, fighting back emotion. "I couldn't keep them out. There were just too many."

Perry's heart stopped. "Was it the Croven?"

Marron shook his head. "No. It was the Rose and Night tribes. They took Delphi."

Perry studied the people with him. Men and women, huddled together. Half of them were children, so tired they swayed on their feet. "The others?" Marron had commanded hundreds of people.

"Forced to stay, some. Others chose to. I don't blame them. I started with twice this number, but many turned back. We haven't eaten—"

Marron's blue eyes filled. He pulled a handkerchief from his pocket. It was folded in a perfect square, but the material was as rumpled and dirty as the rest of his clothing. He frowned at it like he was surprised to find it soiled, and returned it to his pocket.

His ragtag group watched in silence. Their expressions were dead, their tempers muted and lifeless. Perry realized this could happen to the Tides if they lost the compound and were forced into the borderlands. His doubts about the cave began to fade.

"We have nowhere else to go," Marron said.

"You don't need to go anywhere else. You can stay here."

"We're taking them in?" Twig asked. "How're we going to feed them?"

"We are," Perry said, though he didn't know how. He barely had enough food for the Tides. But what could he do? He could never turn Marron away.

"Get them settled," he told Reef.

He took Marron to his house. There, Marron's temper deepened and deepened, becoming something immense, until finally his tears came. Perry sat with him at the table, deeply shaken himself. At Delphi, Marron had had soft beds and the finest food as often as he'd wanted. He'd had a wall protecting him, with archers posted day and night. He'd lost everything.

That night at supper—watered-down fish soup—Perry sat with Marron at the high table and looked across the cookhouse. The Tides wanted nothing to do with Marron's people. They sat apart, at separate tables, glaring at the new-comers. Perry hardly recognized his tribe anymore. People came and people left. Both were unsettling to the Tides.

"Thank you," Marron said quietly. He knew the strain he'd placed on Perry.

"No need for that. Tomorrow I plan to put you to work."

Marron nodded, his blue eyes sparkling, filling with the sharp curiosity Perry remembered. "Of course. Ask any-thing."

22

ARIA

Whatever Aria had expected from the Horns, it hadn't been this. She absorbed their settlement in awe as she and Roar approached on a farm road. She had imagined Rim as a compound, like the Tides', but this was so much more.

The road led them through a valley many times larger than the Tides'. Farmland stepped up mountain slopes that rose to soaring, snowcapped peaks. Here and there she saw the silvery scars of Aether damage. Sable had the same challenges Perry did with growing food. The realization gave her a perverse satisfaction.

In the distance she saw the city: a cluster of towers of varying heights nestled against the sheer side of a mountain. Balconies and bridges connected the towers in a chaotic network, giving Rim a sprawling, jumbled appearance that reminded her of a coral reef. A single structure loomed above the others, with a spired rooftop that looked like a spear. The Snake River skirted the near side of the city, forming a natural moat, with smaller structures and homes spilling along its banks.

Aether currents flowed bright and fast in the late morning sky, enhancing Rim's severe appearance. The storm they'd been running from had followed them there.

Aria lifted an eyebrow. "It's not the Tide compound, is it?"

Roar shook his head, his gaze locked on the city. "No. It's not."

As they neared Rim, the road grew crowded with people coming and going, carrying satchels and pushing carts. She noticed that the Marked wore specific clothing that revealed their arms, making their Senses known—vests for the men, and shirts with slits along the sleeves for the women. Adrenaline prickled in Aria's veins as she ran a hand over her shirt, picturing the botched Marking beneath.

Roar kept close as they reached a wide cobbled bridge and slipped into the flow. Snatches of conversation drifted to Aria's ears.

". . . just had a storm days ago . . ."

". . . find your brother and tell him to get home now . . ."

". . . worse growing season than last year . . ."

The bridge brought them into narrow streets bordered by stone houses that were several stories high. Aria took the lead, following the main road. The way was tight, shadowed as a tunnel and crowded with people, their voices echoing off stone and stone and more stone. Gutters were strewn with filth, and a fetid scent carried to her nose. Rim was large, but she could already tell it was nowhere near as modern as Marron's.

The streets climbed and turned, and then ended abruptly at the tower. Massive wooden doors opened to a stone chamber that flickered with torchlight. Guards in trim black uniforms with red stag horns embroidered on the chest watched the traffic of people who passed inside.

As she and Roar walked up, a hulking guard with a thick black beard blocked their path. "Your business?" he asked.

"We're here from the Tides to see Sable," she said.

"Stay here." He disappeared inside.

It felt like an hour passed before another guard arrived, giving Roar a cursory look. "You're Marked?" he asked. He had close-cropped dark hair, almost shaved, and an impatient look in his eyes. The stag horns at his chest were woven in silver thread.

Roar nodded. "An Aud."

The guard's gaze turned to her, his impatience disappearing. "And you?"

"Unmarked," she answered. It was true, in part. She was Unmarked on one side.

The guard's eyebrows lifted slightly, and then his gaze trailed down her body, settling at her belt. "Pretty pair of knives." His tone was flirtatious and teasing.

"Thank you," Aria answered. "I keep them sharp."

His mouth curled in amusement. "Follow me."

Aria exchanged a look with Roar as they stepped inside. This was it. No turning back now.

Inside, the wide hall smelled faintly of mold and rancid wine. It was cold and damp. Even with the wooden shutters thrown open, and lamps, the stone corridor was gloomy and shadowed. The faint chatter of voices carried to her ears, growing louder.

Roar prowled beside her, searching every person, every room they passed, with hunger in his eyes. Aria couldn't imagine how he felt. After so many months of searching, he'd finally see Liv.

They crossed a wide threshold, entering a hall as expansive as the cookhouse at the Tides' but with high, arched ceilings that reminded her of Gothic cathedrals. A meal was in progress. Dozens of guards were packed around the tables, a sea of black and red spreading out before her. Sable kept his military force close.

A stroke of luck, she thought. She'd been worried about Sable reading her temper. Maybe in such a crowd he'd miss scenting the fear swirling inside her.

"Which one is Sable?"

At the far end of the hall she saw a dais, where several men and women sat above the rest. None of the men wore a Blood Lord chain.

"I don't see him," said the guard. "But you might. He has short hair. Blue eyes. He's about my height. Exactly my height, actually."

The humor in his tone sent a chill crawling down her spine.

She looked at the guard—at Sable—standing beside her.

He was older than she'd expected. In his thirties, she guessed. Average in height and build, with features that were refined and well-proportioned but somehow unremarkable. She'd have thought him bland if it hadn't been for the look in his steel-colored eyes. That look—confident, cunning, amused—catapulted him from forgettable to appealing.

Sable smiled, obviously pleased with the trick he'd played on her. "I know you're from the Tides, but I didn't catch your names."

She cleared her throat. "Aria and Roar."

Sable's eyes moved to Roar and narrowed in recognition. "Olivia has spoken of you."

"Where is she?" Roar asked.

Seconds passed. The hall bustled with noise around them. Her pulse pounding, Aria watched Sable's chest expand and contract with a breath and knew he was scenting Roar's rage. His jealousy. A year's worth of worrying about Liv.

"She's close," Sable said finally. "Come. I'll take you to her now. What a reunion this will be."

They exited the hall and moved back into the shadowed corridors. Aria tried to memorize their path, but the halls twisted and turned and then climbed narrow stairs and turned again. There were doors and lamps along the walls, but no windows or distinguishing marks to help her remember the way. A trapped feeling crawled over her, reminding her of a labyrinth Realm she'd been in once. An image of a dungeon flashed before her eyes, raising the hair on the back of her neck. Where was Sable keeping Liv?

"How is the young Blood Lord of the Tides faring?" Sable asked over his shoulder. She couldn't see his expression, but the tone in his voice was light and casual. Aria had a feeling he knew Perry had lost part of his tribe. The question seemed to be a test more than a search for information.

"Faring," Roar said tightly.

In the darkness Sable laughed, the sound smooth and engaging. "Carefully put." He stopped in front of a heavy wooden door. "Here we are."

They stepped out into a large stone-paved courtyard loud with the cheers of a crowd. Around her the castle—it was the best word she could come up with for Sable's rambling stronghold—rose up hundreds of feet in the same disjointed arrangement of balconies and walkways she'd seen from afar. The sheer gray face of the mountain soared higher still, sharing the sky with the roiling web of Aether.

She followed Sable toward the crowd gathered at the center, her pulse racing, conscious of Roar moving beside her. Above the cheers, she heard the *ting ting* of clashing steel. The spectators parted when they saw Sable, stepping aside to let them through. Aria glimpsed flashes of blond hair up ahead.

And then she saw her.

Liv swung a half-sword against a soldier who was her size—nearly six feet tall. Her hair, dark and light streaks of blond, reached halfway down her back. She had wide-set eyes, a strong jaw, and high cheekbones. She wore leather boots, slim pants, and a sleeveless shirt that showed lean, defined muscles.

She was strong. Her face. Her body. Everything about her.

Her fighting style was all power, no hesitation. She fought like she was diving into the sea with every move. *They're very alike,* Roar had once told her about Perry and Liv. Aria saw that now.

Liv looked comfortable and in control, hardly the captive Roar had imagined finding. Aria glanced at him and found his face ashen. She'd never seen him look so shaken. A surge of protectiveness moved over her.

Liv ducked to avoid a high, slicing blow from her opponent, but he followed with a forearm that caught her flush across the face. Her head whipped to the side. She recovered in an instant and stepped in where almost anyone would have rolled out, stunning the man with a punch to the gut. When he doubled over, she drove an elbow into the back of his head, unyielding, dropping him to his knees, where he stayed, coughing, reeling from the force she'd put behind the blows.

Smiling, Liv nudged his shoulder with her foot. "Come on, Loran. Stand. That can't be all you're good for."

"I can't. You cracked a rib. I'm sure of it." The soldier lifted his head, looking their way. "Talk to her, Sable. She shows no mercy. It's no way to train."

Sable laughed—the same smooth, seductive sound Aria had heard in the corridors. "Wrong, Loran. It's the only way to train."

Liv turned, spotting Sable. Her smile widened for an

instant. Then she saw Roar. Seconds passed, and she didn't move. Didn't look away. Unblinking, she reached up, sheathing her sword at her back.

As she walked over, all Aria could do was stare at a girl she'd been hearing about for months. A girl who controlled her best friend's heart. Who had the same blood as Perry running in her veins.

"What are you doing here?" she asked. The blow she'd taken across the cheek had left a red welt, but the color had drained from the rest of her face. She looked as pale as Roar.

"I could ask you the same." Roar's words were cold, but his voice was hoarse with emotion, and the veins at his neck stood out. He was barely holding himself back.

Sable looked from one to the other, and smiled. "Your friends have come for the wedding, Liv."

Aria's blood went cold.

Sable saw her surprise. "Didn't you know?" he asked, his eyebrows lifting. "I sent word to the Tides. You arrived just in time. Liv and I will be married in three days."

Married. Liv was going to be *married.* Aria didn't know why she was so shocked. It was the deal that had been made between Vale and Sable—Liv's hand in marriage in exchange for food—but something felt terribly wrong.

Then she saw how close Liv and Sable stood. How they stood *together.*

Sable reached up and brushed his thumb along the welt on Liv's cheek. His touch lingered, his fingers sliding down her neck, the gesture slow and sensual. "This will be a perfect shade of purple by then." He slipped his arm around Liv's waist. "I'd punish Loran, but you've done it for me."

Liv's focus hadn't left Roar. "You didn't need to come here," she said, but her meaning was clear: She didn't *want* him there. Liv wanted to marry Sable.

Rage coursed through Aria. She bit the inside of her lip and tasted blood. Roar had turned to stone beside her. She needed to get him out of there. "Is there someplace we can rest? It was a long trip."

Liv blinked, noticing her for the first time. She looked from Aria to Roar, her breathing focused. "Who are you?"

"Excuse my manners," Sable said. "I thought you knew each other. Liv, this is Aria." He motioned one of his men over. "Show them to the guest rooms by my quarters," he said. Then he smiled broadly. "I'll have supper arranged for the four of us later. Tonight we'll celebrate."

Aria's room was cold and spare: a simple cot and a chair with a curling backrest made of stag horns. The only light came through a dingy beveled-glass window recessed deep in the stone wall.

Roar was given the room adjacent to hers, but he followed her inside. Aria pulled the door shut and wrapped her arms around him. His muscles were tense, trembling.

"I don't understand. Liv let him touch her."

She winced at the pain in his voice. "I know. I'm sorry."

She had no better words to give him. She remembered the conversation they'd had days after leaving the Tides. She'd still felt the poison inside her, and she'd been in knots about leaving Perry. Roar had spoken to her of *truth*. He'd lost a truth today, just as she had months ago when she'd learned she was half Outsider. Her life had rested on a pillar that had suddenly vanished, and she still hadn't found her balance. Nothing she said would help him, so she stood with him and held him until he was ready to stand on his own again.

When he drew away, the anger in his brown eyes chilled her. She grasped his hand. *Roar, don't do anything to Sable. He's expecting it. Don't give him a reason to hurt you.*

He didn't answer her. For once she wished she could hear *his* thoughts.

He shook his head. "No. You don't." He moved away, sitting against the door.

She sat on the bed and looked around the small room. She didn't know what to do. For the past two weeks, she'd raced to get here. Now that she was here, she felt trapped.

Roar pulled his knees up, resting his head in his hands. His forearms were flexed, his hands fisted. In hours, they'd have dinner with Liv and Sable. How would it feel to sit across a dinner table from Perry and another girl? To watch him touch her cheek, the way Sable had touched Liv's? How would Roar bear it? In their plans, she and Roar had never spoken about leaving Rim without Liv. Not once had they imagined she'd want to stay.

Aria pulled her satchel into her lap, feeling the small lump inside the lining. Earlier, she'd wrapped the Smarteye in a cloth, with a handful of pine needles to mask the synthetic scent of the device, in case Sable searched their things. She heard the heavy footfalls of guards moving through the corridors, and the door didn't have a lock. While she was there, contacting Hess—or Soren—would be too dangerous.

It was said that Sable despised Dwellers. She didn't want to find out.

She rummaged around until she found the falcon carving. An intense pang of longing hit her as she brought it out. She imagined Perry as he'd been the night of her Marking ceremony, leaning against Vale's door with his thumbs hanging on his belt. She pictured his narrow hips and wide shoulders, and the small tilt of his head. His focus completely on her. Whenever his eyes were on her, she felt so completely *seen*.

She held the image in her mind, and pretended she could speak with him through the figurine the same way she spoke with Roar.

We're here, but it's a mess, Perry. Your sister . . . I really wanted to like her, but I can't. I'm sorry, but I can't. Maybe I was wrong to leave without you. Maybe if you were here, you could talk Liv out of marrying Sable and help us find the Still Blue. But I promise I'll find a way.

I miss you.

I miss you, I miss you, I miss you.

Be ready, because when I see you, I'll never let you go again.

23

PEREGRINE

M y word, Peregrine," Marron said. He craned his neck, staring in wonder at the cavern. "What a place."

Perry had brought him there first thing in the morning, explaining the Tides' situation along the way, holding Marron's arm as they climbed down the bluff. Now he concentrated on breathing evenly as he followed Marron's lead deeper inside.

"It's not ideal," Perry said, raising the torch in his hand higher.

"Ideals belong in a world only the wise man can understand," Marron said quietly.

"That would be you."

Marron met his gaze and smiled warmly. "That would be Socrates. But you're also wise, Perry. I had no plan for losing Delphi. I regret that very much."

They fell into silence. Perry knew Marron was thinking

about the home and the people he'd lost. Months ago, Perry had watched Roar and Aria train with knives on the rooftop at Delphi. He'd kissed her for the first time there.

Perry cleared his throat. His thoughts were slipping to a place he didn't want to go. "I want to bring the tribe here before we're forced out. We should leave the compound on our terms."

"Oh, yes," Marron agreed. "We'll need to start preparing right away. We'll need freshwater, light, and ventilation. Heat and storage for food. The access is poor, but we can improve it. I could design a pulley to lower heavier supplies."

His list continued. Perry listened, finally recognizing the man he knew: gentle, meticulous, brilliant. He wondered how Marron could ever have thought himself a burden.

When he returned to the compound, Perry called a meeting in the cookhouse to tell the tribe about his plan to move them to the cave. As he'd expected, they reeled under the news.

"I don't see how we can survive there for any length of time," Bear said. His face was red, and sweat beaded on his forehead. He was angrier than Perry had ever seen him. "We've managed the Aether during the winters," he continued. "It's like you're expecting the worst. Like you've given up."

"I'm not expecting the worst," Perry said. "The worst is *happening*. If you want proof, go outside and take a look at the sky, or at the acres that have burned over the past month. And this isn't like winter. We won't be able to ride this out.

Sooner or later we'll face another tribe, or another storm, that will level us. We have to make the first move—before that happens. We need to act now, while we still can."

"You said you were going to take us to the Still Blue," said Rowan.

"When I know where it is, I will," Perry said.

Rowan shook his head in frustration. "What if we're forced out of the cave?"

"Then I'll figure something else out."

After an hour of hearing the same complaints, Perry cut off the meeting. He ordered part of Bear's workforce to help Marron with the cave. Then he watched Bear storm out and the rest of the cookhouse empty. In a daze, Perry crossed the clearing to his home, needing a moment alone to think about his decision.

He went to the window, where Talon's carvings rested, and braced himself against the sill. There were seven figurines there. Seven, lined up in the same direction. He turned the one at the center the other way, so it faced outside. As Blood Lord, was his responsibility to follow the will of the majority? Or was it to guide them toward what he knew—what he *believed* to be best for them? He'd chosen the latter. He prayed he was right.

He spent the rest of the afternoon helping at the cave. Marron was organized, efficient, and comfortable handling a large project. Bear didn't show up, but the people Perry had chosen to work there warmed to Marron quickly. As Perry made the hour-long walk back to the compound, he told Marron so.

"They've come around to me because you did first. You're the one who's shown them the way."

Yeah, Perry thought. To a cave.

Their conversation turned to people who'd served Marron at Delphi. Slate and Rose had been held captive. If Perry and Marron could find a way to bring them and any others to the Tides, they would. They talked until Perry spotted Reef rushing toward him on the trail near the compound.

"What's going on?" Perry asked.

Reef scratched his chin. He looked like he was trying not to smile. "Wait until you see what just showed up," he said as they fell in step.

Perry's gaze went immediately across the clearing as they entered the compound. A girl with hair the color of copper stood on the eastern approach. In the last light of day, he saw a caravan of wagons stretching out behind her. Perry estimated roughly forty people either on horseback or on foot. They had the look of warriors—strong and armed with weapons.

"It's the second half of Sable's payment for Liv," Reef said at his side.

Twig jogged over and made a high-pitched sound that was close to a giggle. "Perry, that's all *food*!"

Perry's gaze moved back to the caravan as he walked up. Stunned, he tallied eight horse-drawn carts, ten head of cattle. He heard goats. On a gust he scented herbs, chicken, grain. His mouth began to water as he suddenly felt the full brunt of the hunger he'd grown used to fighting off.

"I'm Kirra," said the red-haired girl. "I bet you're happy to see me. Sable sent a message. He's pleased to honor the agreement he made with Vale for Olivia's hand in marriage, though he didn't have to. He didn't say the last part, but he should have."

Perry hardly listened to her. His heart raced as he realized that everything he saw was for the Tides.

Marron appeared at his side, his cheeks flushed with excitement. "Oh, my goodness. Peregrine, this will help."

Bear and Molly walked up with Willow and Old Will. Others were coming out of the cookhouse, gathering around. The air filled with their elated tempers, slashes of vibrant color shimmering at the edges of his vision. The relief was so potent—his own, the tribe's—that Perry's throat tightened with emotion.

The girl lifted an eyebrow. Her red hair whipped in the wind, fire in the glow of sunset. "Still time to get a meal together if we unpack now."

Perry's gaze fell to the Marking on her arm. He blinked. Blinked again as it sank in. A Scire. She was like him. He looked at her, curious now. Apart from his sister, he'd never known a female Scire. Theirs was the rarest Sense. It was one of the reasons Liv's marriage had needed to be arranged.

"What was your name?" he asked.

"Kirra. I told you that already."

"Right . . . I missed it before."

She had a full, round face that gave her an innocent look, but the curves of her body erased that impression. So did the teasing glint in her eyes. She looked a few years older than him, he guessed, and her scent was mellow and slightly cool, reminding him of autumn leaves.

"Did you say my sister *married* Sable?" he asked.

"I'm sure by now."

Perry turned back to the wagons. Liv had always been *his*. As the oldest, Vale had been groomed by their father for Blood Lord. But he and Liv had been left to themselves. Perry couldn't believe it. She belonged to someone else now. Liv, who was quick to laugh, quick to anger, quick to forgive. Liv, who did nothing in part and everything in full, was *married*.

As much as he'd believed she should do her duty to the Tides by marrying Sable, he'd never expected that she actually would. His sister had always been unpredictable, but this was her greatest surprise of all. She'd run off, disappeared, and then ended up doing what had been asked of her all along.

Perry's stomach clenched as he thought of Roar. How would he react when he found out?

"Well?" said Kirra, pulling him from his thoughts. "It's getting late. Should we unpack?"

Perry ran a hand over his jaw, and nodded.

It was done. Liv was married. He couldn't change it now.

24

ARIA

That night, Aria and Roar were escorted to a wide dining room. Candlelight and silver glimmered on a long dinner table. A centerpiece of twisting willow branches rose out of a huge vase, casting spindly shadows across the ceiling. Along one side of the room, doors opened to a balcony. Rust-colored drapes stirred in the wind, revealing glimpses of the churning Aether sky.

Roar scanned the room. "Where's Liv?" he asked as they stepped inside.

Sable rose from the table. He wore his Blood Lord chain now, a fantastic, shining collar spotted with sapphires that sparkled against his deep gray shirt. The chain transformed him, enhancing the blue in his eyes and the confidence in his smile. Aria wondered how she'd ever mistaken him for ordinary. He looked comfortable with the chain. At ease with power. She realized she'd never had the same thought about Perry.

"Liv is running late," Sable said. "She seems to like making me wait."

"Maybe she's avoiding you," Roar said.

Sable's mouth lifted in a small smile. "I'm happy you're here. It'll be good for Liv to have a childhood friend at our wedding."

"She told you we're *friends*?" Roar asked with a smirk. He couldn't seem to stop himself.

Sable replied smoothly, but his stare was cruel. "I know what you *were*. That's what she said you *are*."

A gust blew into the room and lifted a corner of the tablecloth, upsetting a pewter goblet. It clattered onto the stone floor. Neither Sable nor Roar moved.

Aria stepped between them. "It looks like the storm will break soon," she said, striding to the balcony. It was a blatant attempt at diversion, but it worked. Sable followed her.

The wind lifted her hair off her shoulders as she stepped past the drapes. She walked to the low stone wall that edged the balcony, hugging herself against the cold. The rugged exterior of the fortress dropped several stories to the Snake River directly below. Aether light shimmered across its dark surface.

Sable appeared beside her. "It's beautiful from a distance, isn't it?" he said, staring at the Aether. The flows were taking on a twisting, spooling shape. Soon the funnels would drop. "Very different when you're right beneath it." He looked at her. "You've been in a storm before?"

"Yes."

"I thought so. I scent your fear, but I could be wrong. Maybe you fear something else. Are you afraid of heights, Aria? It's a long way down."

A shiver ran through her, but her voice was even when she answered. "I'm fine with heights."

Sable smiled. "That doesn't surprise me. You said you were from the Tides?"

He was prodding her with questions. Scenting her tempers and seeking her weakness. "I came from there, yes."

"But you didn't know Liv before today."

"No."

He watched her again, going still, intent. She could see his thoughts turning, his curiosity honing on her. She didn't think she could stand it any longer when Liv's voice drew his attention back inside. Sable shifted slightly, but he didn't go to her.

"Where's Sable?" Liv asked Roar.

Aria saw her through the gap in the drapes. Liv looked like a different person from the girl she had seen earlier. She wore a Grecian dress in a burnished orange color that enhanced the bronze of her complexion. A green rope looped around her waist, and she'd swept her thick blond mane up off her shoulders.

"What happened to you?" Roar asked her.

"I couldn't figure out the belt," Liv answered blithely.

"I wasn't talking about the dress."

"I know."

"Then why are you—"

"Roar, *stop*," Liv said sharply. She moved to the table and sat.

Roar followed, crouching at her side. "Are you going to ignore me? Are you going to act like there's nothing between us?" He'd lowered his voice, but Aria could hear everything he said. The stone room was like a stage, amplifying the sounds and pushing them outside to where she and Sable stood, watching in the darkness. She wondered if Sable could hear him too.

"Olivia," Roar said urgently, passionately. "What are you *doing* here?"

"I'm waiting for food," she said, staring straight ahead. "And Sable."

Roar cursed, jerking away from her like he'd been pushed.

Sable laughed softly at Aria's side. "Shall we?" he said, returning inside. He went to Liv and kissed her on the lips.

"You're beautiful," he whispered before he straightened.

A blush crept over Liv's cheeks. "You're embarrassing me."

"Why?" said Sable, taking a seat by her side. He looked at Roar, amusement in his eyes. "I doubt anyone here would disagree."

Aria's stomach twisted. Roar looked ready to spring forward and rip Sable to pieces. Pulse racing, she glanced at the guards standing by the door. Both men locked eyes with her. They were watching everything.

When Roar took the seat beside her, she brushed her arm

past his and sent him a quick warning. *Roar, stay with me. Stay calm—please.*

Across the table, both Sable and Liv noticed the gesture. The room had no secrets. Every whisper was heard. Every shift in emotion scented.

Darkness settled in Liv's green eyes. Was it *jealousy*? How could she dare feel that? She was marrying Sable. She had no right to feel possessive over Roar.

Servants brought out platters of roast ham and vegetables. Aria somehow felt both hungry and nauseated. She took a piece of bread.

They ate in uncomfortable silence for a few moments. Aria's gaze kept returning to Roar's hand on the knife beside her. Roar and Liv wouldn't look at each other. Sable watched everything.

"Was Perry happy with the food we sent?" Liv asked finally.

"The other half of the payoff?" Roar said, surprised.

"It's called a dowry," Liv said sharply. "You sent it, didn't you, Sable?"

"The day I promised," Sable said. "The Tides have received it, I'm sure. It must have arrived after your friends left. I sent forty of my best warriors there as well. They'll stay and help however your brother needs them."

Liv looked at him. "You did?"

Sable smiled. "I know you worry about him."

Aria felt her last trace of hope for Roar fade. The deal was done. Liv belonged to Sable. They just needed the wedding ceremony now. It seemed like a formality.

"Did Perry send a message for me?" Liv asked.

Roar shook his head. "We had to leave quickly, so he didn't have a chance. Even then, I'm not sure he would have sent word."

"Why?" Liv said. "Has he lost his tongue?"

"He blames himself for what happened to Vale, Liv."

She scowled. "I *know* what Vale did. I *know* who my brother was. How hard is it to send a message?"

"That's a good question," Roar said. "How hard *is it* to send a message? Perry hasn't heard from *you* in a year. Maybe he's afraid he's lost you. Maybe he thinks you don't care about him anymore. Do you, Liv?"

Liv and Roar stared at each other, unblinking. Obviously, this was no longer about Perry. Aria felt like she and Sable had disappeared from the room.

"Of course I love him," Liv said. "He's my brother. I'd do anything for him."

"Touching, Liv." Roar pushed back from the table. "I'm sure Perry will be happy to hear that." His steps were silent as he left.

Alone with Liv and Sable, Aria suddenly felt like an intruder. The wind had blown out the candles at their end of the table. In the weaker light, Liv's dress looked cold, like red clay. Everything looked gray and cold.

"I'll have your brother brought here," Sable said, reaching for Liv's hand. "We can hold the wedding until then. Tell me what you want, and I'll do it."

Liv smiled at him, a quick, shaky flash. "I'm sorry . . . I'm not hungry," she said, and left the room.

Aria waited for Sable to go after her. He didn't. He plucked a fig from his plate and ate it, watching her as he chewed.

"I know why Roar is here," he said. "Why are *you*?"

His words were casual, but the look in his eyes was penetrating. Aria glanced at the door, gauging the distance, instinct telling her to leave *now*.

Sable's hand shot out and clasped her wrist. With her free hand, Aria snatched a knife from the table. She held it facing down, ready for the strike she'd make at his neck. A killing strike. There would only be one shot against someone like him. But that wouldn't help her. She needed him to talk.

Sable smiled and gave a slight shake of his head. His eyes were pale as glass at the center, and ringed with dark blue. "You don't need that. I won't hurt you unless you give me reason to."

He slid his hand up her arm, pushing up her sleeve. His thumb ran over her skin, slow and firm, as he studied the ruined half Marking. Chills shot down her spine at the cold feel of his touch.

Sable stared deep into her eyes. "You're a puzzle, aren't you?"

Aria's breath was caught in her throat. Sounds sharpened. The flap of the drapes, and the rush of the Snake River. The approaching footsteps in the hall. Was he seeing her hearing ability? Her life in Reverie and in the Realms, and everything else that she hid?

A guard with stringy blond hair entered. "The storm's holding on path to Ranger's Edge."

Sable paid him no attention. "What do you want from me?" he said, his voice low and menacing.

She couldn't lie. She couldn't. "The Still Blue."

Sable's grip loosened. He let out a slow exhale and sat back. "And here I thought you so unique," he said simply. Then he rose from his chair and left.

Aria couldn't move for long minutes afterward. She hadn't felt repulsed at being touched in months, since she'd first been cast out of Reverie. Pain woke in her arm. His grasp had been tighter than she'd realized. She set the knife down at last, returning it to its place beside the empty plate, fingers aching from gripping it.

Now what? Sable was suspicious of her. He'd pry until he learned the truth about who she was. Her life was in danger. Her mission was in danger. She drew a breath and stood. She wouldn't let herself fail.

Aria passed the guards at the door, making her way back to her room. She noted the guards at posts and roaming the halls. Moving unseen would be difficult, but not impossible. She froze when she heard Sable's voice. He sounded close, but she couldn't tell for certain. Sounds bounced in strange ways along the meandering corridors. Heart thundering, she listened to him ordering the outskirts of Rim evacuated. Maybe the storm would spur him to discuss the Still Blue tonight.

Later, she told herself. She'd sneak out and learn what she could.

She wasn't surprised to find someone waiting when she stepped into her room.

She'd expected Roar, but it was Liv.

25

PEREGRINE

That night, Perry sat at the high table, awed by the food passed before him. Ham served with raisins as gold as the sunrise. Walnut bread with warm goat cheese. Carrots cooked in honey and butter. Strawberries. Cherries. A platter with six kinds of cheeses. Wine or Luster, for those who wanted it. The aromas filled the cookhouse. Tomorrow the tribe would return to rations, but tonight they feasted.

He ate until his hunger cramps became the aches of a stuffed stomach. Every bite reminded him of the sacrifice Liv had made for the Tides. When he finished, he sat back and watched the people around him. Marron buttered a piece of bread with the same precision with which he did everything. Bear attacked the mountain of food before him, while Molly bounced River on her knee. Hyde and Gren vied for Brooke's attention, Twig barely getting in a word between them.

Only hours earlier, he'd been in the same place, listening

to them lash at him in anger.

Across the table, Willow elbowed Cinder. "Look. There's not a single piece of fish anywhere."

"Thank the skies," Cinder said. "I thought I was going to grow gills."

Willow laughed. Then Perry laughed, seeing Cinder's ears turn red beneath his cap.

At the far end of the hall, Kirra ate with her group. They were a raucous bunch, big in their gestures. Every one of them seemed to have an explosive laugh. Perry's eyes kept returning to Kirra. He'd set up a meeting with her later to learn of news from the other territories. Coming from the Horns, she might also know something about the Still Blue.

When they finished eating, Kirra's group pushed aside a few tables, clearing space. Then the music began, guitars and drums playing lively tunes. Their good cheer caught like wildfire. The Tides joined in eagerly, and soon the hall filled with song and dancing.

"Did Cinder tell you about his birthday?" Willow asked.

Cinder shook his head. "Willow, no. I was joking about that."

"I wasn't," Willow said. "Cinder doesn't know when his birthday is, so it could actually be *any* day. And since it can be *any* day, then why not today? We're already celebrating."

Perry crossed his arms and tried not to laugh. "Today seems like the perfect day to me."

"Maybe you could say something, you know, to make it official?"

"I can do that." He looked at Cinder. "How old do you want to be?"

Cinder's eyes went wide. "I don't know."

"How about thirteen?" Perry suggested.

"All right." Cinder shrugged, but his temper warmed with emotion. This meant more to him than he was letting on, and how couldn't it? He deserved to know his own age. To have a day to measure his life by. Perry was only sorry he hadn't thought to do something like this sooner.

"As Lord of the Tides, I name this day your birthday. Congratulations."

A grin spread over Cinder's face. "Thanks."

"Now you have to dance," Willow said. She pulled him up, ignoring his halfhearted objections, and towed him into the crowd.

Perry sat back and scratched Flea under his muzzle, watching everything, relishing the lightness in his heart. Kirra hadn't just brought food. She'd brought a reminder of better times. This was the hall as it should be. The Tides as he always wanted to see them.

It was late when the tribe disbanded for their homes. No one had wanted the night to end. Reef pulled Perry aside in the darkened clearing. Lamps were lit around them, swinging gently in a cool ocean breeze.

"Twenty-seven men and eleven women," he said. "Ten Seers and five Auds among them, and you know about Kirra. Every one of them can handle a weapon, as far as I can tell."

Perry had suspected the same thing. "You worried?"

Reef shook his head. "No. But just the same, I'll stay back tonight."

Perry nodded, trusting Reef to keep an eye on the new-comers. He almost ran Molly over as he turned to go. Marron had fallen ill, she told him. Nothing more than indigestion, but he'd be resting for the night. With Reef and Marron out, he'd be meeting with Kirra alone. Perry crossed the clearing to his house, not sure why that made him nervous.

A short while later, she knocked on his door and stepped inside. Perry rose from the chair by the fire. Kirra froze and scanned the empty room. She seemed surprised that no one else was there. "I gave my people the night to themselves. It's been a long journey."

Perry moved to the table and poured two cups of Luster, handing one to her. "They've earned their rest, I'm sure."

Taking the drink, Kirra sat across the table, her eyes smiling as she watched him. She wore a tight shirt the color of wheat, the neck unbuttoned lower than it had been during supper. "We showed up at the right time," she said. "Your tribe was hungry."

"They were," Perry agreed. He couldn't deny that their situation was dire, but he didn't like it being pointed out by a stranger.

"When will you return to Rim?" he asked. He wanted to send a message to his sister. How was Liv? He had to know that she was all right.

Kirra laughed. "You want to see me go already? I'm hurt,"

she said with a small pout. "Sable wants me to stay. We're here to help out as long as you need us."

That caught him off guard. He took a drink, giving himself a moment to recover as Luster warmed his throat. Sable was rumored to be ruthless, and this wasn't a time for generosity. Had Liv pressed him for more aid? He wouldn't put it past his sister. Liv could be ruthless too.

Perry set down his cup. "Sable might want you to stay, but he doesn't make decisions around here."

"Of course not," Kirra said, "but I don't see why it's a problem. We brought our own food, and you have plenty of room to board us. Sable is your brother now. Consider our help a gift from him."

A gift? Help? Perry's grip tightened on the cup. "Sable's not my brother."

Kirra took a sip of Luster, amusement glinting in her eyes. "I can imagine why you wouldn't feel so, having never met him. Regardless, the advantage should be clear to you. I have the strongest fighters you can find, and my horses are trained to hold steady during storms and raids. We could help protect the compound for you. You won't have to retreat to a cave."

She'd heard. Though it was his choice and the best thing for the Tides, shame crept over him, heating his face. Kirra leaned forward and breathed in deeply, her gaze fixed on him. Her eyes were the color of amber—the same fiery color he scented in her temper. She was reading him, just as he was reading her.

"I've heard about you," she said. "They say you broke into the Dweller Pod and that you defeated a tribe of Croven. They say you're twice Marked—a Seer, but you see in the dark."

"Talkative, whoever they are. In all this chatter you've been hearing, has anyone mentioned the Still Blue? Has my brother Sable told you where it is?"

"The land of sunshine and butterflies?" she said, sitting back again. "Don't tell me you're looking for it too. It's a fool's hope."

"Are you calling me a fool, Kirra?"

She smiled. It was the first time he'd called her by name. Because she noticed, he did too. "A hopeful fool."

Perry smirked. "The worst kind." He was starting to wonder if *everything* she said would streak him. "You don't think the Still Blue exists? Don't you have any desire to live?"

"I *am* living," she said. "I won't be chased by the sky."

They fell silent, watching each other. Her scent bristled with excitement. She didn't look away, and he realized he couldn't either.

"You're in a vulnerable position," she said, finally. "There's nothing wrong with accepting a little help."

Help. That word again. He was done. He couldn't hear it one more time. "I'll consider the offer," he said, standing. "Is there anything else?"

Kirra blinked up at him. "Do you want there to be?" Her meaning couldn't have been any clearer.

Perry went to the door and opened it, letting in the night

air. "Good night, Kirra."

She rose to her feet and walked over. Stopping less than a foot in front of him, she stared into his eyes as she inhaled.

Perry's stomach clenched. She'd stirred his pulse, something he hadn't felt in weeks. She'd know, but there was nothing he could do to hide it.

"Sleep well, Peregrine of the Tides," she said, and then slipped out into the darkness.

26

ARIA

"What are you doing here, Liv?" Aria asked, stepping into her room. She couldn't keep the anger from her voice.

Liv rose from the bed. "I was looking for Roar. He wasn't in his room." The Greek dress looked rumpled now, falling off her shoulder, and she'd taken her hair down, but she looked stronger and more at ease than she had during dinner.

Aria crossed her arms. A lamp flickered by the bedside, lighting the chilly, cramped room. "He's not here. As you can clearly see."

"Just give him a message for me—"

"I'm not telling him anything for you."

Liv smirked. "Exactly who *are* you?"

"A friend of Roar's and Perry's." Aria bit the inside of her lip as soon as the words left her mouth. *Friend* felt like such a weak way to describe herself. She was much more than that—to both of them.

A smile spread across Liv's face. "Ahh . . . you're a friend of Perry's. I should've guessed. You look like someone my brother would be *friends* with."

"Time for you to leave."

Liv gave a small laugh, making no move to go. "Does that surprise you? You can't really think you're the only girl who's fallen for him."

Aria felt her face heat with anger. "I know I'm the only girl he's rendered to."

Liv went perfectly still. Then she stepped close, her eyes boring into Aria. The welt from earlier disappeared against the redness of her cheeks. "I will kill you if you hurt him," she said, her voice calm, unemotional. It wasn't a threat. It was information. A consequence.

"I was thinking that same thing earlier."

"You don't know *anything*," Liv said. "Tell Roar he has to leave. Right away. Before the wedding. He can't stay here."

"How can you act like he's an *inconvenience*?" Aria spat, thinking of all the nights she'd spent talking with Roar about Liv. Hearing how wonderful she was. This girl was horrible. Selfish. Rude. "*You* ran off! *You* left him! He's been looking for you for a year."

Liv waved a hand, gesturing around the room. "Do you think I chose this? Do you think I want to be here? My brother *sold* me! Vale took away everything I wanted." She glanced at the door, staring at it like she was deciding something, and then stepped closer. "You want to know what

I've done for the past year? I worked *every day* at forgetting Roar. I shut out every smile, every kiss, every stupid, perfect thing he ever said to make me laugh. I buried *all* of it. It took me a year to stop thinking about him. A year to stop missing him enough to come here and face Sable.

"Roar is ruining everything by being here," Liv continued. "I'm not strong enough. How can I forget him when he's right in front of me? How can I marry Sable if all I'm thinking about is *Roar*?"

Tears brimmed in Liv's eyes, and she breathed raggedly. Aria didn't want to feel sympathy for her. Not when she'd hurt Roar as much as she had. "He's here to bring you back, Liv. There has to be a way you can come back to the Tides."

"Go back?" Liv said with a thin laugh. "Perry can't repay the dowry. And I can't run away from this any longer. I know what it's like out there. I know the Tides need help, and Sable can give it. He'll *keep* helping if we marry. How can I walk away from that? How can I leave if it means my family could starve—or *die*?"

Aria shook her head. She didn't know. She let out a breath and sat on the bed as a sudden wave of exhaustion swept over her. Aether flashed through the small window, making the room flicker softly with blue light.

Liv's problem felt uncomfortably familiar. Aria had been so focused on finding the Still Blue for Hess and on getting Talon back that she hadn't let herself think about what would happen *afterward*. Would there ever be a way she and Perry could be together? The Tides had rejected her, and

Reverie wasn't even an option. Everyone, and everything, was against them.

Aria pushed away the thoughts. Worrying wouldn't help anything. She looked up at Liv. "What about Sable?" She rubbed her wrist, feeling the echo of his grip.

Liv shrugged. "He's not terrible. . . . I know . . . it's not much of a way to think of the man I'm marrying, but it's better than I'd hoped. I thought I'd hate him, and I don't."

She bit her bottom lip, hesitating, like she was deciding whether to say anything more. Then she came to the bed, sitting beside Aria. "When I got here earlier this spring, he was going to let me leave. He told me I could go whenever I wanted, but that since I'd finally arrived, we might as well get to know each other. I didn't feel as trapped after he said that. It helped me feel less like a *thing* that was being passed around."

Aria wondered if Sable had said that on purpose. Scires were known for manipulating people. But shouldn't Liv have seen that?

"I don't fawn over him," Liv continued, "and he likes that. I think he sees me as a challenge." She fiddled with the green rope around her waist. "And he's attracted to me. The scent he gives off when I enter a room . . . it's not something you can fake."

Aria stared at the door, listening to footsteps outside fade. "Do you feel the same way about him?" she asked when it was quiet again.

"No . . . not the same." Liv tied the ends of her belt into

an elaborate knot as she thought. "When he kisses me, he makes me nervous, but I think it's because it feels different." She met Aria's eyes. "I've never kissed anyone other than Roar, and that's—"

She shut her eyes, wincing. "This is what I can't have. I can't sit here and remember how it feels to kiss Roar when I'm marrying someone else in days. He has to leave. It's too hard for me like this, and I can't stand to see him hurting." She shook her head. "I hate that he makes me feel weak."

Aria sat back against the iron headboard, remembering Perry on their last night together, bruised and beaten after a fight that had happened because of her. The next day, he lost part of his tribe. She didn't feel weak because of him. She felt too powerful, like every choice she made had the potential to hurt him, and that was the last thing she wanted.

"Roar will move on," Liv said quietly. Her eyes had softened, and Aria knew she'd read her temper. "He'll forget about me."

"You can't really believe that."

Liv bit her lower lip. "No," she said. "I don't."

"Will you tell him the truth? Roar needs to know what you're doing. He needs to know why."

"You think it will help?"

"No. But you owe it to him."

Liv watched her for a long moment. "All right. I'll talk to him tomorrow." She scooted higher on the bed, drawing the blanket over her legs. The sounds of the storm filtered into the room, and a cold draft flowed in beneath the bedroom door. "How is my brother really doing?"

Just a short while ago, she had threatened Aria. Now she was close and relaxed. Lost in her thoughts. *Hot and cold*, Aria thought. She wondered if there was anything in-between with Liv.

Aria pulled the other side of the blanket over her. The last time she'd seen Perry, he'd been bruised and abandoned by so many people. By *her*. She hated knowing she'd added to his pain. "It hasn't been easy."

"It's so much to do. So much to take care of," Liv said. "He must be out of his mind missing Talon."

"He is, but we're getting Talon back," Aria said before she could stop herself.

Liv frowned, her green eyes roaming over Aria's face. "Where are you from?"

Aria hesitated. She had the feeling her answer would shape their relationship from that moment on. Should she risk telling Liv the truth? She wanted trust between them, and here, late at night and in the quiet of her room, she just wanted to be herself. She drew a breath and answered. "I'm from Reverie."

Liv blinked at her. "You're a *Dweller*?"

"Yes. . . . Well, a half Dweller."

Liv smiled, a small laugh bubbling out of her. "How did *that* happen?"

Aria shifted to her side and rested her head on her arm, mirroring Liv. Then she explained how she'd been cast out of the Pod in the fall and met Perry. She told Liv everything

232

that had happened at the Tides', and how she needed to find the Still Blue to get Talon back. When Aria finished, Liv was silent, and the sounds of the Aether funnels had faded. Rim had seen the worst of the storm.

"I've heard Sable mention the Still Blue a few times," Liv said. Her eyes were heavy with sleep. "He knows where it is. We'll find out and get Talon back."

We. Such a small word, but it felt huge. Aria felt a grounding, settling sort of thrill. Liv would help.

Liv studied her for a long moment. "So you don't care what happened at the Tides'? That you were poisoned? You're going back to my brother?"

Aria nodded. "I care, but I can't imagine *not* going back to him." Lyrics sprang into mind, well-worn in her singer's memory. "'Love is a rebellious bird that nobody can tame,'" she said. "It's from an opera called *Carmen.*"

Liv narrowed her eyes. "Are you the bird, or is my brother?"

Aria smiled. "I think the bird is the connection between us. . . . I'd do anything for him," she said, and realized that it really was that simple.

Liv's gaze grew distant. "It's a good saying," she said after a long while. She yawned. "I'm going to sleep here. Sorry if I snore."

"Sure, why don't you stay? There's plenty of room if neither one of us moves."

"That won't be a problem. I can't move anyway. This dress is like wearing a tourniquet."

"You tied the belt wrong. I've worn that style of dress before in the Realms. I could show you the right way."

"No need. It's a stupid dress."

Aria laughed. "It's not *stupid*. You look amazing in it. Like Athena."

"Yeah?" Liv yawned again and closed her eyes. "I thought Roar would like it. All right. Show me how to tie the stupid dress tomorrow."

Soon, as promised, Liv snored. It wasn't loud. Just a soft purr that wove with the sound of the wind, lulling Aria to sleep.

27

PEREGRINE

W hat's she doing up there?" Perry asked.

He stopped in the clearing and looked to the roof of his house. Kirra's hair caught his eye like a red flag flapping in the breeze. The sound of hammers pounding carried down to him.

He'd spent the morning at the cavern with Marron, going over plans to grade the bluff that led to the cove. If they could create a switchback path, they'd be able to bring carts and horses down the slope. It would be far better than steps, so it was worth a try, but they'd need more help.

"You don't know about this?" Reef said, beside him.

"No. I don't." Perry climbed the ladder to the roof. Kirra stood a dozen paces away, watching two of her men, Forest and Lark, rip up roof tiles. As he walked over, Perry's anger built with every step. He felt more protective over this space than he did about his house. This was *his* perch.

Kirra turned to face him, smiling. She rested her hands on her hips and tipped her head to the side.

"Good morning," she said. "I saw the crack in the ceiling last night. I thought we'd take care of it."

She'd spoken louder than necessary, letting her voice carry. Her men looked over, sizing him up. They'd pulled off a section of stone tiles, exposing the battens beneath. Perry knew a dozen Auds in the clearing had heard her as well. It was no mystery what the tribe would think. Everyone knew that gap was above his loft.

He drew a breath, forcing down his rage. She was changing something that didn't need to be changed. He'd watched the Aether through that gap for as long as he could remember, but he couldn't stop the work now. The sliver that had been a few inches wide had grown to a hole more than a foot across, exposing the inner beams. Through it, he could see the blankets in his loft below.

"Bear told me about a few other things we could take care of while we're here," Kirra said.

"Take a walk with me, Kirra," he said.

"I'd love to." The sound of her voice—sweet as nectar—chafed at his nerves.

Perry felt the eyes of people on them as they came down the ladder and crossed the clearing together. He took the trail to the harbor, knowing he'd find it empty. It was too early in the day for the fishermen to be back.

"I thought we'd make ourselves useful," Kirra said when they stopped.

It streaked him that she'd spoken first. "If you want work, come to me, not Bear."

"I tried, but I couldn't find you." She lifted an eyebrow. "Does that mean you want us to stay?"

Perry had considered it all morning as he'd listened to Marron describe the work needed at the cave. He saw no reason to turn away a band of able-bodied people. If he was right about the Aether, they were on borrowed time.

"Yes," he said. "I want you to stay."

Kirra's eyes widened in surprise, but she recovered quickly. "I was expecting you to fight me a little more. I wouldn't have minded, actually."

Her words were flirty, but her temper was difficult to read, an odd mixture of warm and cool. Bitter and sweet.

She laughed, tucking a stray lock of her hair behind her ear. "You make me nervous, staring at me with those eyes."

"They're the only ones I have."

"I didn't mean that I don't like them."

"I know what you meant."

She shifted her weight, her scent warming. "Right," she said, her gaze wandering to his chest and then to the chain at his neck.

Her attraction to him was real—there was no hiding that—but he couldn't shake the feeling that she was trying to bait him.

"So where do you want us to work?" she asked.

"Finish the roof. I'll show you the cave tomorrow." He turned to go.

She touched his arm, rooting him in place. A shot of adrenaline pulsed through his body. "Perry, it'll be easier if we can find a way to get along."

"We are getting along," he said, and walked away.

At supper, Kirra's group was as rowdy as the previous night. The two men who had fixed the hole in Perry's roof, Lark and Forest, came from the deep south, like Kirra did. They carried on loudly, telling jokes and stories back and forth in a battle of wits. By the time supper ended, they had the Tides cheering for more.

Kirra fit right in with the Tides. Perry watched her laughing with Gren and Twig, and then later with Brooke. She even spent time talking with Old Will, turning his face red beneath his white beard.

Perry wasn't surprised by how quickly she gained the Tides' acceptance. He understood how relieved they were to have her there and wished he felt the same way, but everything she said and did made him feel like a target.

Bear came over when the cookhouse had almost emptied, sitting across from Perry and wringing his huge hands. "Can we talk, Peregrine?"

Perry straightened his back at the formal tone in his voice. "Of course. What's going on?"

Bear sighed and wove his fingers together. "Some of us have been talking, and we don't want to move to the cave. There's no reason for it now. We've got food—enough to get us on our feet again—and Kirra's people to help defend us. It's all we need."

Perry's stomach churned. Bear had questioned his decisions before, but this felt different. This felt like something more. He cleared his throat. "I'm not changing my plan. I swore an oath to do what's right for the tribe. That's what I'm doing."

"I understand," Bear said. "I don't want to go against you. None of us do." He stood, his thick eyebrows knotted together. "I'm sorry, Perry. I wanted you to know."

Later, at his house, Perry sat around the table with Marron and Reef as the rest of the Six played dice. They were in high spirits from another night of music and entertainment, their hunger sated for the second day in a row.

Perry listened absently as they passed around a bottle of Luster, joking with one another. The conversation with Bear had left him uneasy. As much as Wylan's departure had hurt, watching Bear turn against him would be worse. He liked Bear. Respected him. It was much harder failing someone he cared about.

Perry shifted the chain around his neck. Suddenly, loyalty felt like such a fragile thing. He'd never thought he would need to earn it day in and day out. Though he didn't forgive his brother for what he'd done, Perry was beginning to understand the pressure that had forced Vale to sell off Talon and Clara. He'd sacrificed a few for the good of the whole.

Perry tried to imagine trading Willow to the Dwellers for solutions to his problems. Just the thought made him sick.

"Snake eyes again. Damn dice," Straggler said. He lifted the cup to reveal two ones on the table.

Hyde smirked. "Strag, I didn't think it was possible to be as unlucky as you are."

"He's so unlucky it's almost *lucky*," Gren said. "It's like he has reverse luck."

"He's reverse good-looking, too," said Hyde.

"I'm going to reverse punch you," Strag said to his brother.

"That was reverse smart, man. It means you're going to punch *yourself.*"

Beside Perry, Marron smiled softly as he made notes in Vale's ledger. He was designing portable furnaces that would provide both heat and light for the cave. It was just one of the things he had thought of that impressed Perry.

Reef sat back in his chair with his arms crossed, eyes heavy. Ignoring the game, Perry told him what Bear had said.

Reef scratched his head, pushing back his braids. "It's because of Kirra," he said. "She's changed things around here."

It wasn't just because of Kirra, Perry thought. It was because of Liv. By marrying Sable, she'd given the Tides a chance. He wondered if she knew how much they'd needed it. He felt a sharp pang in his chest, missing his sister. Grateful for her. Sorry for the sacrifice she'd had to make. Liv had a new life now. A new home. When would he see her again? He shook the thoughts from his mind.

"So you agree with Bear?" he asked Reef. "You think we should stay here?"

"I agree with Bear, but I follow you." Reef tipped his chin at the others around the table. "We all do."

Perry's stomach dropped. He had their support, but it was based on fealty. On a promise they'd made to him months ago on bended knee. They followed blindly, without seeing any wisdom in his thinking, and that didn't feel right either.

"I agree with you," Marron said quietly. "For what it's worth."

Perry nodded in thanks. It was worth a lot just then.

"What about you, Per?" Straggler asked. "You still think we should move?"

"I do," Perry said, resting his arms on the table. "Kirra's brought food and fighters, but she hasn't stopped the Aether. And we have to be ready. For all I know, she could pack up and leave tomorrow."

Instantly, he regretted his words. The game of dice halted, and an awkward silence fell over the group. He sounded paranoid, like he thought everyone ran off.

He was relieved when Cinder called down from the loft, breaking the silence. "I don't like Kirra either."

"Because she patched up the roof?"

Cinder peered over the edge, holding on to his hat to keep it from falling. "No. I just don't."

Perry had figured as much. Cinder knew Scires could scent the Aether on him. But with its sting always in the air now, he had nothing to worry about in Kirra.

Twig rolled his eyes and rattled the dice in the cup. "The kid doesn't like anyone."

Gren jabbed him with an elbow. "That's not true. He likes Willow—don't you, Cinder? And you're one to talk, frog kisser."

When the house was filled with sounds of six men—and one boy—croaking at the top of their lungs, Marron closed the ledger. Before he left, he leaned toward Perry and said, "Leaders need to see clearly in darkness, Peregrine. You already do that."

An hour later, Perry rose from the table and stretched his back. The house was quiet, but outside, the wind had picked up. He heard its low whistle and saw the embers in the hearth glowing, struggling to rekindle.

Looking up to the loft, he searched in vain for the sliver of light that had always been there. Cinder's foot hung over the edge, twitching in sleep. Perry climbed over Hayden and Straggler, opened the door to Vale's room, and stepped inside.

It was cooler and darker in there. With the floor in the other room packed, it made no sense to leave this one unused, but he couldn't do it. He'd never been able to bear being within those walls. His mother had died there, and Mila, too. The room brought only one good memory to mind.

He lay down on the bed, letting out a slow breath, and stared at the wooden beams of the ceiling. He'd gotten used to fighting against the pull, but now he didn't. Now he let himself remember the way Aria had felt in his arms just before the Marking Ceremony, smiling as she asked if he ever missed anything.

His answer hadn't changed. The truth was that no matter how hard he tried not to, he did miss her. Always.

28

ARIA

L iv smoothed her hands over the ivory silk of her wedding dress. "What do you think?" she asked. Her hair hung in tangled golden waves around her shoulders, and her eyes were puffy with sleep. "Is it all right?"

They were in Liv's room, a large chamber with a balcony like last night's dining room, just a few doors down along the same corridor. A fire crackled in a huge stone hearth to one side, and thick fur rugs covered the wooden floorboards.

Aria sat on the plush bed, watching a stout woman pin the hem of Liv's dress. She was tired and wished she and Liv had fallen asleep here, instead of on her bed. A crisp morning breeze drifted in from outside, carrying the scent of smoke—a reminder of last night's storm.

"Much better than all right," Aria answered. The simple lines of the dress complemented Liv's long, muscular figure and enhanced her natural beauty. She looked stunning. And nervous. Since she'd put the dress on half an hour earlier, Liv hadn't stopped drumming her fingers against her legs.

"Hold still or I'll prick you." The seamstress spoke with pins pressed between her lips, her voice muffled and irritated.

"That's not much of a threat, Rena. You've pricked me ten times already."

"'Cause you're wriggly as a fish. Hold *still*!"

Liv rolled her eyes. "I'm tossing you into the river once you're finished."

Rena huffed. "I may toss myself in well before then, dear."

Liv was joking, but she looked paler by the second. Aria couldn't blame her. She was getting married in two days, bound forever to someone she didn't love. To *Sable*.

Aria glanced toward the door, her stomach knotted with anxiety. Roar still hadn't reappeared since he'd left dinner last night.

The sound of voices out in the hall thrummed through the thick wood. She was learning her way around the twisting corridors. Sable's chamber was nearby. Now that he knew she was after the Still Blue, it would be harder than ever for her to break away and search for information, but she would try later.

"What you said last night about the rebellious bird?" Liv said suddenly. "I agree with you."

Aria sat up. "You do?"

Liv nodded. "There's no taming it. . . . Do you think I'm too late?"

Too late to tell Roar she loved him? Aria almost let out a laugh of pure happiness. "No. I don't think you could ever be too late." For the next ten minutes, as the seamstress finished, she fidgeted as much as Liv, fighting to keep the smile from her lips. When Rena left and they were finally alone, she jumped off the bed and rushed to Liv's side. "You're sure?"

"Yes. He's the only thing I've always been sure about. Help me get this thing off. I have to find him." In seconds she changed out of the dress into worn brown pants, leather boots, and a white long-sleeved shirt. She twisted her hair behind her back, and pulled the leather holster with her half-sword across her shoulder.

They checked Roar's bedroom and then Aria's, finding both empty. Discreetly, Liv asked a few guards about Roar. No one had seen him.

"Where do you think he is?" Aria asked as Liv led her through the corridors.

Liv smiled. "I have some ideas."

Aria's ears tuned to the voices around her as they stepped outside and took to the shadowed city streets. She could gather information while they searched for Roar.

People took notice of Liv as they walked, recognizing her, nodding in greeting. Her height made her hard to miss. In a few days, she'd be a powerful woman—a leader, alongside Sable—and they admired her for it. Aria wondered how that would feel. Would she ever stand beside Perry, strong in her own right and accepted for who she was?

Everyone seemed to be speaking of last night's storm. The

southern fields of Rim still burned, and everyone wondered what action Sable would take. Aria asked herself the same questions. If his land was burning—if he was suffering under the Aether like everyone else—why hadn't he left yet for the Still Blue? Why was he waiting?

"How big is the Horns tribe?" she asked Liv as they wove through a crowded market.

"Thousands in the city and more in the outer reaches. He has colonies, too. He likes to have the best and the most of everything. That's why he doesn't like Dwellers." She looked at Aria, her shoulders rising in a small apologetic shrug. "He can't buy your medicines or weapons, and he hates that. He despises anything that he can't have."

That made more sense than Wylan's theory about a centuries-old grudge.

Aria's mind whirred as she followed Liv. How would Sable move his entire tribe of thousands to the Still Blue? Not just people, but the provisions they'd need, while staying nimble enough to avoid Aether storms? She couldn't figure out how he'd manage it. Maybe that was why he hadn't done it yet.

Liv stopped in front of a slanted door with peeling red paint. The din of conversation drifted to Aria's ears. "If Roar's anywhere, he's here."

As they stepped inside, Aria took in the long tables packed with men and women. The honey-sweet smell of Luster hung in the musty air. "A bar." She shook her head, but had to admit it was a good place to start. The first time she'd met Roar, he'd had a bottle of Luster in his hand. She'd seen the same thing many times since.

Roar wasn't there, but they found him just two stops later. He sat at a table in a dark corner, alone. When he saw them, he winced and dropped his head.

He was still slouching as Aria walked up, his hands in fists on the table.

She sat down across from him. "You made me worry," she said, striving for levity. "I hate worrying."

He peered up at her with bloodshot eyes and flashed a quick, tired smile. "Sorry." Then he glared at Liv, who'd taken a seat beside him. "Aren't you supposed to be getting married?"

Liv could barely keep the smile from her lips. She reached over and rested her hand on top of Roar's. He jolted, drawing away, but she held him in a tight grip.

Seconds passed. Roar went from staring at her hand to staring into her eyes, his face transforming from lost to found. From broken to whole.

Aria felt her throat tighten, and she couldn't look at him anymore. Across the dimly lit bar, a man with sallow skin met her eyes, his gaze holding for a moment too long.

"Liv," she warned quietly. They were being watched.

Liv drew her hand away, but Roar didn't move. His eyes glossed with tears. He was holding his breath. Holding on to the last of his self-control.

"You almost killed me," he whispered hoarsely. "I hate you, Liv. I hate you."

It was such a lie. It was as far from the truth as words could be. Here, among Sable's people, it was all he could say.

"I know," Liv said.

A sour-faced older woman by the bar cut her eyes at Aria. Suddenly everyone seemed to be watching and listening. "We have to get out of here," she whispered.

"Liv, *you* need to leave," Roar said quietly. "Right now. It's too much of a risk for you to stay. He'll know how you feel."

Liv shook her head. "It doesn't matter. It won't change anything. He knew the minute you showed up."

Aria leaned toward them. "Let's go," she said, just as Sable's guards burst through the door.

Aria and Roar were stripped of their knives and hauled back through the city streets. Seeing them treated like captives, Liv yelled and flew into a fury that fell just short of drawing her half-sword, but the guards didn't relent. Sable's orders, they told her.

Aria exchanged a worried look with Roar as they approached Sable's looming fortress. Liv had said that Sable knew the truth of her feelings for Roar. She hadn't seemed concerned. Their marriage was arranged; it had never been about love. But a hard pit of worry settled in Aria's stomach.

They were taken past the great hall—now empty and silent—and through the winding corridors to the dining room with the bramble centerpiece and the rust-colored drapes. Sable sat at the table, talking with a man Aria recognized. He was bedraggled, spoons and trinkets hanging from his clothes. His teeth were few and crooked.

He looked vaguely familiar, like a figure she'd seen in a dream—or a nightmare. Then she remembered. She'd caught a glimpse of him during her Marking Ceremony. He was the gossip who'd been there the night she'd been poisoned.

A single thought blared inside her mind.

This man knew she was a Dweller.

When he saw them, Sable pushed back his chair and stood. He looked briefly at Liv and Roar, his expression even, almost disinterested, before turning to focus on her.

"Sorry to spoil your fun this afternoon, Aria," he said as he walked toward her, "but Shade here has just shared some interesting facts about you. It seems I was right. You *are* unique."

Her heart slammed against her ribs as he stopped in front of her. She couldn't look away from his piercing blue eyes. When he spoke again, the cutting tone in his voice sent a chill up her spine. "Did you come here to steal what I know, Dweller?"

She saw only one possible move. One chance. She had to take it.

"No," she said. "I'm here to offer you a deal."

29

PEREGRINE

I hate this," Kirra said.

Perry watched Kirra brush sand off her hands as he took a drink from his water skin. "You hate *sand*? I've never heard anyone say that."

"You think it's ridiculous."

He shook his head. "No. More like impossible . . . like hating trees."

Kirra smiled. "I'm indifferent toward trees."

Along the dunes, their horses tugged at the sea grass.

They'd spent most of the day with Marron, assigning Kirra's people to different tasks. Then Perry had shown Kirra his northern borders—he could use her people's help on watch as well. Now they'd stopped for a quick rest along the coast before returning to the compound.

They needed to get back soon—a storm was building from the north—but he wanted just a few more minutes of not being Blood Lord.

Kirra had been easier to be around that morning. And with plenty of work to be done, she had a point about them getting along. He'd decided to give her a chance.

She leaned back on her elbows. "Where I come from, we have lakes. They're quieter. Cleaner. And it's easier to scent without all the salt in the air."

It was the opposite for him. He preferred the way scents carried on moist ocean air. But then, that was what he'd always known. "Why did you leave?"

"We were forced out by another tribe when I was young. I grew up in the borderlands until we were brought in by the Horns. Sable's been good to me. I'm his favorite for missions like this. I don't complain. I'd rather be on the move than stuck in Rim." She smiled. "Enough about me." Her gaze fell to his hand. "I've been wondering how you got those scars."

Perry flexed his fingers. "Burned it last year."

"Looks like it was bad."

"It was." He didn't want to talk about his hand. Cinder had torched it. Aria had bandaged it. Neither were things he wanted to share with Kirra. Quiet stretched out between them. Perry looked across the ocean, to where the Aether flashed deep on the horizon. Storms were constant now, out at sea.

"I didn't know about the girl—the Dweller—when I first got here," Kirra said after a while.

He resisted the urge to change the subject again. "So

there's something you hadn't heard about me."

She tipped her head to the side, mirroring him. "It sounds like I just missed her," she said. "What if we're the same person? Maybe I'm her in disguise."

That surprised him. He laughed. "You're not."

"No? I bet I know you better than she did."

"I don't think so, Kirra."

She lifted her eyebrows. "Really? Let's see. . . . You worry about your people, and it's a deep worry, more than the responsibility of wearing the chain. Like taking care of other people is something you need to do. If I had to guess, I'd say protection and safety are things you never knew yourself."

Perry forced himself not to break eye contact with her. He couldn't blame her for knowing what she did. She was like him. It was the way they took in people. Down to the core of their emotions. Down to their deepest truths.

"You have a strong bond with Marron and Reef," she continued, "but your relationship with one is harder on you than the other."

True again. Marron was a mentor, and a peer. But sometimes Reef seemed more like a father—a connection that had never felt easy.

"Then there's Cinder," she said. "You're not rendered to him, as far as I can tell, but there's something powerful between you." She paused, waiting for him to comment, and continued when he didn't. "What's really interesting is your temper around women. You're obviously—"

Perry gave a choked laugh. "All right, that's enough. You

can stop now. What about you, Kirra?"

"What about me?" She sounded calm, but a vibrant green scent reached him, shimmering with anxiety.

"For two days you've been trying to draw me in, but today you're not."

"I'd still try to draw you in if I thought I stood a chance." She said it plainly, no apology. "Anyway, I'm sorry about what you're going through."

He knew he was being baited, but he couldn't help himself. "What I'm going through?"

She shrugged. "Being betrayed by your best friend."

Perry stared at her. She thought Aria and Roar were *together*? He shook his head. "No. You heard wrong. They're just friends, Kirra. They both had to go north."

"Oh . . . I guess I just assumed, since they're both Auds, and they left without telling you. Sorry. Forget I said anything." She looked up at the sky. "That's looking bad." She stood, brushing off sand from her hands. "Come on. We should head out."

As they rode back to the compound, Perry couldn't block out the images.

Roar lifting Aria into a hug that first day, at his house.

Roar standing at the top of the beach, joking after Perry had been kissing Aria. *That was killing me too, Per.*

A joke. It had to have been a joke.

Aria and Roar singing in the cookhouse the night of the

Aether storm. Singing *perfectly*, like they'd done it a thousand times before.

Perry shook his head. He *knew* how Aria felt toward him—and how she felt toward Roar. When they were together, he *scented* the difference.

Kirra had done this to him on purpose. She'd planted the idea to throw him into doubt, but Aria hadn't betrayed him. She wouldn't do that, and neither would Roar. That wasn't why she had left.

He didn't want to think about the real reason why. He'd pushed it back, where he'd kept the thought for weeks, but it wouldn't stay. Wouldn't stop. Wouldn't let him go.

Aria had left because she'd been poisoned. She had left because there—in his home, right under his nose—she'd almost been killed. She had left because he'd promised to protect her, and he hadn't. That was why.

Because he'd failed her.

~ 30 ~

ARIA

I t's called a Smarteye," Aria said, holding the device in her trembling hands. She sat at the dining table with Sable, a steady rain pattering outside on the stone balcony. Night was falling, and she heard the Snake River, swollen with rainwater, rushing far below.

"I've heard of them," Sable said.

Aria remembered the look in his eyes from the last time they'd sat at that table. He'd snatched her wrist then. He'd hurt her with no hesitation.

Liv sat in silence beside him, her face emotionless. At the far end of the room, Roar looked calm, leaning against the wall, but his gaze moved from Sable to the guards by the door, calculating and intense.

Aria swallowed, her throat tight and dry. "I'll contact Consul Hess now."

She'd never felt more self-conscious as she applied the device. Even the guards by the door stared at her. At least Sable had sent the scraggly gossipmonger away.

When she fractioned, she appeared in Hess's office again. He stood by the wall of windows behind his desk. Like before, she saw the even levels of the Panop and felt the same twist of homesickness.

"Yes?" he said impatiently.

"I'm here with Sable."

"I *know* where you are," Hess said, his irritation plain.

"I mean he's *here*," she said. "Sable is in front of me right now."

Hess came around his desk, suddenly focused. Alert. She continued. "He knows where the Still Blue is, but he needs transportation. He says he's open to a trade."

Aria heard herself speaking, the sound of her own voice oddly far away. In the real, she felt the wooden back of the chair pressed against her spine, the sensation dull and distant. She was in Sable's dining room and Hess's office, but *everything* felt unreal. She couldn't believe this was happening.

"Sable *offered* to negotiate?"

Aria shook her head. "No. It was my idea. I took a guess at what he needed, and I know what we have." She'd seen the hangar lined with Hovercraft months ago in Reverie, the day she'd been left on the outside. "I followed a hunch," she said. "I had to—and I was right."

Hess watched her for a long moment, eyes narrowing.

"Transport to where and for how many?"

"I don't know," she said. "Sable wants to talk with you directly."

"When?" he asked.

"Now."

Hess nodded. "Give him the Eye. I'll do the rest."

Aria fractioned out, but she didn't take the Smarteye off yet. In the real, Sable's gaze held on her. Keeping her breathing steady, she chose the Phantom mask.

Soren spoke as soon as she joined him at the opera hall. "I'm on it."

"You'll record their meeting? I want to know *everything* they say, Soren. I want to see it myself."

"I already said I would." A grin spread across his face. "Not bad, Aria. Not bad."

Aria fractioned out and took off the Smarteye, holding it in the palm of her hand. Her fingers still shook, and she couldn't get them to stop. "It's set up," she said to Sable. "Hess is waiting for you."

Sable held out his hand, but she hesitated, suddenly feeling possessive over the device. She'd helped Perry into the Realms willingly last fall, but this felt different. Like she was inviting a stranger into something private. She had no choice. Sable would give Hess the location of the Still Blue in exchange for transport. Her part of the deal would be done. She'd be able to get Talon back and be free of Hess.

She handed it to Sable. "Place it over your left eye, like I did. It'll pull tight to your skin. Stay calm, breathe slowly, and you'll adjust. Hess will bring you into a Realm once the device is activated."

Candlelight reflected on the device as Sable examined it. Satisfied, he applied it over his eye. Aria saw his shoulders stiffen as the biotech worked, and then relax as he adjusted to the gentle pressure. Moments later he grunted softly, his focus growing distant, and she knew he'd fractioned to the Realms. He was with Hess. There was nothing to do now but wait.

Aria relaxed in her chair and imagined the negotiations happening right then between Sable and Hess. Who would hold the upper hand? She'd see everything later, thanks to Soren. She'd never have expected to have him as an ally on the inside.

Minutes passed in silence before Sable jerked upright. He looked around the room, and then removed the Smarteye. "Unbelievable," he said, staring at the device in his hand.

"What did Hess say?" she asked.

Sable drew a few slow breaths. "I told him what I need. He's looking into it."

"So we wait?" Aria asked. "How long?"

"A few hours."

She gasped. That was soon. She couldn't believe the plan was working. She felt like she'd just taken her first step back toward the Tides. Toward Perry.

Sable rose from the table. "Let's go, Olivia," he said, walking to the door.

Aria shot to her feet. *"Wait,"* she said. "The Smarteye. I'll bring it back when it's time."

He turned back to her. "No need. I'll keep it."

Liv came to her side. "Sable, it's hers."

"Not anymore," he said, and then spoke to the guards by the door. "Keep them here overnight. I might still have need for the Dweller. Then see them out of the city at first light." Sable's steel-blue eyes moved to Liv. "You understand, I'm sure, why your friends can't stay."

Liv glanced at Roar, who stood a few feet away, frozen. "I understand," she said. Then she followed Sable from the room without a backward glance.

Hours later, Aria sat at the table with Roar, watching the rust-colored drapes stir in the wind. The dining room was cloaked in darkness, the only light coming through the open balcony doors. Every so often, she heard the muffled voices of the guards posted in the corridor.

She rubbed her arms, feeling numb. Sable had surely met with Hess again by now. He had used her and discarded her. She shook her head. He was just like Hess.

Outside, the rain had stopped, leaving the stones on the balcony slick, reflecting the glow of the sky. From where she sat, she could see currents of Aether. Bright rivers, flowing against the darkness. They'd see another storm soon. It didn't shock her anymore. Eventually, the storms would come every day, and it would be just like the Unity. Decades of constant funnels crashing across the earth, coating it in destruction. But it wouldn't spread over everything.

In her mind, she pictured an oasis. A golden place that

shimmered in the sunlight. She imagined a long pier, with seagulls wheeling in the blue sky above. She pictured Perry and Talon together, fishing at the end, content and relaxed. Cinder would be there too, watching them, holding his hat to keep it from blowing away. She imagined Liv and Roar nearby, whispering to each other, planning some kind of mischief that would lead, inevitably, to someone being tossed into the water. And she would be there. She'd sing something gentle and pretty. A song that would hold the sway of the waves and the warm feel of the sun. A song that would capture how she felt for all of them.

That was what she wanted. It was her Still Blue, and every breath she took, every second that passed, she could choose to fight for it, or not.

She realized it was no choice at all. She would always fight.

Aria stood and motioned for Roar to follow her to the balcony. As she stepped outside, the ghostly moan of the wind raised the hair on her arms. Below, she saw the Snake River, its black water rippling with Aether light. Smoke lifted up from the chimneys of homes along the banks, and she could see the bridge she and Roar had crossed only yesterday. In the darkness it stood as an arc dotted with points of firelight.

Roar stood beside her, his jaw tense, his brown eyes tight with anger.

She reached for his hand.

We're going to steal the Eye back. We can take the ledge to the next balcony and slip inside. I can get us to Sable's room. I need the

Still Blue for Talon. For Perry. If it's on the Eye, then we'll have what we came for. We'll get Liv and get out of here.

It was a desperate plan. Flawed and dangerous. But their window for action was closing by the minute. In hours, they'd be thrown out of Rim. The time for risks was now.

"Yes," Roar whispered urgently. "Let's go."

Aria peered over the low wall that bordered the balcony. A small ledge ran to the next balcony, about twenty feet away. It was just a small lip of stone, barely four inches wide. She looked down. She wasn't afraid of heights, but her stomach clenched like she'd been punched. The drop to the Snake was sixty feet, she guessed. A fall from this height could be lethal.

She swung her legs over the wall and stepped onto the ledge. A gust set her shirt flapping. She gasped, curling her back at the chill that raced up her spine. Digging her fingers into the grooves, she drew a breath and took her first steps away from the balcony. Then another step. And then another.

She skimmed her hands over the stone blocks, grasping cracks and edges as she kept her gaze on her feet. She heard the soft brush of Roar's feet behind her, and the drift of a woman's laughter from somewhere above.

Her gaze darted over. Halfway there.

Her boot slipped. Her shin smacked the ledge. She grasped desperately at stone, fingernails lifting, tearing. Roar's fingers clamped onto her arm, steadying her. She pressed her cheek against the stone wall, every muscle in her body clenching. As close as she pushed herself to the wall, it wasn't enough. She breathed, forcing her mind away from the feeling of falling backward.

"I'm right here," Roar whispered. His hand splayed on her back, firm and warm. "I won't let you fall."

She could only nod. She could only keep going.

One step at a time, she inched toward the other balcony. As she neared, she saw a pair of double doors. They were open, but there was only darkness beyond. She waited, forcing back her eagerness to be off the slippery ledge, letting her ears tell her what awaited inside.

She didn't hear anything. Not a sound.

Aria hopped over the low wall and dropped into a crouch. She set a hand down, needing just a quick connection with solid ground. Roar landed soundlessly beside her.

Together, they skimmed across the balcony. A quick testing glance through the doors showed an empty, darkened room. They stepped inside, silent, weaponless.

Only the Aether light flowing through the doors illuminated the chamber, but it was enough to see that the space was bare—possessing no more furniture than a few chairs pushed to the corner. Roar moved swiftly toward them. She heard two muffled snaps. He returned and handed her something. A broken horn spur. Aria tested the feel of it in her hand. It was roughly the same length as her knives. Not as sharp, but it would do as a weapon.

Moving to the door, they listened for sounds in the hall. Silence. They slipped outside and hurried toward Sable's room. Lamps flickered along the way, creating pools of shadow and light. She firmed her grip on the horn handle. She'd spent the winter practicing her fighting skills with Roar. Learning speed. Momentum. Stealth. She felt ready, the rush in her blood on the edge between eagerness and fear.

Liv's room was close, and Sable's wouldn't be much farther.

Aria heard footsteps. She froze. Ahead of her, Roar tensed. Two strides echoed to her ears. Both heavyset, the knock of their heels firm against the stones. The sound bounced—in front of her one instant, behind the next. She saw the same uncertainty in Roar's eyes. Which way? There was no time.

They surged forward together, feet gliding, devouring the stone hall. They'd either avoid the guards or run right into them.

They reached the end just as a pair of guards came around the corner, and then they moved like they'd rehearsed it. Roar lunged for the largest man, closest to him. Aria sprang on the other.

She rammed the horn into the guard's temple. The strike was solid, the impact jarring, shooting up her arm. The man rocked back, stunned. She grasped the knife at his belt and drew it, ready for her second strike. Ready to cut. But his eyes rolled back, and he was fading. She jammed the hilt of the knife into his jaw, knocking him out, and still had time to grasp the sleeve of his uniform, softening the sound of his fall.

For an instant she stared at the guard—at his ruddy complexion and slack mouth—soundly defeated on the floor, and she felt a confidence that a tattoo could never give her. She turned to see Roar straighten over the other guard's body. He slid a knife into his belt, his dark eyes flicking to hers, cool and focused. He tipped his chin, gesturing down the hall, and then hoisted the man he'd slain up over his shoulder.

Aria couldn't carry the other guard alone, and there was no time to second-guess. She sprinted for Liv's room. Pulling herself short at Liv's door, she grasped the iron handle, and stepped inside.

Light from the hall spilled into the darkened room. Liv lay on her bed, awake, on top of the covers. When she saw Aria, she shot to her feet, landing on the floor with a quiet thump. She wore her day clothes, down to her boots.

Liv looked from Aria to the door. Then she bolted into the hall without uttering a word. Aria shot after her. They passed Roar, carrying the guard over his shoulder. Silently, Liv held the man Aria had knocked out beneath the arms. Aria took him by his feet. Together, they carried him into Liv's room and set him down against the wall, where Roar had set the other man. Aria darted back to the open door. Carefully, she eased it closed, listening to the hardware click softly into place.

Then she turned and saw Roar and Liv locked in an embrace.

31

PEREGRINE

Perry sat in the cookhouse after supper in a daze, his mind stuck on Aria. She hadn't betrayed him. She wasn't with Roar. He hadn't lost her. The thoughts ran through his mind in an endless cycle.

The Aether had built all day, leaving everyone anxious, waiting for the storm to hit. Reef and Marron sat at his sides, both of them quiet. Nearby, Kirra talked with her men, speaking in quiet tones.

Only Willow carried on normally. She was across from Perry at the table, chattering to Cinder about the day she'd found Flea.

"It was four years ago," she said, "and he was even scrabblier than he is now."

"That's scrabbly," Cinder said, trying not to smile.

"I know. Me and Perry and Talon were coming back from the harbor when Talon spotted him. Flea was lying on his side, just off the trail. Right, Perry?"

He heard his name and surfaced to answer. "That's right."

"So we got closer and saw a nail speared through his paw. You know the soft webby part between his toes?" Willow splayed her fingers, pointing. "That's where the nail was. I was scared he'd bite, but Perry went right up and said, 'Easy, fleabag. I'm just going to take a look at your paw.'"

Perry smiled at Willow's imitation of him. He didn't think his voice was that deep. As she prattled on, he looked down at his own hand, flexing it. Remembering the feel of Aria's fingers in his.

Did she hate him? Had she forgotten about him?

"What's going on?" Reef asked quietly.

Perry shook his head. "Nothing."

Reef watched him for a long moment. "Right," he said, irritated, but as he rose to leave, his hand came down on Perry's shoulder in a quick, reassuring grip.

Perry fought the urge to knock it away. Nothing *was* wrong. He was fine.

On his other side, Marron pretended not to notice. He had Vale's old ledger open on the table to a diagram he'd made of the cave. When he turned the page, Perry saw a tally of food from a year ago, written in his brother's hand. They'd thought they had so little in those days. They had less now. The stash of food Kirra had brought wouldn't last forever, and Perry didn't know how they'd replenish it.

Marron sensed him watching and looked up, a soft smile on his face. "Fine time to be Blood Lord, isn't it?"

Perry swallowed. It wasn't pity. It wasn't. He nodded. "It'd be worse without you here."

Marron's smile grew warmer. "You've assembled a good team, Perry." He went back to the ledger, creating three lines, studying them, and then sighing. He closed the book. "I'm of no use. Might as well try to rest." He tucked it under his arm and left.

His departure inspired the others. One by one people made their way out, until it was only Reef and Kirra, leaving together. Perry watched them go, his heart pounding for no reason that he could understand. Then he was finally alone. He drew the candle closer and played with the flame, his eyes blurring as he tested his threshold for pain, until it guttered and went out.

When he finally stepped outside, the air smelled ashy and carried the sting of Aether. It smelled of ruin. The sky churned dark and bright. Marbled and shifting. In hours, the storm would break, and the tribe would come flooding into the cookhouse for shelter.

Flea trotted over from across the clearing, his ears bouncing up and down. Perry knelt and scratched his neck. "Hey, fleabag. You watching over things for me?"

Flea panted at him. In a flash Perry remembered him the same way weeks ago, leaning against Aria's leg. Suddenly he was overwhelmed by the urge to feel sharp and clear again. To get her out of his head.

He shot toward the beach trail, sprinting when Flea tore ahead, turning it into a race. Perry pushed himself and jumped off the last dune, thinking of nothing more than diving into the sea.

He landed on the soft sand and froze.

Flea trotted toward a girl who was down by the shore. She was facing the water. Taller than Willow, Perry saw, with a woman's body and hair he could tell was red, even in the blue night.

Kirra saw Flea. Then she turned around and spotted him. She lifted her hand in a small wave.

Perry hesitated, knowing he should wave good-bye and head back to the compound, but the next thing he knew, he was standing in front of her, no memory of walking across the sand or choosing to stay.

"I was hoping you'd show up," she said, smiling.

"I thought you didn't like the beach." His voice sounded deep and hoarse.

"It's not as bad when you're here. Can't sleep?"

"I . . . No." Perry crossed his arms, fisting his hands. "I was going to swim."

"But now you're not?"

He shook his head. The waves were huge. Pounding on the sand. He needed to be there. In the water. Or home in his bed. Anywhere but here.

"About what I said earlier," she said. "I should mind my own business."

"It doesn't matter."

Kirra lifted an eyebrow. "Really?"

Perry wanted to say yes. He didn't want to be a fool who'd

given his heart to a girl who'd left him. Didn't want to feel weak anymore.

He didn't answer, but Kirra came nearer anyway. Closer than she should have. He couldn't ignore the shape of her body any longer, or the smile on her lips.

He tensed when she touched his arm, though he'd expected it. She slid her hand down to his wrist. Pulling gently, she uncrossed his arms. Then she wrapped them around her back and stepped in, closing the space between them.

32

ARIA

O livia, what are you doing to me?" Roar spoke in a low rush, staring into Liv's eyes. "How could you come here?"

"I'm sorry, Roar. I thought I could help the Tides. I thought I could go through with it. I thought I could move on from you."

As she spoke, Roar kissed her cheeks, her chin, her forehead. Aria spun and darted for the balcony, passing Liv's wedding dress hanging by the opened doors. She kept going until her legs bumped against the low wall and her fingers gripped the cold stones and she was staring down. Down at the dark water in the distance.

She didn't want to listen, didn't want to hear them, but her ears were sharp—so much sharper when her adrenaline was going.

Liv's voice. "I was wrong. I was so wrong."

And then Roar. "It's all right, Livy. I love you. No matter what. Always."

Then it was quiet, and Aria heard only the wind breathing over the balcony, and their breaths, Liv's and Roar's, uneven and catching. Aria shut her eyes as her heart twisted and twisted. She could almost feel Perry's arms around her. Where was he now? Was he thinking about her, too?

Seconds later, Roar and Liv appeared on the balcony together, eyes sparkling. Liv's half-sword peeked over one shoulder. Over the other, she carried her satchel and Aria's.

"I was coming for you tonight," Liv said, and handed the leather pack over. She reached into her bag and brought out the Smarteye. "Sable hid it in his room. I snuck in while he slept. I'd scented pine on it earlier. I went right to it." She handed it to Aria. "Go. Use it quickly."

Aria shook her head. "Now?" How long until someone noticed the guards missing? "We have to get out of here."

"You have to do it now," Liv said. "He'll come after us if we take it."

"He'll come after you regardless, Olivia," Roar said. "We need to go."

"He won't," Liv said. "Get the Still Blue. If we don't have that, we don't have Talon."

There was no time to argue. Aria applied the device, and her Smartscreen appeared. She chose the Phantom icon. Soren would know whether Sable and Hess had discussed the Still Blue. She waited, expecting to fraction into the opera hall. She didn't. Instead, two new icons appeared, generic, bearing only time counters. Soren had left her the recordings.

She chose the one with the shortest running time, growing more nervous with every passing second. Roar was in Liv's room, listening by the door for sounds in the hall.

An image expanded on her Smartscreen. She was viewing a scratch Realm. A blank space with nothing more than darkness, broken by a single spotlight from above. Sable stood to one side, Hess to the other, the planes of their faces cut sharply by light and shadow.

Hess was wearing his official Consul uniform. Navy, trimmed with reflective slashes along the sleeve and collar. He stood rigid, straight, hands down at his sides. Sable wore a fitted black shirt and pants, and the Blood Lord chain sparkled at his neck. He had a relaxed stance, his eyes wrinkled in amusement. One man looked dangerous; the other looked deadly.

Sable spoke first. "Charming, your world. Is it always this appealing?"

Hess's mouth lifted into a smirk. "I didn't want to overwhelm you earlier."

Aria realized she'd chosen the recording of their second meeting. There was no time to change. She let it play on.

"Would you prefer this?" Hess asked.

In a quiet lurch, the Realm changed. Now they stood in a thatch-roofed hut with open sides, set up high like it was on stilts. A golden savannah rolled out to the horizon, the grass undulating in waves under a warm breeze.

Hess had no idea. He had meant it as an insult. A jab at the primitive man he believed Sable to be. But for a long moment all Aria could do—all Sable could do—was stare in wonder at the sun-doused scenery. At an open, still sky. At earth that was gently baked, not cruelly burned by Aether.

Sable turned his focus back to Hess. "I do prefer it, thank you. What have you learned?"

Hess sighed. "My engineers assure me that the craft will travel over any kind of terrain. They have shields, but their effectiveness is limited. Any intense concentration of Aether will overpower them."

Sable nodded. "I have a solution for that. What's the total, Hess?"

"Eight hundred people. And that will be pushing their capacity."

"That's not enough," Sable said.

"We were never intended to leave Reverie," Hess said, his words clipped with frustration. "We're not prepared for an exodus of this magnitude. Are you?"

Sable smiled. "We wouldn't be having this conversation if I were."

Hess ignored the jab. "We split the number evenly or the deal is off."

"Yes. Fine," Sable said impatiently. "We've been through the terms."

In the real, Roar returned to the balcony. "We have to go," he whispered, tugging on her arm. Aria shook her head.

She couldn't stop listening now.

"How soon can you be ready?" Sable asked Hess.

"A week to fuel and load the craft, and to organize the . . . the survivors. The Chosen."

Sable nodded as he stared thoughtfully across the grassy plain. "Eight hundred people," he said to himself. Then he faced Hess. "What will you do with the rest of your citizens?"

The color drained from Hess's face. "What *can* I do with them? They'll be told to wait for the second deployment."

Sable's lips lifted into a smile. "You know there won't be a second deployment. It's a single crossing."

"Yes, I know that," Hess said tightly. "But they won't."

Aria's knees softened, her shoulder bumping against Liv's. Hess and Sable were going to pick and choose who went. Who *lived* and who *died*. She couldn't catch her breath, and she felt nauseous. Sickened by how coldly they discussed leaving people behind.

Roar's grasp on her arm tightened. "Aria, you have to stop!"

Sounds erupted in the hall. She tensed, racing through the commands to shut off the Eye.

"In here!" someone yelled.

Roar drew his knife. Aria heard the thud of a shoulder driving open the door, and then the crash of wood against stone. In the darkness of Liv's room, she saw a rush of movement. A black tide crashing toward them.

She backpedaled, fumbling with her satchel. Her legs slammed against the balcony wall as she shoved the Eye deep inside the leather pack. Footsteps pounded closer, and then guards appeared, shouting for them to stand down, steel flashing in the dimness.

Liv drew her half-sword from its sheath, stepping around Roar.

"Liv!" he yelled.

The guard at the helm raised a crossbow, stopping her. She stood a few paces in front of Aria and Roar, poised to slash. Sable's guards filed in, forming a wall of red and black across the wide threshold. They were trapped on the balcony.

Everything was still, silent, except for the even, unhurried tread of footsteps. Sable's men stepped aside as he came forward. Aria saw no trace of surprise on his face.

"The girl has the eyepiece," one of the guards said. "I saw her put it in her bag."

Sable's gaze moved to her, cold and focused. Aria firmed her grip on the satchel.

"I took it," Liv said, still in her fighting stance.

"I know." Sable took a step forward, his chest working as he scented the air. "I knew you'd had a change of heart, Olivia. But I'd hoped you wouldn't act on it."

"Let them go," Liv said. "Let them leave, and I'll stay."

Roar tensed beside Aria. "No, Liv!"

Sable ignored him. "What makes you think I want you to stay? You stole from me. And you've chosen another." He looked to Roar. "But there might be a solution. Maybe you have too many options."

Sable snatched the crossbow from the man at his side and trained it on Roar.

"You think that'll change anything?" Roar said, his voice hard. "It doesn't matter *what* you do. She'll never be yours."

"You think so?" Sable asked. He firmed his grip on the weapon, readying to fire.

"No!" Aria thrust the satchel out over the wall. "If you want the Smarteye back, swear you won't hurt him. Swear in front of your men you won't, or I'll drop it."

"If you do that, Dweller, I will kill you *both*."

Liv surged forward, sword swinging. Sable adjusted his aim and fired. The bolt left the crossbow. Liv flew backward and fell.

Her body struck the stones with a sickening thud, like a heavy sack of grain heaved to the ground. Then she lay still.

The real was broken. It had a glitch, like the Realms. Liv wasn't moving. She lay just a pace away from Aria's feet. From Roar's. Her long blond hair spilling over her chest. Through the golden strands, Aria saw the bolt that had struck her, blood seeping up, spreading deep red over her ivory shirt.

She heard Roar exhale. A singular sound. A sigh like a last breath.

Then she saw what would happen next.

Roar would attack Sable, no matter that it wouldn't bring Liv back. No matter that half a dozen armed men stood beside their Blood Lord. Roar would try to kill Sable. But he would be the one killed, if she didn't do something *now*.

She lunged. Wrapping Roar in her arms, she flung herself back, pulling them over the balcony wall. Then they were weightless and falling, falling, falling through the darkness.

～ 33 ～

PEREGRINE

F orget about her," Kirra whispered, staring up at him. "She's gone."

Her scent flowed into Perry's nose. A brittle autumn scent. Leaves that crumbled into jagged pieces. The wrong scent, but he felt his fists unfold. His fingers spread on the small of Kirra's back. On flesh that didn't feel the way he wanted. Did she feel his fingers shaking?

"Perry . . . ," Kirra whispered, her scent warming. She licked her lips and stared up at him, her eyes glinting. "I didn't expect this either."

A fierce hunger rolled through him. Heartache that pounded inside his chest like the breaking waves. "Yes, you did."

She shook her head. "It's not why I came here. We could be good together," she said. Then her hands were on him. Fast, cold hands running over his chest. Skimming his stomach. She moved closer, pressing her body to his, and leaned up to kiss him.

"Kirra."

"Don't talk, Perry."

He took her wrists and drew her hands away. "No."

She settled onto her heels and stared at his chest. They stayed that way, not moving. Not speaking. Her temper lit like fire, crimson, searing. Then he scented her resolve, her control, as it cooled and cooled, icing over.

Perry heard a bark along the beach trail. He'd forgotten about Flea. He'd forgotten about the storm roiling above them. He'd forgotten, for a second, how it felt to be left behind.

Strangely, he felt calm now. It didn't matter if Aria was hundreds of miles away, or whether she'd hurt him, or said good-bye, or anything else. Nothing would change the way he felt. Not ignoring his thoughts of her, or being with Kirra. The moment Aria had taken his hand on the roof at Marron's, she'd changed everything. No matter what happened, she'd always be the one.

"I'm sorry, Kirra," he said. "I shouldn't have come here."

Kirra lifted her shoulders. "I'll survive." She turned to go, but stopped herself. She looked back, smiling. "But you should know that I always get what I'm after."

34

ARIA

Aria had flown before, in the Realms. It was a glorious thing, soaring with no weight and no care. Flying felt like becoming the wind. This was nothing like that. It was an ugly, grasping, panicking thing. As the Snake River blurred closer, her only thought—her *every* thought—was *hold on to Roar.*

The water slammed into her, hard as stone, and then everything happened at once. Every bone in her body jarred. Roar tore out of her grip, and darkness swallowed her, driving every thought from her mind. She didn't know if she was still there—still alive—until she saw the wavering light of the Aether calling her to the surface.

Her limbs unlocked, and she kicked, pushing through the water. Cold pierced into her muscles and her eyes. She was too heavy, too slow. Her clothes filled, dragging her down, and she felt the strap of her satchel looped around her waist.

Aria grasped it and swam, every stroke thick, like cutting through mud. She broke the surface and sucked in a breath.

"Roar!" she screeched, scanning the water. The river looked calm on the surface, but the current was brutally strong.

Filling her lungs, she went under, searching desperately for him. She couldn't see more than a few feet in front of her, but she spotted him floating close by, his back to her.

He wasn't swimming.

Panic exploded inside of her. She'd thrown him over the balcony.

If she'd killed him—

If he was gone—

She reached him, grasped under his arms, and towed him up. They surfaced, but now she had to kick harder. His weight was immense, and he was limp in her arms, a dead weight pulling her down.

"Roar!" she gasped, struggling to keep him above water. The cold was beyond anything she'd ever experienced, stabbing like a thousand needles into her muscles. "Roar, help me!" She swallowed water, and started coughing. They were still sinking. Still falling together.

She couldn't talk. Aria reached up, fumbling, finding the bare skin at his neck. *Roar, please. I can't do this without you!*

He jolted like he'd woken from a nightmare, wrenching out of her arms.

Aria surfaced and retched river water, fighting to catch a breath.

Roar swam away from her. She had to be losing her mind. He'd never leave her. Then she saw a dark shape floating toward them on the current. For an irrational second, she thought Sable had come after them, until her eyes focused and she saw the fallen log. Roar latched onto it.

"Aria!" He reached for her and pulled her in.

Aria grabbed hold, broken branches jabbing into her numbed hands. She couldn't stop shaking, shaking from her core. They passed beneath the bridge and raced past homes along shore, everything dark and still in the dead of night.

"Too cold," she said. "We have to get out." Her jaw was trembling so much her words were unrecognizable.

They kicked toward shore together, but she didn't know how they made it. She could barely feel her legs anymore. When their feet thudded against the gravelly riverbed, they released the driftwood. Roar's arm came around her, and they waded on, clinging to each other, reality returning with every step.

Liv.

Liv.

Liv.

She hadn't looked at Roar's face yet. She was afraid of what she'd see.

As they trudged out of the river and onto land, she suddenly weighed a thousand pounds. Somehow, she and Roar hobbled up the shore, carrying each other, stumbling arm in arm. They passed between two houses and crossed a field, plunging into the woods beyond.

Aria didn't know where they were heading. She couldn't keep a straight line. She was beyond thinking, and her steps were weaving.

"Walking can't cold anymore." It was her voice but slurred, and she didn't think she'd made sense. Then she was on her side in the tall grass. She couldn't remember falling over. She drew into a ball, trying to stop the pain that stabbed into her muscles, her heart.

Roar appeared above her. There for an instant, then he was gone, and all she saw was Aether, flowing in currents above her.

Aria wanted to go after him. She didn't want to be alone, and all she felt was *aloneness*. She needed a place with falcon carvings on the sill. She needed a place to belong.

When she opened her eyes, spindly tree branches swayed above her, and the first light of dawn colored the sky. Her head was resting on Roar's chest. A thick, coarse blanket covered them, warm and smelling of horse.

She sat up, every muscle in her body aching, quivering with weakness. Her hair was still damp from the river. They were in the fold of a small gully. Roar must have moved her while she was asleep. Or unconscious. A fire smoldered nearby. Their jackets and boots were set out to dry.

Roar slept with a soft smile on his lips. His skin was a shade too pale. She memorized the way he looked. Aria wasn't sure when she'd see him smile again.

He was beautiful, and it wasn't fair.

She drew a shaky breath. "Roar," she said.

He rolled to his feet without a word. The suddenness of his movement startled her, and she wondered if he'd ever been asleep.

He stared at her with unfocused eyes. Stared *through* her. She remembered feeling that way when her mother died. Detached. Like nothing she saw looked the same. In one day, her entire life had changed. Everything—from the world around her to the way she felt inside—had become unrecognizable.

Aria stood. She wanted to hold him and sob with him. *Give it to me,* she wanted to scream. *Give me the pain. Let me take it from you.*

Roar turned away. He picked up his jacket, banked the fire, and began to walk.

As they hurried to put the Snake behind them, clouds moved in, casting a mottled darkness over the woods. Aria's right knee throbbed—she must have sprained it on the fall from the balcony—but they had to keep going. Sable would be after them. They needed to get away from Rim and find safety. It was all she let herself think about. All she could manage.

They traveled along the crest, stopping in the afternoon in a dense pocket of pines. The Snake curved along the valley below, the water rippling like scales. In the distance she saw a wall of rising black smoke. Another stretch of land decimated by a storm. The Aether was growing more powerful. No one could be in any doubt.

Roar dropped his satchel and sat. He hadn't spoken once yet today. Not a word.

"I'm going to look around," she said. "I won't go far." She left to scout their position. They were protected on one side by a shale slope. On the other by an impassable cliff. If anyone came after them, they'd have fair warning.

When she came back, she found Roar hunched over his knees with his head in his hands. Tears streamed down his cheeks and rolled off his chin, but he wasn't moving. Aria had never seen anyone cry that way. So still. Like he didn't even realize he was doing it.

"I'm right here, Roar," she said, sitting by him. "I'm here."

He shut his eyes. He didn't respond.

Seeing him that way made her hurt. It made her want to scream until her throat was raw, but she couldn't force him to talk. When he was ready, she'd be there.

Aria found a spare shirt in her satchel and tore it into strips. She wrapped her knee and put her things away, then had nothing else to do except watch Roar's heart bleed out before her eyes.

An image sprang to her mind, of Liv smiling sleepily and asking, *Are you the bird, or is my brother?*

Aria clamped her hand over her mouth and scrambled away. She darted past shrubs and trees, needing distance because she couldn't cry silently and she wouldn't make it worse for Roar.

Liv should've been married tomorrow, or she should have

run away with Roar. She should have seen Perry as a Blood Lord, and she should've been Aria's friend. So much had vanished in a second.

Aria remembered being in the dining room with Sable. She'd had a knife in her hand, and a clear shot at his neck. She hated herself for not having done it. She should have killed him then.

Eyes swollen, her head pounding, she limped back to Roar. He was asleep, his head resting on his satchel.

She found her Smarteye and fought back a wave of fresh tears. If Liv hadn't stolen it, would she still be alive? Would she be alive if Aria had given the Eye back to Sable on the balcony?

It nauseated her to think of Hess and Sable's meeting. Their deal to go to the Still Blue together meant turning their backs on countless innocent people. She thought about Talon and Caleb and the rest of her friends in Reverie. Would they be chosen to go? And what about Perry, and Cinder, and the rest of the Tides? What about *everyone else*? The Unity was happening again, and it was more horrific than anything she'd imagined.

The thought of seeing Hess made her stomach turn, but she needed to. She'd connected him with Sable. She had done her part in helping him find the Still Blue. Now he needed to follow through on his part of the deal—and if he failed her, she'd contact Soren. She didn't care *how* it happened. She needed Talon back.

Pulse racing, she applied the Smarteye. The biotech worked, attaching to her eye socket. She saw that the recordings were gone. Only the icons for Hess and Soren remained on her screen. She tried Hess and waited. He didn't come. She tried Soren next. He never showed either.

35

PEREGRINE

L ater, Perry climbed up to the roof of his house and watched the Aether coiling in the sky. He'd plunged into the ocean after Kirra left, needing to wash her scent from him. He'd cut through the waves until his shoulders burned, then returned to the compound, his body tired and numb, his mind clear.

As he rested his head against the roof tiles, he could still feel the movement of the ocean. Closing his eyes, he drifted on the blurry edge of a memory.

He remembered the time his father took him hunting, just the two of them, on the afternoon Talon was born. Perry had been eleven years old. A warm day, the breeze as soft as a breath. He remembered the sound of his father's stride, heavy and sure, as they'd walked through the woods.

Hours passed before Perry realized his father wasn't tracking, wasn't paying attention to scents. He stopped abruptly and knelt, looking Perry in the eyes in a way he seldom did, spots of sunlight dancing on his forehead. Then he told Perry that love was like the waves in the sea, gentle and good sometimes, rough and terrible at others, but that it was endless and stronger than the sky and the earth and everything in between.

"One day," his father had said, "I hope you understand. And I hope you'll forgive me."

Perry knew how it felt to be haunted by a mistake whenever he lay down to sleep. There was nothing more painful than hurting someone you loved. Because of Vale, Perry realized he *understood*. No matter how hard he tried, there would be times when he couldn't stop the rough and terrible from happening. To his tribe. To Aria. To his brother.

Shifting his back on the roof tiles, he decided that the *one day* his father had spoken of was today. Tonight. Right now. And he forgave.

The storm struck before dawn, wrenching him from a deep, restful sleep. The Aether turned in spirals, brighter than he'd ever seen. Perry climbed to his feet, his skin prickling, the acrid smell sharp and suffocating. To the west, a funnel wove down from the sky, turning toward the earth. The shrieking sound roared in his ears as it struck and spooled back up. He saw another funnel to the south, and then another. Suddenly the night was alive, pulsing with light.

"Perry, get off there!" Gren yelled from the clearing

below. People rushed out of their homes, terrified, running for the cookhouse.

Perry sprinted for the ladder. Halfway down, everything turned shocking white, and the air shuddered. His legs tensed. He missed a rung and fell, tumbling to the dirt.

Across the clearing, an Aether funnel whirled down, striking Bear's house. Shaking the earth beneath his feet. Perry watched, unable to move, as roof tiles exploded and popped. The funnel spooled back up, and the roof rumbled and toppled to one side. He shot to his feet and sprinted, knocking people over.

"Bear!" he yelled. "Molly!" He saw only a tumble of rock where the front door and window had been. Smoke seeped from the rubble. Fire burned somewhere inside.

Twig appeared beside him. "They're in there! I hear Bear!"

People gathered around, watching in shock as flames licked up from the cracks in the sloping roof. Perry caught Reef's eyes. "Get everyone in the cookhouse!"

Hayden pumped water from the well. Kirra's people stood behind her, clothes whipping in the hot, swirling wind.

"What do you want us to do?" she asked, their time on the beach forgotten.

"We need more water," he told her. "And help move rubble!"

"If we move any of this, the rest of the roof could fall," Gren said.

"We don't have a choice!" Perry yelled. Every second they lost, the fire spread. He grasped the stones of the collapsed wall, heaving them away one at a time, panic setting in as the heat of the fire seeped through the rubble into his hands. He sensed his own men beside him and Kirra's.

Seconds felt like hours. He looked up and saw an Aether funnel slash down to the cookhouse. The impact threw him sideways, down to his knees. When the funnel wove back to the sky, he stayed for silent, dizzying seconds, regaining his bearings. Twig stared at him vacantly, a trail of blood running down his ear.

"Perry! Over here!" Straggler called from a dozen paces away. Hyde and Hayden pulled Molly through a gap in the rubble.

Perry ran to her. Blood seeped from a gash on her forehead, but she was alive. "He's still in there," she said.

"I'll get him, Molly," he promised. He wouldn't let Bear die.

The brothers carried her to the cookhouse, where she could get treated. Everywhere Perry looked, funnels lashed the ground.

Nearby, Kirra called her people into the cookhouse. "We tried," she told him. She shrugged and walked away. That was how easily she gave up on someone who needed help. Whose life was on the line.

Perry turned back to the house just as the rest of the roof folded inward. The air rushed from his lungs, and screams of terror erupted around him.

"It's over, Perry." Twig grasped him by the arm, tugging him toward the cookhouse. "We have to get inside."

Perry shook him off. "I'm not leaving him!" He spotted Reef across the clearing, running with Hyde. He knew they'd haul him away.

Then Cinder ran up with Willow, Flea barking at their feet. He looked at Perry, a fierce intensity in his eyes. "Let me help!"

"No!" Perry wouldn't risk Cinder's life too. "Get in the cookhouse!"

Cinder shook his head. "I could do something!"

"Cinder, no! Willow, get him out of here!"

It was too late. Cinder was somewhere else. His stare was empty, oblivious to the chaos around him. As he backed away, moving to the middle of the clearing, his eyes began to glow, and veins of Aether spread over his face and hands. Shocked curses and shouts broke around Perry as others took notice of Cinder—and of the sky.

Above, the Aether melded into a single, massive whirlpool. A funnel twisted down, forming a solid brilliant wall that circled Cinder, engulfing him. Perry couldn't find his voice. He couldn't move. Didn't know how to stop Cinder.

A blast of light sent piercing pain into his eyes, blinding him. He flew back on the earth, landing on his side, and shielded his head. Waited for his skin to burn. A hot gust whipped past him, pushing him back for long seconds; then a sudden silence fell over the compound. He peered up and saw no Aether. The sky was blue and calm as far as he could see.

He looked to the center of the clearing. A small figure was curled in a circle of glittering embers. Stumbling to his feet, Perry ran to him. Cinder lay deathly still and bare, his hat gone, his hair gone, his chest unmoving.

36

ARIA

I have to find us another way to the Tides," Aria said the next morning, hugging her growling stomach. The snare trap she'd set the previous night had been empty. "I hurt my knee when we fell."

Roar looked up from the flames with lifeless eyes. He hadn't spoken yet. She tried to remember: had he said her name when they were in the Snake River? She'd been so out of her mind with cold that now she wondered if she'd imagined it.

"We could go part of the way by boat on the Snake," she continued. "It'll be a risk, but so is being out here. And at least it'll get us there faster."

She spoke quietly, but her own voice seemed loud. "Roar . . . please say something." She moved beside him and took his hand. *I'm here. I'm right here. I'm so sorry about Liv. Please tell me you can hear me.*

He looked at her, his eyes warming for a moment before he drew away.

They returned to the Snake while heading west, away from Rim. That afternoon, they reached a fishing town, where she found them passage on a wide barge heading downriver. The hold was cluttered with crates and burlap sacks filled with goods. She'd been ready to fight, ready for anything in case Sable had people looking for them, but the captain, a leather-faced man named Maverick, didn't ask any questions. She paid their way with one of her knives.

"Nice blade, ladybug," said Maverick. His eyes flicked to Roar. "You give me the other one and I'll give you the cabin."

She was anxious and hurting and had no patience. "Call me ladybug again and I *will* give you the other one."

Maverick smiled, showing a mouth full of silver teeth. "Welcome aboard."

Before they cast off, Aria listened closely to the gossip at the busy wharf. Sable had amassed a legion of men and was preparing to take them south. She heard different reasons for it. He wanted to conquer a new territory; he was on a quest for the Still Blue; he sought revenge against an Aud who had slain his bride only days before their wedding.

Aria imagined Sable spreading this last rumor himself. She hadn't thought it possible to hate him any more, but after hearing that, she did.

Once aboard, she and Roar settled themselves between

sacks filled with wool, rolls of leather, and salvaged goods like tires and plastic pipes from before the Unity. It amazed her that trade carried on as usual. It seemed futile.

She felt like she possessed a terrible secret. The world was coming to an end, and if Hess and Sable got their way, only eight hundred people would live on. Part of her wanted to scream a warning from the top of her lungs. But how would that help? What could anyone do without the location of the Still Blue? The other part of her still couldn't accept that what she'd seen—what she'd heard planned by Sable and Hess—could possibly be true.

She closed her eyes when they moved onto open water, listening to the crew's voices and the creak of the wooden ship. Every sound made her feel worse for Roar.

When it was quiet, Aria pulled her coat over her head and tried the Smarteye again. She hadn't given up hope of reaching either Hess or Soren. She couldn't give up on bringing Talon back to Perry.

Neither Hess nor Soren responded. She stuffed the Eye back into the satchel. Had they turned their backs on her, or had something happened to Reverie? She couldn't stop thinking of the glitches in the Realms. What if she'd lost contact because the damage in Reverie had gotten worse? What if it was crumbling? She couldn't deny the possibility. She'd seen what happened to Bliss in the fall, when she'd found her mother.

Unsettled, Aria rested her head against Roar's shoulder and watched the Aether turn above. A cold wind blew along the Snake, numbing her ears and her nose. Roar put his arm around her. She gathered close, reassured by this small sign that he was still there, somewhere beneath the shell of silence and grief. She found his hand, speaking to him without speaking, hoping at least this way he could hear her.

She told him she'd do anything to make him hurt less, and then waited for him to take his hand away. He didn't. His fingers threaded through hers, his grip familiar, comfortable, so she spoke to him some more.

As they floated down the Snake River, she told him about Hess and Sable's arrangement, and about her fears of Reverie's condition. She talked about the Realms—her favorites and least favorites—and all the ones she thought he'd like. She told him about her most frightening experience: a tie between when she thought Perry had been captured by the Croven in the fall, and when she couldn't find Roar in the Snake River. And her saddest: when she found her mother in Reverie. She told him about Perry. Deeper things than she'd ever shared before. *Don't ever spare me,* Roar had said once. Now she didn't. She couldn't, even if she'd wanted to. Perry was on her mind always.

She thought to Roar so much that it became natural and she stopped thinking about thinking and just thought. Roar heard everything. He knew her mind fully, openly, the same way Perry knew her tempers. Between the two of them, she thought, she was known completely.

She'd been seeking the comfort of a place. Of walls. A roof. A pillow to rest her head on. Now she realized that the people she loved were what gave her life shape, and comfort, and meaning. Perry and Roar were home.

Two days later, they reached the end of their river journey. The Snake had brought them far and given her knee a chance to heal, but now it forked west and they'd need to walk the last stretch to the Tides.

"A day and a half south," Maverick told her. "Maybe more if that slows you up." He tipped his head to a massive Aether storm brewing in the distance. Then he glanced at Roar, who waited on the dock. Maverick had never heard him speak a word. He'd only seen Roar stare vacantly at the water, or at the sky. "You know, you could do a lot better than him, ladybug."

Aria shook her head. "No. I couldn't."

They traveled well that day, stopping at night to rest. The following morning, Aria couldn't believe that after nearly a month away, she'd be back at the Tides that afternoon.

She felt like a failure. She hadn't discovered the location of the Still Blue, and they didn't have Liv. Her heart tore in half, the ache to see Perry colliding with the dread of what she'd have to tell him.

Aria rummaged in her satchel for the Smarteye and applied it. The Eye had barely gripped her skin when she fractioned to the opera house. Right away, she knew something was wrong. The rows of seats and balconies wavered, like she was seeing them through a sheet of water. Soren stood a few feet away, red-faced and panicked.

"I only have a few seconds before my father traces me. It's ending, Aria. It's shutting down. We got slammed by a storm and lost another generator. All the Pod's systems are failing. They're just containing the damage now."

Aria sucked in a breath. She felt like she'd been punched in the stomach. "Where's Talon?" she asked. In the real, Roar tensed at her side.

"He's with me. My father's been in contact with Sable."

"How did he—"

"He could tell by tracking your Smarteye that you'd taken it, so he sent men to Rim with another one after you left," Soren said, interrupting her. "Hess and Sable are both getting ready to leave for the Still Blue. My father's chosen who he's taking, and separated them into one of the service domes. No one with DLS is allowed to go. He's locked the rest of us in the Panop."

Aria tried to process his words. "He locked you in there. Your father *left you*?"

Soren shook his head. "No. He wanted me to go, but I couldn't leave. I can't let all these people just stay here and die. I thought I could unlock the Panop doors from inside, but I can't. Talon's in here. Caleb and Rune—everyone. *You* need to get us out of here. We're on auxiliary power. It won't last more than days. That's it. Then we run out of air."

"I'm coming," she said. "I'll be there. Keep Talon safe."

"I will, but *hurry*. Oh—and I know where they're going. I've been watching my father's comms with Sable—"

A surge of light blinded her, and pain exploded deep

300

behind her eye, shooting down her spine. She screamed, pulling at the Smarteye, wrenching desperately until it came off in her hand.

Roar knelt in front of her, gripping her arms. His eyes held more depth than she'd seen in days. Aria's head pounded, and tears streamed from her eyes, but she staggered to her feet.

"We have to go, Roar!" she said. "Talon's in danger. We need to get to Perry now!"

37

PEREGRINE

Perry swept the falcon carvings off the windowsill and put them into a linen bag. His things had already been moved to the cave, but now he packed Talon's clothes, toys, and books. Maybe it was foolish to move his nephew's belongings, but he couldn't leave them behind.

He picked up the small bow from the table and smiled. He and Talon used to spend hours shooting socks at each other from across the room. He drew the string, testing it. Would the bow still suit Talon—or had he had a growth spurt? He'd been gone half a year. Perry didn't miss him any less.

Twig came through the front door. "Storm's moving in," he said, taking the stuffed bag. "Is this ready?"

Perry nodded. "I'll be right out."

Only a few days had passed since the last storm, but another one was already building from the south, a massive, churning front that promised to be even worse. It had taken almost losing Bear and Molly to convince the Tides to leave the compound. It had almost cost Cinder's life, but they were going.

Perry went to Vale's room and crossed his arms, leaning against the door frame. Molly sat in a chair by the bed, watching over Cinder. His sacrifice had bought the Tides time to reach the cave in safety. Because of him, they'd been able to dig Bear out of the rubble alive. Cinder was as much Molly's now as he was Perry's.

"How's he doing?" Perry asked.

Molly caught his eye and smiled. "Better. He's awake."

Perry stepped into the room. Cinder's eyes fluttered open. He looked gray and hollow-boned, his breath rasping and shallow. He was wearing his usual cap, but his head was bald beneath. Perry scratched his chin, remembering. The only thing Cinder had said when he'd come to the night of the storm was *Don't let anyone see me.*

"I'll head up and make sure everything is set for him," Molly said, leaving them.

"You ready to go?" Perry asked Cinder. "I've got one more trip before I'm coming back for you."

Cinder licked his lips. "I don't want to."

"Willow's going to be there. She's been waiting to see you."

Cinder's eyes filled with tears. "She knows what I am."

"You think she cares that you're different? You saved her life, Cinder. You saved the Tides. Right now I think she likes you better than Flea."

Cinder blinked. Tears rolled down his face, seeping into the pillow. "She'll see me this way."

"I don't think she gives a damn what you look like. I know I don't. I won't force you, but I think you should come. Marron has a special place set up for you, and Willow needs her friend back." He grinned. "She's driving everyone crazy."

Cinder's mouth twitched in a brief smile. "All right. I'll go."

"Good." Perry rested his hand on Cinder's hat. "I'm grateful for you. Everyone is."

Gren waited outside with a horse. "I'll keep an eye on him," he said, handing Perry the reins.

The compound was quiet, but across the clearing Perry saw Forest and Lark packing up their own mounts. They looked over, tipping their heads at him.

Since the night of the storm, Kirra had no longer flirted or pushed him. In the span of a week, she'd gone from interested to indifferent, and he was fine with it. He regretted every second he'd spent with her on the beach. He regretted every second he'd ever spent with her.

Perry swung up into the saddle. "I'll be back in an hour," he told Gren.

Marron had transformed the cave. Fires cast golden light across the vast space, and the smell of sage floated through the air, softening the dampness and salt. He had organized the sleeping areas with tents for each family around the perimeter, to match the setup of the compound. Lamps lit a few from inside, and the material glowed soft white. The wide space at the center had been left open for gatherings, with the exception of a small wooden platform. In adjacent caverns, there were areas for cooking, washing, and even for keeping livestock and storing food. People wandered from one place to the next, wide-eyed as they oriented themselves in their new home.

It looked a thousand times more inviting than anything Perry had imagined. He could almost forget he was beneath a mountain of rock.

He spotted Marron by the small stage with Reef and Bear, and walked over to join them. Bear leaned on a cane, and both of his eyes were black.

"What do you think?" Marron asked.

Perry rubbed the back of his head. As much as Marron had done, it was still a temporary shelter. Still a cave. "I think I'm lucky to know you," he said finally.

Marron smiled. "Likewise."

Bear shifted his weight, peering at him. "I was wrong to doubt you."

Perry shook his head. "No. I don't know anyone who doesn't doubt. And I want to know what you think—especially when you think I'm wrong. But I need your trust. I always want the best for you and Molly. For everyone in the Tides."

Bear nodded. "I know that, Perry. We all do." He held out his hand, his grip crushing when Perry took it.

Bear wasn't the only one in the Tides who had changed toward Perry since the storm. They didn't argue with him anymore. Now, when he spoke, he sensed them listening and felt the power of their attention. He'd become Blood Lord day by day, through every act, every success, and even through his failures. Not by taking the chain from Vale.

Perry looked around, and a seed of suspicion took root. It was difficult to tell in this new space, but they seemed too few in number. People were missing.

"Where's Kirra?" he asked. He didn't see her, or any of her people.

"Didn't she tell you?" Marron said. "She left this morning. She told me they were going back to Sable."

"When?" Perry demanded. "When did they leave?"

"Hours ago," Bear said. "First thing this morning."

That couldn't be right. Perry had just seen Lark and Forest. Why would they have stayed behind?

Fear shot through him. He spun, running back to the horse he'd left outside with Twig. Ten minutes later, he thundered up to his house. The front door gaped open. He didn't see a soul anywhere.

Perry stepped inside, his heart pounding. Gren lay on the floor with his hands and feet bound by rope. Blood streamed from his nose, and his eye was swelling shut.

"They took Cinder," he said. "I couldn't stop them."

Half an hour later, Perry stood on the beach outside the cave with Marron and Reef. He pulled the Blood Lord chain over his head and held it in his fist.

Marron's blue eyes widened. "Peregrine?"

Nearby, Reef stared at the sea, arms crossed, unmoving.

"I can't take this with me." Perry didn't need to say why. With storms striking so often and the borderlands teeming with dispersed, leaving would be more dangerous than ever. "The Tides trust you," he continued. "Besides, you like jewels better than I do."

"I'll keep it," Marron said. "But it's yours. You'll wear it again."

Perry tried to smile, but his mouth twitched. He wanted to wear the chain more than ever, he realized. He wasn't the Blood Lord that Vale or his father had been, but he was still worthy. He was the right leader for the Tides now. And he knew he could carry the weight—his own way.

He handed the chain to Marron and headed up the beach with Reef. Twig waited at the trail with two horses. The only ones Kirra had left behind.

"Let me go," Reef said.

Perry shook his head. "I have to do this, Reef. When someone needs me, I dive."

After a moment, Reef nodded. "I know," he said. "I know that now." He ran a hand over his face. "You've got a week before I come after you."

Perry remembered the day he'd gone after Aria. Reef had given him an hour that lasted ten minutes. He smiled. "Knowing you, that means a day," he said, clasping Reef's hand. He pulled his satchel over his shoulder, and picked up his quiver and bow. Then he mounted up and set off with Twig.

Perry's throat tightened as they rode away. Weeks ago, he'd planned to leave his tribe behind, but now it was much harder than he'd expected. Harder than it had ever felt before.

His thoughts turned to Kirra as the afternoon wore on. She'd been after Cinder all along. Her questions about the Croven and his scarred hand hadn't been about him. She'd been probing him for information, waiting for the right time—the right way—to snatch Cinder. She'd deceived Perry, just like Vale had.

Sable was behind this. Perry didn't want to think about what use he had in mind for Cinder. He should've trusted his instincts. He should've sent Kirra away the day she'd shown up.

Kirra's tracks moved north on a well-worn trader's route. They'd been riding a few hours when Perry glimpsed movement in the distance. Adrenaline sparked through him. He spurred his horse, shooting forward, hoping to cut off Lark and Forest.

His stomach seized when he saw that it wasn't either of Kirra's men.

Twig pulled his horse alongside. "What do you see?"

Waves of numbness rolled through Perry. He couldn't believe his eyes. "It's Roar," he said. "And Aria."

Twig cursed. "Are you serious?"

Perry's impulse was to call out to them. They were both Auds. If he raised his voice, they'd hear him. It was what he would have done once. Roar was his best friend. And Aria was . . .

What was she to him? What were they to each other?

"What do you want to do?" Twig asked.

Perry wanted to run to her, because she'd come back. And he wanted to hurt her, because she'd left.

"Perry?" Twig said, jarring him back.

He urged his horse on. They rode closer, and the moment came when Aria heard the horses. Her head turned in his direction, but her eyes remained unfocused, unseeing in the dark. He watched her lips form words he couldn't hear and then heard Twig's answer beside him.

"It's me, Twig." He paused, sending Perry a worried glance. "Perry's with me too."

Messages passed between Auds. Heard only by Aud ears.

Perry watched as Aria looked at Roar, her face tensing in a look of plain regret. No. It was more than regret. It was dread. After a month of being apart, she *dreaded* seeing him.

She reached out and took Roar's hand, and he knew they were passing a message between them. Perry couldn't believe his eyes. They didn't think he could see them, but he did. He saw *everything*.

He was in fog as they reached each other. He dismounted and felt like he was floating. Like he was seeing everything from a distance.

He didn't know what was happening. Why Aria wasn't in

his arms. Why there was no greeting or smile on Roar's face. Then Aria's temper hit him, and it was so heavy and dark that he felt himself sway, overcome by it.

"Perry . . ." She looked at Roar, her eyes blurring.

"What is it?" Perry asked, but he already knew. He couldn't believe it. Everything Kirra had said—everything he'd tried not to believe about Roar and Aria—was true.

He looked at Roar. "What did you do?"

Roar wouldn't meet his eyes, and his face was white.

Rage ignited inside of him. He lunged and shoved Roar, swinging, curses pouring out of him.

Aria shot forward. "Perry, stop!"

Roar was too quick. He gave ground, and trapped Perry by the arms. "It's Liv," he said. "Perry . . . it's Liv."

~ 38 ~

ARIA

Finally Roar spoke, and Aria's heart broke at his words.

"I couldn't do anything. I couldn't stop Sable. I'm sorry, Perry. It happened so fast. She's gone. I lost her, Perry. She's gone."

"What are you talking about?" Perry said, shoving Roar away. He looked at Aria, confusion flashing in his green eyes. "Why is he saying that?"

Aria didn't want to answer. She didn't want to make it real for him, but she had to. "It's the truth," she said. "I'm sorry."

Perry blinked at her. "You mean . . . my *sister*?" The tone in his voice—vulnerable, tender—destroyed her. "What happened?"

As quickly as she could, she explained Hess and Sable's deal to reach the Still Blue together, and about Talon as well. She hated to do it, but he needed to know Talon's life was in danger. Liv, she saved for last. She felt light-headed as she spoke, breathless and detached, like when she'd been invisible in the Realms.

She hadn't spoken for long, but when she finished, the woods felt darker, fading into the night. Perry looked from her to Roar, tears brimming in his eyes. She watched him battle with himself, struggling for focus. Struggling to keep himself together. "Talon is trapped in Reverie?" he said finally.

"Talon and thousands of people," she answered. "They'll run out of oxygen if we don't get them out. We're their only chance."

He was moving to his horse before she'd finished speaking. "Go after Cinder," Perry told Twig.

Aria had forgotten Twig was there. "What happened to Cinder?"

Perry swung into his saddle. "The Horns took him." He rode up and held his hand down to her. "Let's go!"

Aria glanced at Roar. Whatever she'd expected of today, leaving him hadn't been part of it.

"I'll go with Twig," he said to her. The tension between him and Perry was still there.

Quickly she hugged Roar. Then she took Perry's hand. He pulled her up behind him, and the horse began to move before she'd settled her weight.

Aria reached out instinctively, wrapping her arms around him as the horse galloped into the woods. Liv was forgotten for now. Roar and Cinder, too. Everything except Talon.

She could feel the ridges of Perry's ribs through his shirt. The shift of his muscles. He was real and close, just as she'd wanted him to be for weeks—for *months*. But nothing had changed. He still felt far away.

~ 39 ~

PEREGRINE

Perry pushed the horse toward Reverie beneath a night sky writhing with Aether. Snatches of the horizon showed through the trees, pulsing with the light of funnels. They were heading south, right into the heart of a storm, but he had no choice. Talon was trapped.

Images of his sister flashed before his eyes. Senseless things. Liv pinning him down, when they were young, to run a brush through his hair. Liv wrapped in Roar's arms at the beach, laughing. Liv arguing with Vale over the arrangement with Sable, almost going to blows. He couldn't accept that he'd never see her again.

Talon was all he had now. He was the only family Perry had left. He glanced at Aria's arms, wrapped tight around him. Maybe he was wrong. Maybe he had more.

As they neared Reverie, a sharp scent carried on a warm gust, rustling through the trees. It brought a chemical taste to his tongue that he remembered from the night he'd broken into the Pod in the fall. Though he couldn't see Reverie yet, he knew it was burning.

Soon after, the horse locked beneath him as they crested a hill, rearing up, nickering in terror. The broad valley that spread before him was a sight unlike anything Perry had ever seen. They'd ridden for hours—it was sometime in the middle of the night—but Aether lit up the flat expanse. Hundreds of funnels lashed down from the sky, leaving bright red trails across the desert. Perry tightened his grip on the reins as the horse stamped and tossed its head. No amount of training would quiet its instincts now.

Terror speared through him as the rounded form of the Pod came into focus. It sat directly beneath the thick of the storm, spewing clouds of smoke as black as coal. Much of it was concealed, but he remembered its shape from other times he'd been there. An enormous central dome like a hill, surrounded by smaller domes that branched off like the rays of the sun. Somewhere in there, he'd find Talon.

The horse wouldn't settle. Perry turned in the saddle. "We can't ride any farther."

Aria jumped to the ground, no hesitation. "Come on!"

Perry grabbed his bow and ran after her, legs heavy from hours in the saddle. As they tore across the desert, he tried not to think of their odds, running miles through an Aether storm, with no shelter, no place to take cover.

Funnels struck down, each one louder, closer, sending

searing waves across his skin. A sudden shriek exploded in his ears; then a flash of light blinded him. Forty paces away, a funnel of Aether twisted down, ripping across the earth. Every muscle in his body clenched, pain shuddering through him. Unable to soften his fall, he thudded onto the ground, the wind driven out of his lungs.

Aria crouched a few paces away, tucked in a ball, her hands jammed over her ears. She was screaming. The sound of her pain carried above the Aether, cutting through him. He couldn't stop it. Couldn't move to her. How could he have brought her here?

The brightness receded suddenly as the funnel spooled back up. Quiet roared in his ears. He fought to bring his feet beneath him and stumbled toward her. Aria shot toward him at the same time. They collided, slamming together, grasping for each other as they found their balance. Their eyes locked, and Perry saw his own terror mirrored on her face.

An hour passed in a heartbeat. Perry didn't feel his weight. Didn't hear his steps as he ran. Brilliant slashes of light surrounded them, and the deafening roar of the storm was constant.

They closed in on the Pod's massive form, stopping half a mile away. Smoke billowed around them. Perry's eyes and lungs burned. He couldn't scent anything anymore. From where he stood, he could see that much of Ag 6, the dome he'd broken into months ago, had collapsed. Flames spewed a hundred feet in the air. He'd hoped to enter Reverie through it again. Now he saw they had no chance.

"Perry, look!"

The smoke shifted with the wind, drawing back like a veil. He saw another dome shimmering with blue light and spotted a vast opening. As he watched, two Hovercrafts streamed out of it, looking small as sparrows against the dome's massive scale. They cut a seam through the desert, their lights fading into the smoky, flashing darkness.

"That has to be Hess," Aria said. "He's abandoning it."

"That's our way in," he said.

They ran closer, huddling together at the side of the opening, which soared hundreds of feet tall. Inside, he saw Dweller ships lined in rows. He recognized the smaller craft from when they'd taken Talon. Bodies shaped like teardrops, sleek and shimmery as abalone shells. Beyond them loomed a ship that dwarfed the others, its form segmented like an earth crawler. Armed soldiers moved in controlled chaos, loading supply crates, directing the flight of one Hover after another in a rush to leave the Pod.

As he watched, a craft nearby sparked to life. Wings spread from its underbelly, a set of four like a dragonfly. Lights shot down their length, and then the air thrummed as the craft lifted off the ground. He flinched as it shot past with a deafening, buzzing sound.

Aria met his eyes. "The airlock into Reverie is at the other end."

Perry saw it. The entrance was hundreds of yards away. He honed in on a group of men close by, his gaze finding the compact pistols at their belts.

"We can sneak past them," Aria said. "They're focused on leaving, not on defending the Pod."

He nodded. It was their only shot. He pointed to a cluster of supply crates on palettes halfway down the hangar. There was a gap between them and the wall. "When the next Hover powers up, run for those crates. We can take cover behind them."

Aria shot forward as soon as the Hover lifted off the ground. Perry sprinted, staying with her. They were almost to the crates when a cluster of soldiers saw them. Bullets struck the wall behind him, the sound quiet compared to the buzz of the Hovers. He reached the crates and pulled his bow off his back.

"We need to keep going!" he yelled. They couldn't give the soldiers a chance to get organized. Aria drew her knife as they sprinted along the narrow corridor.

When they came through the other side, he saw a group of soldiers standing between them and the entrance. Three men. Two had drawn their weapons; the other one looked around in confusion. The only way he'd reach Talon was by getting past them.

Perry fired as they ran. His arrow struck the first man in the chest, sending him flying to the ground. Slashes of red cut past him as the Guardians shot back. The steel crates behind him clanged loudly. He fired at the second man, but it wasn't enough. Aria surged ahead. She threw her knife at the third man, hitting him in the stomach. The man reeled back, firing his pistol.

"Aria!"

Perry's heart seized as he watched her fall to the ground. He put an arrow clean through the man who'd shot her. Then he dashed to her, grabbing her by the waist and scooping her off the ground. She held her arm as they ran, blood running through her fingers. Perry pulled her with him, stooping to the floor to grab a pistol that had fallen by one of the downed soldiers. Across the hangar, people shouted in confusion as an alarm sounded.

More soldiers opened fire at them, but Perry noticed that most barely paused in their evacuation efforts. Perry's finger found the trigger. He fired again and again, a distant part of his mind amazed at the ease and speed of the weapon.

With each step she took, Aria leaned more of her weight on him. They tore up a ramp and into the airlock chamber as people yelled behind him, their voices fading in and out of the alarms. He jammed at the door's controls. It slid open, revealing stunned soldiers on the other side.

Perry pushed past them into a wide, curving corridor, the sounds of the alarm receding behind him. He didn't know where he was going. Knew only that he needed to find safety. Take care of her. Find Talon.

Aria stopped suddenly. "Here!" She pressed her fingers into the control pad of a door, opening it, and they darted inside.

40

ARIA

Aria fell back against the wall. Dizziness rolled over her in waves. She needed to catch her breath. Her heart was beating too fast. She needed it to slow down.

Perry stood by the door, listening to the sounds in the hall. She had the fleeting thought that he looked comfortable with the gun in his hand, like he'd been using one for years instead of minutes. The shouts of Guardians grew louder.

"Forget it!" Aria heard outside. "They're gone." Then their footsteps faded.

Perry lowered the gun. He looked at her, his eyebrows drawn with worry. "Stay right there."

She closed her eyes. The pain in her arm was immense, but her head was clear, unlike when she'd been poisoned. Oddly, the feeling of blood rolling down her arm and dribbling from her fingertips bothered her the most. She could function with pain, but losing blood would make her weak and slow her down.

The room was a supply repository for emergency evacuations. She'd learned of storerooms like this from Pod safety drills. Metal lockers ran in rows down the length. In them she saw hazard suits. Oxygen masks. Fire extinguishers. First-aid supplies. Perry ran to the nearest one, bringing back a metal case. He knelt and popped it open.

"There should be a blue tube," she said through gasps, "for stopping bleeding."

He rifled through it, coming up with the tube and a bandage. "Look at me," he said, straightening. "Right at my eyes."

He drew her hand away from the wound.

Aria sucked in a breath at the burst of pain that shot down her arm. She'd been hit on her bicep, but strangely, the worst pain was in her fingertips. The muscles in her legs began to shake.

"Easy," Perry said. "Just keep breathing, nice and slow."

"Is my arm still there?" she asked.

"Still there." His lips pulled into a quick smile, but she saw the worry behind it. "When it heals, it's going to match my hand perfectly."

With firm, efficient movements, he applied the coagulant and then wrapped the bandage tightly around her arm. Aria kept her gaze on his face. On the blond stubble across his jaw, and the bend in his nose. She could look at him forever. She could spend her life watching him just blink and breathe that near to her.

Her eyes blurred, and she wasn't sure if it was from the pain or from the relief of being with him again. He brought a sense of rightness. She felt it every moment she spent with him. Even the wrong ones. Even the painful ones, like now.

Perry's hands stilled. He looked up, and his gaze told her everything. He felt it too.

A tremor thrummed through the soles of her boots, and then the lockers rattled. The rumbling sound built. It kept going, growing louder and louder. The lights shut off. Aria searched the darkness, panic rising inside of her. A red emergency light above the door pulsed a few times and turned on, holding steady. Slowly, the noise faded.

"This place is coming down," Perry said, tying off the bandage.

She nodded. "The corridor circles the Panop. If we stay on it, we should find an access door." She pushed herself off the wall. The bleeding had slowed, but she still felt light-headed.

Perry peered through the door. The corridor had fallen into darkness, lit only by emergency lights every twenty paces. "Stay close to me."

They ran along the curving corridor together, the wail of fire alarms echoing off the cement walls and filling her ears. Aria smelled smoke, and the temperature had spiked. The fires had moved inside the Pod. Her strength was draining rapidly, just as she'd feared. She felt like she was running underwater.

"Here," she said, stopping at wide double doors marked PANOPTICON. "This is where Hess locked them in." She pressed at the control board next to it. NO ACCESS flashed up on the screen. She tried again, stabbing at the panel in anger. They couldn't be this close and not get inside.

She didn't hear the Reverie soldiers rounding the bend toward them. The alarms had swallowed the sounds of their approach. But Perry saw them. A staccato of bright bursts exploded beside her as he fired. Down the corridor, the Guardians fell. Perry broke into a run, covering the distance to the soldiers with a shocking surge of speed. He wrenched one of the Guardians off the ground by the collar and returned with the struggling man, who'd been shot in the leg.

"Open the door," he commanded, holding the Guardian in front of the panel.

"No!" The man twisted his body to break loose. In a flash, Aria saw her mother's face. Lifeless, as she'd last seen her. She couldn't fail again. Talon was in there. Thousands of people would die if they couldn't get in.

With her good arm, she drew her knife and slashed it across the Guardian's face. She caught him across the chin, the steel blade scraping against bone. "Get us in there!"

The man screamed and jerked back. Then he pressed desperately at the panel, entering an access code as he begged to be let go.

The doors slid open, revealing a long hallway.

She ran, her feet pounding on the slick floor, and froze as she came through the other side, into the Panop. Into her home.

She absorbed it instantaneously, feeling like a stranger. Rising up in a perfect spiraling corkscrew around the central atrium were the forty levels where she'd slept, eaten, attended school, and fractioned to the Realms.

It looked bigger, bleaker than she remembered. The gray color, which had once seemed almost invisible to her, now struck her as lifeless, suffocating in its coldness. How had she ever been happy here?

Then her eyes moved past the familiar and latched onto everything that was wrong. The smoke tumbling from the higher levels. Pieces of concrete crumbling, falling to where she and Perry stood. Flashes of people running—or chasing one another. The hair-raising screams of terror, fading in and out with the blare of the fire alarms. Hardest to believe were the groups of people sitting in the atrium lounges socializing normally, like nothing unusual was happening.

Aria spotted Pixie's short black hair and sprinted over.

Pixie startled when she ran up, blinking in confusion. "Aria?" A smile spread over her face. "It's so good to see you! Soren told us you were alive, but I thought he was just acting strange again."

"Reverie is breaking! You need to get out of here, Pixie. You have to leave!"

"Leave to where?"

"To the outside!"

Pixie shook her head, fear flashing across her features. "Oh, no . . . I'm not going *there*. Hess told us to stay here and enjoy the Realms. He's fixing everything." She smiled. "Sit down, Aria. Have you seen the Atlantis Realm? The kelp gardens are champ this time of year."

"We're running out of time, Aria," Perry said beside her.

Pixie seemed to notice him for the first time. "Who's he?"

"We need to find Soren," Aria said quickly. "Can you message him for me?"

"Sure, I'll do that right now. But he's not far. He's just in the southern lounge."

Aria turned to Perry. "This way!" As she ran to the other end of the atrium, an explosion shook the air and sent her staggering. Pieces of concrete fell around them, disintegrating as they struck the smooth floors. She covered her head, fear pushing her on. The only solution—their only hope of surviving—was to get out of there.

Up ahead, she saw a group running toward her. She spotted a familiar face, and then several others. She wanted to cry at the sight of them. Caleb was there, his eyes wide and disbelieving. Rune and Jupiter, running together. She saw Soren at the center of the pack, and then the boy beside him.

Perry broke away from her side. He covered the distance in long, powerful strides and swept Talon into his arms. Over Perry's shoulder, she caught a glimpse of Talon's smile before he buried his face in Perry's neck.

She'd waited for months to see that sight. She wanted to savor it, if only for an instant, but Soren barreled up, his gaze boring into her.

"Took you long enough," he said. "I kept my part of the bargain. Now you keep yours."

41

PEREGRINE

I'm all right. Really, I'm all right," Talon said. Perry held him as tight as he could without hurting him. "Uncle Perry, we have to go."

Perry set him down and grasped his small hand. He took in his nephew's face. Talon was healthy. And *here*.

Brooke's younger sister, Clara, ran up and hugged his leg. Her face was red, and she was crying. Perry knelt. "It's all right, Clara. I'm going to get you both home. I need you and Talon to hold hands. Don't let go of each other, and keep close. Right next to me."

Clara ran a sleeve over her face, wiping away tears, and nodded. Perry straightened. Aria stood with Soren, the Dweller who he'd fought months ago. Dozens of people had run up with him. They were alert and terrified, unlike the dazed people he had seen moments ago. He noticed they weren't wearing Smarteyes.

"You brought the *Savage*?" Soren said.

Across the atrium, a sudden burst of flames spewed from a corridor. A second later, the wave of heat hit him. "We need to move, Aria. Now!"

"The transport hangar," she said. "This way!"

They raced back to the Panop door, Soren and his group following. Aria called out as she ran, yelling to anyone who would listen to leave Reverie, but the peal of fire alarms and the thunder of smashing concrete swallowed even her voice. The people sitting in groupings on the ground floor didn't move. They stayed blank-faced, oblivious to the chaos around them. Aria stopped in front of the girl she'd spoken to before and grabbed her by the shoulders.

"Pixie, you have to get out of here now!" she yelled. This time the girl didn't respond at all. She stared ahead, unresponsive. Aria turned to Soren. "What's wrong with them? Is it DLS?"

"It's that. It's leaving her for the outside. It's everything," Soren answered.

"Can't you shut off their Smarteyes?" she asked desperately.

"I've tried!" Soren said. "They have to do it themselves. There's no getting through to them. They're scared. This is all they've ever known. I did everything I could."

An explosive boom filled Perry's ears. "Aria, we have to leave."

She shook her head, tears spilling from her eyes. "I can't do this. I can't leave them."

Perry stepped toward her, taking her face in his hands. "You have to. I'm not leaving here without you."

He felt the truth of his words settle like cold over him. He'd do anything to change it. Give anything. But no matter what they did, they couldn't save everyone.

"Come with me," he said. "Please, Aria. It's time to go."

She looked up, her gaze moving slowly across the crumbling Pod. "I'm sorry . . . I'm sorry," she said. He put his arm around her, his heart breaking for her. For all the innocent people who deserved to live, but wouldn't. Together they ran for the exit, leaving the Panop behind.

They raced back into the outer corridors, leading the pack of Dwellers. Black smoke poured from air ducts, and the red emergency lights pulsed slowly, stuttering on for a second, off for a few more. Perry kept track of Talon and Clara, but Aria worried him more. She held her arm close and was struggling to keep up.

They reached the transport hangar and darted inside. It looked abandoned, nothing like the teeming hub Perry had seen earlier. He didn't see any soldiers, and only a handful of Hovers remained.

"Can you pilot any of these?" Aria asked Soren. The color had drained from her face.

"I can in the Realms," Soren said. "These are *real*."

People streamed in around them. Through the vast opening at the other end, the desert still flashed with the full power of the storm.

"Do it," Perry said. He and Aria had barely survived the

journey there. He saw no way of leading dozens of scared people—Dwellers who'd never set foot outside—into the wrath of an Aether storm.

Soren wheeled on him. "I don't take orders from you!"

"Then take them from me!" Aria yelled. "Move, Soren! There's no time!"

"There's no way this works," Soren said, but he ran to one of the Hovers.

The ship was immense up close, the material of the body seamless and pale blue, with the shimmer of a pearl. Perry grabbed Talon's and Clara's hands, pulling them up the ramp.

The cabin inside was a wide, windowless tube. To one side, through a small doorway, he saw the cockpit. The other end was packed with metal crates. A supply craft, he realized, though one that had only been partially loaded. The middle of the hold where he stood was empty, but quickly filling with people.

"Move all the way back and sit down," Aria instructed them. "Hold on to something, if you can."

He noticed the Dwellers wore the same gray clothes Aria had when he'd first seen her that night in Ag 6. They were fair-skinned and wide-eyed, and though he couldn't scent their tempers through the smoke, their reactions to him were blatant, plain on their stunned faces.

He looked down at himself. He had blood and soot covering his battered clothes, and a gun in his hand. Besides that, he knew he'd look hard and feral in their eyes, just as they looked soft and terrified to him.

He wasn't helping anything by being there.

"In here," he told Talon and Clara, ushering them into the cockpit.

He bumped his head on the door as he entered and flashed on Roar, who would've made a wisecrack. Who should be there. Who Perry had treated awfully earlier. He couldn't believe he'd questioned Roar's loyalty. Suddenly, he remembered Liv. The air rushed from his lungs and his stomach twisted. At some point he'd think about his sister and end up on his knees, but not now. He couldn't now.

The cockpit was small and dim, no bigger than Vale's room, with a rounded window that curved along the front. Perry saw the exit at the far end of the hangar. Outside, thick black smoke flashed with Aether, concealing the desert.

Soren sat in one of the two pilot seats, cursing as he swiped at a smooth bank of controls. He must have sensed Perry's attention, because he glanced back, hatred in his eyes. "I haven't forgotten, Savage."

Perry's gaze went to the scar on Soren's chin. "Then you remember the outcome."

"I'm not afraid of you."

A small voice spoke up beside Perry. "Soren, he's my uncle."

Soren looked at Talon, his expression softening. Then he turned back to the controls.

Perry glanced at his nephew, surprised at the influence he had over Soren. How had that happened? He stashed the gun on a shelf beside a handful of other weapons, and had

Talon and Clara sit against the back wall. Then he crouched, studying his nephew's face. "You all right?"

Talon nodded, smiling tiredly. Perry saw traces of Vale in his deep green eyes, and noticed his front teeth had grown in. Suddenly he felt all the months they'd lost, and the full weight of his responsibility. Talon was his now.

He straightened as the engines buzzed to life. The panel in front of Soren lit up, the rest of the cabin falling into darkness.

"Hold on!" Soren yelled.

A murmur of alarm came from the people in the main cabin. Aria slipped through the door beside Perry, stepping into the cockpit just as the Hover rose with a lurch. He grabbed her by the waist, catching her as she stumbled. The craft surged forward, pushing Aria's back against his chest. He locked his arms around her, holding tight as the walls of the hangar blurred past, the Hover gaining speed by the second. They shot outside and plunged into the smoke. Perry couldn't see anything through the window but noticed that Soren navigated by the screen on the console in front of him.

In seconds they broke into clear air, and he stared in awe at the earth streaking past. He'd taken his name from a falcon, but never in his life had he thought he'd fly. Funnels lashed down across the desert, but they were fewer now. The pale light of dawn spread across the sky, softening the glare of the Aether. He felt Aria's weight relax against him. Because he could, he rested his chin on top of her head.

As the Hover banked west, adjusting its course, Perry spotted Hess's fleet, a trail of lights moving across the valley in the distance. He recognized the shape of the immense craft he'd seen earlier. Reverie came into view next, crumbling, consumed by smoke.

Aria watched, silent in his arms. His gaze trailed over the curve of her shoulder, the slope of her cheek. The dark flick of her eyelashes as she blinked. His heart filled with hurt. Hers. His. He understood exactly what she felt. He'd lost his home as well.

"Whenever you're ready, Aria, maybe you could tell me where I'm going."

Perry's hands curled into fists at Soren's tone. Aria turned and peered up at him in question. The bandage on her arm had bled through. She'd need medical care—and soon.

"The Tides," he said, not as much suggesting it as saying what felt right. He had plenty of shelter to offer. And after what he'd just seen, he had a feeling the Dwellers would adapt to the cave faster than the tribe.

Aria's gray eyes sparkled in the dim cabin. "The crates in the back are loaded with supplies. Food. Weapons. Medicine."

He nodded. It was a simple decision. An obvious alliance. They were stronger together. And this time, he thought, the Dwellers would be welcome. Perry glanced at Soren. Most of them would be, at least.

"Head northwest," Aria said. "Beyond that range of hills."

Soren adjusted the steering control, pointing the craft

toward the Tide Valley. Perry glanced down, eager to finally bring Talon home to the tribe. His nephew's eyes were just drifting closed. Beside him, Clara slept.

Aria took his hand, leading him to the open pilot seat. Perry sat and pulled her into his lap. She turned and nestled against him, resting her forehead against his cheek, and for a moment he had everything he needed.

42

ARIA

"Are you trying to make me crash?" Soren glanced at her from the other seat. The light of the controls made his face look sharper. Crueler. More like his father's. Soren's gaze moved to Perry. "Because that's disgusting."

Aria's arm throbbed with pain, and her eyes burned from smoke and tiredness. She wanted to close them and fade into unconsciousness, but they'd reach the Tides soon. She had to stay focused.

Behind her, she heard the murmuring of the others in the cabin. Caleb was back there. She hadn't even had a chance to talk to him yet. Rune and Jupiter were also there, and dozens of others—every one of them scared.

They needed her. She'd brought them out of Reverie. She knew how to survive on the outside. They'd need her guidance. It was her responsibility to watch over them now.

Perry brushed her hair over her shoulder and whispered

by her ear, "Rest. Ignore him."

The sound of his voice, deep and unhurried, traveled through her, settling warm in her stomach. She lifted her head. Perry watched her, his face drawn with worry. She brushed her fingers over the soft scruff on his jaw and then buried them in his hair, wanting to feel all the textures of him. "If you don't like what you see, Soren, then don't look."

She saw the flash of Perry's smile just before their lips met. Their kiss was gentle and slow, and full of meaning. They had hurried through every moment since he'd met her in the woods. While they'd been at the Tides'. On the race to Reverie. Now they finally had a moment together without hiding or rushing. There was so much she wanted to say. So much she wanted him to know.

Perry's hand settled on her hip, his grip firm. She felt their kiss shift into something deeper as his mouth moved with more urgency over hers. Suddenly there was real heat between them, and she had to force herself to draw away.

When she did, a soft curse slipped through Perry's lips. His eyes were half-lidded, unfocused. He looked as overcome as she felt.

Aria leaned by his ear. "We'll pick that up when we're alone."

He laughed. "That better be soon." He took her face in his hands and drew her close so their foreheads touched. Aria's hair fell forward, making a wall, a space that was just theirs. That close, all she could see were his eyes. They were glossy, shining like coins beneath water.

"You broke me in half when you left," he whispered.

She knew she had. She'd known then, when she'd done it. "I was trying to protect you."

"I know." He exhaled, his breath soft on her face. "I know you were." He ran the back of his fingers over her cheek. "I want to tell you something." He smiled, but the look in his eyes was mellow and tempting.

"You do?"

He nodded. "I've been wanting to tell you for a while. But I'm going to wait until later. When we're alone."

Aria laughed. "That better be soon." She lay back against his chest and couldn't remember feeling any safer than she did then.

Outside, the hills blurred past. She was surprised by how far they'd gone. They'd reach the Tides soon.

"I swear that almost made me sick," Soren muttered.

Aria remembered their last hurried exchange through the Smarteye.

"What?" Soren said, scowling at her. "Why are you looking at me that way?"

"You said you knew where the Still Blue was." Their connection had been cut off, just before he could tell her.

Soren grinned. "That's right, I do. I saw everything Sable and my father talked about. But I'm not saying a word in front of the Savage."

Perry's arms tensed around her. "Call me that again, Dweller, and it'll be the last thing you ever say." He shifted his back, relaxing again. "And you don't need to tell me anything. I know where it is."

Aria looked up at Perry. She moved too quickly, and pain shot down her arm. She bit the inside of her lip, waiting for it to subside. "You know where the Still Blue is?"

He nodded. "That fleet was moving dead west. There's only one thing in that direction."

The realization struck her before he'd finished speaking. "It's at sea," she said.

Perry made a low sound of agreement. "I was never closer to it than when I was home."

Soren's mouth twisted in disappointment. "Well, you don't know everything."

Aria shook her head, in no mood for Soren's games. "Just say it, Soren. What did you find out?"

Soren's lip curled like he was ready to say something snide, but then his expression relaxed. When he replied, his voice was even, and lacked its usual bitterness. "Sable says he has to go through a solid wall of Aether before he reaches open sky." He made a dismissive sound, low in his throat. "He says he can do it, but it's a lie. No ship can do that."

No ship could, Aria thought, but there was another way. She spoke at the same time Perry did.

"Cinder."

43

PEREGRINE

The Hover passed the Tide compound and glided north along the coast. Soren had to take them over the open ocean to reach the protected cove outside the cave, the bluff too steep for the craft to negotiate. Perry noticed that the ride was rougher over water. As Aria dozed in his arms, he looked across to the horizon and felt a surge of hope. They didn't have Cinder, or the might that Hess and Sable would have together, but the Still Blue was somewhere at sea, and no one knew the sea like the Tides did. The ocean was their territory.

Talon and Clara woke as the Hover put down on the beach. Perry had an explanation ready as to why they'd needed to leave the compound, but seeing the huge smiles on their faces, he decided he'd explain later.

"Tell me I didn't just land in front of a cave," Soren said.

Aria stirred in Perry's arms. Slowly she unfolded her legs

and rose from his lap. "We can get rid of him any time."

"I wish you weren't joking," Perry said. He already missed the feeling of her weight against him.

Soren pushed the steering console away and stood. "That's some kind of gratitude for saving your lives. You're both welcome, by the way."

Aria smiled. She held her hand out to help Perry up, her injured arm tucked against her side. "Who said I was joking?"

Perry rose and followed her into the main cabin, ignoring the gasps of the Dwellers huddled there. Resting his hand on Talon's shoulder, he stood beside Aria as she pressed a control by the door. The hatch opened with a rush of air that carried the sound of the waves, lowering to the sand.

In the morning light, he saw the Tides stream out of the cave, filling in along the beach. They gaped at the ship, caught between disbelief and panic. Behind him, dozens of Dwellers stared at the world outside, their fear palpable, strong enough to scent even with his smoke-blunted nose.

Perry spotted Marron and Reef. Bear and Molly. His gaze moved past the brothers—Hyde, Hayden, and Strag. Past Willow and Brooke. In search of Roar and Twig. Regret hit him as he realized that neither of them was there. He had to find them—and Cinder—but first he and Aria had to settle the Dwellers into their temporary home.

Flea trotted to the bottom of the ramp, whining at the sight of Talon and wagging his tail. Wagging his entire body. Talon looked up, his green eyes shining with eagerness. "Can I go?"

"Sure," Perry said, and watched him run down the ramp with Clara.

Talon didn't get far before Flea jumped on him, knocking him to the sand. Clara shot past them and jumped into Brooke's arms. The tribe rushed forward, surrounding them, until Perry lost sight of them both.

He looked at Aria beside him. There were still so many problems to solve, but they had brought Talon and Clara home, and rescued who they could from Reverie. It was a good beginning.

They would need to form a new tribe now, and find the Still Blue.

Perry held out his hand, remembering his approach to the Tides with her weeks ago. Their awkward silence and the distance they'd put between them. They'd taken their greatest strength and hidden it like a weakness.

"Should we try this again?" he asked.

Aria smiled. "The right way," she said, and wove her fingers through his. "Together."

ACKNOWLEDGMENTS

First and foremost, thank you, Barbara Lalicki, for your support and guidance through the creation of this book. You steered me right many times with encouragement and sage advice. I am so fortunate to have an editor with the soul and talent of an artist. Thank you.

Andrew Harwell provided additional editorial input and helped in countless other ways. Andrew, you do it all with such a fantastic attitude. It is truly a pleasure to work with you. To Karen Sherman, my copyeditor: Thank you for your insight and thoroughness. You make me look good, and I would be nowhere without you. My gratitude also goes to the marketing, design, and sales folks at HarperCollins. There's so much work behind the scenes. I appreciate your efforts very much.

Thank you to my ninja agents, Josh and Tracey Adams, for handling the business side so I can focus on the fun—I mean *creative*—side of things. You are wonderful. Thanks also to Stephen Moore for running the show in Los Angeles.

Lorin Oberweger, Eric Elfman, Lia Keyes, and Jackie Garlick were always available to brainstorm, read, or critique or just support me as I wrote *Through the Ever Night*. You are all invaluable to me.

The YA Muses—my home team of Katy Longshore, Talia Vance, Bret Ballou, and Donna Cooner—this wouldn't be half as fun without you. Thank you so much for sharing this journey with me. YAH-Muses!

One of the most rewarding aspects of being a writer is belonging to the writing community. Thank you, Apocalypsies, for bringing me great friendships and much support during my debut year. A few years ago, the SCBWI opened a door for me. In particular, thanks to Kim Turrisi. I aspire to be like you by someday opening a few doors for others, too.

My family is my greatest treasure. My parents, in-laws, brothers, sisters, cousins, aunts and uncles, nieces and nephews . . . I could write another book or two or ten telling you how much I love you. Thank you for believing in me. To Michael, Luca, and Rocky: You are the point of everything.

Last, but certainly not least, to the bloggers and readers out there—to *you*—thank you for sharing your time with Perry and Aria. Many of you have reached out to me and touched me deeply with your support and enthusiasm. Thank you.

Now, are you ready? It's time to head Into the Still Blue. . . .